THE BOOKCASE OF SHERMAN HOLMES

A Holmes and Garden Collection

A Matter of Business
A Matter of Honour
The Haunting of Sherman Holmes
The Adventure of the Dead Wild Bore
The Bespangled Fur

ANDREA FRAZER

Published by JDI Publications 2022

ISBN 9798366333344

Copyright © **Andrea Frazer** 2015

The right of **Andrea Frazer** to be identified as the author of this work has been asserted by the author in accordance with the Copyright, Designs and Patents Act 1988.

The story contained within this book is a work of fiction. Names and characters are the product of the author's imagination and any resemblance to actual persons, living or dead, is entirely coincidental.

All rights reserved. No part of this book may be reproduced, stored in a retrieval system, or transmitted in any form or by any means, electronic, electrostatic, magnetic tape, mechanical, photocopying, recording or otherwise, without the written permission of the publishers: JDI Publications, Chiang Mai, 50130, Thailand

A MATTER OF BUSINESS

Chapter One

John Garden pulled himself together and got to his feet, and Sherman Holmes drew himself almost to attention. Standing beside her son, Shirley Garden smiled politely across her own desk and invited the weeping woman to move into the inner office.

Holmes and Garden were now officially in business as private investigators and the terribly upset woman was their first client.

Sherman Holmes, having inherited a large fortune, had finally found himself able to indulge his dream of emulating his near-namesake hero Sherlock by setting up a detective agency. His partner, Garden, he had first encountered by chance, when both men had been staying at the Black Swan Hotel and had become caught up in a series of murders. They had found common ground in their love of Conan Doyle's hero and Garden, looking for an escape from his mundane existence, had readily agreed to join Holmes in his venture.

Holmes had pictured himself like his fictional hero and imagined an exciting life as a consulting detective, solving all those hitherto unsolvable cases. However, there were two problems with this. One: although he was obviously the daring leading man to Garden's sidekick, he wasn't actually the brains of the outfit (that was Garden, although Holmes didn't see it that way). Two: the good people of Hamsley Black Cross had far more mundane problems than had Conan Doyle's Victorian Londoners.

As he was about to find out.

Holmes gently moved the distressed woman into the

inner office and settled her in the chair on the other side of his desk, and Garden mouthed the words 'cup of tea' to Shirley before shutting the door between the offices for the sake of confidentiality.

Holmes had the appearance of one who could be confided in, being on the plump side, middle-aged, respectably dressed, and sporting a fine old-fashioned moustache such as one's uncle might have worn in one's childhood. He sat now, behind his desk, smiling a kind smile at their very first live client, absolutely oozing charm and reliability.

'Allow us to introduce ourselves,' he said in his cultivated, reassuring tones, held out his hand to be shaken and continued, 'My name is Sherman Holmes, and this is my business partner' – here, he extended a hand to indicate Garden – 'John Garden. How may we be of service to you, madam?'

After hands were shaken, the woman extracted a handkerchief from her handbag, dried her eyes, and informed them, 'I am Petula Exeter. I live here in Hamsley Black Cross, in a very respectable area, but there have been a lot of pets disappearing recently, and my neighbours and I think that a cat-napper is at work. My own darling little Princess Leia disappeared three days ago.

'At first I thought she'd just wandered off or got shut in someone's shed or garage, but I've gone round the whole neighbourhood and all I can conclude is that someone has made off with her. She's a pedigree, you know – a prize-winner as a kitten, and worth quite some money.'

'I'm so sorry to hear that, Ms Exeter.' Holmes had actually remembered to use the title Ms and not fallen into the trap of addressing a single woman as married, or vice versa. 'Do you have a snapshot of her that we could look at?'

As she fumbled, once more, in her capacious handbag,

Garden put a cup and saucer in front of her, his face a picture of dismay. Was this what their future held? Misplaced pussycats? With his other hand he put a sugar bowl and spoon beside her cup and saucer and declared, 'I took the liberty of assuming that you took milk, but I've brought the sugar in for you to help yourself. If you should want anything else, don't hesitate to ask.' He suddenly felt like a fool. What was she going to request, a burger and fries? Pulling himself together for the second time in a few minutes, he approached his own desk, deciding that he would have to achieve the right mind-set before he could pretend to be a proper private investigator. It would be just like being Joanne, sort of.

Although it was not public knowledge, in his free time Garden was a cross-dresser of some considerable skill, his alter ego being called Joanne. Just as he had to concentrate on walking, talking, and sitting like a female when he was in this guise, so would he have to do when he was John H. Garden, PI. He had had a vision, as Holmes had ushered this first client into the inner office, that most of their clients would be female, and most of them would be in some degree of distress. Men sorted out their problems with their fists on the most basic level, or with their power, as they moved up the business or family hierarchies. Women didn't.

'Have any of your neighbours told you that they have, er, mislaid a pet?' asked Holmes as he stared at the photograph of a cat with a most supercilious expression. Garden, now achieving his goal of adopting the necessary sympathetic attitude, stuffed his knuckles into his mouth for fear of bursting into unforgiveable laughter at the sight of Holmes' serious face.

'A lady in the next street said that her Siamese has been gone for four days now, but that she expected he'd be back when he'd got whatever it was that was bugging him out of his system. She didn't seem at all worried. How she could have been so hard-faced about the disappearance of a beloved pet I have no idea.'

Mrs Exeter held her handkerchief up to her eyes again as they filled with fresh tears. 'Is there anything else you can tell me?' enquired Holmes, slipping the photograph into the top drawer of his desk. 'Has anyone been seen lurking around the area, either on foot or in a vehicle? Have other pets gone missing, apart from your Princess ...' – Garden shot off into the tiny cloakroom downstairs to give vent to his mirth, flushing the lavatory and turning on both basin taps to cover the noise of his sniggers – 'Leia and this Siamese?'

'An elderly lady across the road said she had seen a van a couple of times, but I've noticed no one myself. And a lady on the corner said her little Shih Tzu had run away, but may have been taken.'

'Did your neighbour give any description of the van – make, model, colour, description of its driver?' Inside the cloakroom, Garden had to sit down. There were tears pouring down his cheeks, and he was in danger of wetting himself. This was obviously a bad case of first-day nerves that was getting the better of him.

'She has very limited eyesight, and could only say that it was a van, and that the colour was very pale – perhaps cream, grey, or white. She's actually registered blind, so I couldn't realistically expect any more of her.' Garden was glad he had automatically taken down his lower garments, as a fresh wave of mirth rolled over him. Of all the vehicles in all the world, they were going to be looking for a van – possibly white, make unknown.

Still behind his desk, Holmes opened a new notepad and asked for Mrs Exeter's address and telephone number, noting them carefully in his most immaculate writing. He then asked for the names and addresses of both the lady who had seen the van and the ladies whose dog and cat had disappeared.

'Is there any other information, no matter how inconsequential' – in the cloakroom, Garden thought that he would suffocate from lack of air, so much was he laughing and trying to keep quiet – 'that you might be able to add to what you have already told me?'

'She had a little blue collar round her neck; for f-l-e-a-s you know, with a little bell on it, to stop her killing any dear birdies.'

'Thank you very much for your business, dear lady. May I give you one of our business cards and assure you that we will do our very best to help you in any way we can in this time of distress.' Holmes could be very pompous when the situation required it. 'My partner and I will get straight on to this, and hope to restore your dear kitty to you in next to no time.'

Holmes rose, and Mrs Exeter followed suit. 'I'm so grateful. My little darling's only six months old; still a baby. I got her after my husband died, and she's such good company for me that I don't feel at all lonely when she's around.

'Did I mention that she's a silver-spotted Bengal? As a breed they're quite close to the Asian leopard cat, and so inquisitive and mischievous. I really don't know what I shall do without her. Please do your best to locate her, gentlemen.'

'We shall do everything within our power to return her to your no doubt excellent care in next to no time. A very good day to you, madam,' Holmes positively chirped, hoping that his voice would drown out the sounds coming from the cloakroom.

'Oh, I told the lady whose doggy's gone missing about you, so she might pay you a visit too.'

'Thank you so much. So kind of you,' said Holmes, ushering his client out of the door and into the outer office. 'Please call in or telephone at any time.'

As she vacated the premises, Holmes shot back through

the door to the inner office, pulled open the cloakroom door viciously, and yelled, 'Garden, what the hell do you think you're playing at? That was a paying customer and our very first case.'

As Holmes was upbraiding the disgraceful behaviour of his partner, the street door opened again, letting in what seemed like a tuneless wail from the bagpiper booked by Garden to attract customers to the opening day of their joint business venture, and their very second customer shuffled up to Shirley Garden at her reception desk.

Holmes immediately fell silent, put on a serious face, and returned behind his desk, where he tried to look busy and business-like at the same time. A much-chastened Garden did likewise, now thoroughly sobered up from his bout of the nervous giggles – a form of stage fright, he understood.

After a couple of minutes, there was a discreet knock at the door, and Shirley Garden, in her most formal manner, introduced Miss Jemima Jerome, who wished to consult with them over a little problem. Holmes invited their new client to take a seat, this time at Garden's desk, and sat in his swivelling captain's chair watching with interest to see how Garden handled what would probably turn out to be a similar experience to the last case. Let's see how funny he finds this one, he thought.

Garden smiled across at the elderly woman, and introduced himself and his partner, opening an identical brand new notebook and asking her to explain how they could be of assistance to her.

'It's my little doggy, Prince Rupert,' she started. 'He's gone missing and I presume he has been doggy-napped. I was given your name by Mrs Exeter whose pussy's gone astray. She called on me and we had a little chat, which ended with her telling me she was going to consult with you, and I decided that that was the best course of action for me, too, so here I am.'

'Do you have a photograph of, um, Prince Rupert?' asked Garden with a straight face, noticing that Holmes was the one now looking fit to burst.

'He's a pedigree, you know. He was awfully expensive, but I felt it was worth it when my old pussy passed over. A dog gives you so much more loyalty and keeps you fit, too. You also get to know new people when you bump into other dog-walkers.'

Taking the proffered photograph, Garden wondered just how much exercise one got from taking a toy poodle for a walk, but he held his peace. It was his job to find this missing gem, not question its owner's motives in purchasing it. 'How long has his Highness been gone for?' Garden asked, with a sly wink at the animal's owner that made her crack a small smile.

'His Highness wandered off about four days ago. I've searched all the streets where we usually go walkies, showing everyone I meet his photograph, but no one seems to have seen him.'

'Let me note down your name and address, and may I keep this photograph for now, just until we locate Prince Rupert?'

'Of course you may,' replied Jemima Jerome while Garden slipped the photograph out of sight and glanced over at his partner's desk, behind which had issued a sort of smothered snorting noise. Holmes' chair made no sound as he pushed himself back from his desk and disappeared into the tiny cloakroom.

'We'll pull out all the stops,' Garden promised in all seriousness, only to hear what sounded like a fit of coughing coming from behind the flimsy door of the cramped *toilette* facilities. 'Here is my card. Don't hesitate to call or telephone at any time. Good day to you, madam.' Garden rang a bell on his desk, promptly producing his mother, who ushered their second client off the premises.

'Holmes!' he hissed, dragging the door to the lavatory open and glaring at his mirthful partner, trying desperately to suppress his laughter.

'Sorry, old chap. I didn't realise it sounded so funny to a third party,' he managed, through a gale of inadequately suppressed laughter. 'I promise it won't happen again.'

'I should hope not; and after telling me off so thoroughly.'

'I'm going to nip off and call on the lady whose Siamese has gone walkabout, and the old dear who saw the van,' said the senior partner, pulling himself together.

'That suits me fine. I've got some telephone calls to make,' responded Garden, a determined glint in his eyes.

As Holmes left the office, he found the bagpiper sitting in the clients' chair sharing a cup of tea and biscuits with Shirley Garden. 'And don't be too long about it,' he warned the man, who was wearing enough tartan to model for a shortbread tin. The poor man had been piping for some time now, and was red in the face and puffed, for the weather had turned warm, and his tartan was of a heavy weave. Evidently he was sorely in need of a break.

As soon as Holmes had departed, excited at having something to do, Garden got out the telephone directory and began his very first mission as a bona fide private investigator, as excited as Holmes had been at the thought of visiting a possible witness.

Holmes' enthusiasm was somewhat dampened when he tried to get an answer at the door of Mrs Mary Wilton, the woman who had noticed the van. He had rung the doorbell long and hard several times, and had actually resorted to banging the knocker as hard as he could, when a quavering voice called from inside instructing him to wait a minute, and not be so impatient.

When the door finally cracked open on a security chain, all he could see was a beady eye, magnified enormously through one lens of a pair of strong spectacles, and a glimpse of a white head. Before she had the chance to challenge him, he had his business card through the slit and into her conveniently positioned claw.

There was another long interval as she inspected it, actually walking away at one point to fetch what he later discovered was a magnifying glass, before he could introduce himself and ask if she could spare him a few minutes of her no doubt valuable time in pursuance of his current investigations into the disappearance of local pets.

There was another long pause as she considered his entreaty, then she unclipped the chain, shuffled away from the door, and asked him to enter. She was using a walking frame, and this explained why it had taken her so long to answer the door, as did her response when he asked her if they should take a seat.

He had automatically raised his voice when speaking through the tiny crack available to him through the only slightly open door, but when he used his normal volume, she didn't respond at all. Speaking again rather more loudly, she put a hand up to her ear, staring at him with eyes as big as saucers and asked him to, 'Say again?'

'IS THERE ANYWHERE WE COULD SIT TO TALK?' he positively yelled, at which enquiry she cracked a smile, and ushered him very slowly into the front room of the property.

'CAN YOU GIVE ME ANY DETAILS OF THE VAN YOU SAW THAT MIGHT BE INVOLVED IN THE THEFT OF VALUABLE PETS?' he bellowed, taking his notebook out of his pocket and a pen out of his jacket breast pocket.

'Eh?' she replied, once more cupping her ear with a hand.

'*IS THERE ANYTHING YOU CAN TELL ME ABOUT THE VAN YOU SAW THAT MIGHT BE INVOLVED IN THIS BUSINESS?*' he repeated, even louder. This was going to be harder than he thought.

'What van?' she asked, looking puzzled. Sigh!

'*THE VAN THAT YOU TOLD* ...' – here, he consulted his notebook – '*MRS PETULA EXETER ABOUT WHEN SHE TOLD YOU HER PEDIGREE CAT HAD DISAPPEARED,*' he roared.

It was a long and frustrating visit from which he gleaned precisely nothing, and when he got back into his car, against all his rules, he lit up a pipeful of tobacco, and puffed away in impotent, mutinous rage. What a waste of time that had been, and all he had got was a sore throat.

Determining to get more from the woman whose Siamese had also disappeared, he consulted his notebook once more for the lady's name and address, and drove off in high dudgeon, even stalling his car, so cross was he, before he managed to drive off.

Inside the house, Mary Wilton, realising it was time for her favourite Australian soap opera, removed her hearing aids from the bureau drawer, slickly fitted them and turned them on, then switched on the television set and settled down to a good helping of scandal and neighbourly skulduggery, well satisfied with her performance for that interfering busybody with the ridiculous moustache. He wouldn't be back in a hurry, and it would count as her bad deed for the day.

At Holmes' next port of call, the door was answered by a spry woman, probably in her mid-sixties, about whose ankles a Siamese cat wove itself in and out. Looking down at it with a jaundiced eye, Holmes handed over a card, saying, 'I was here to ask about your cat's disappearance but, as I can see, he has returned.'

'Just this morning,' replied the woman with a broad, beaming smile. 'Little tinker had been setting up home in next door's works van. Neighbour didn't notice him getting in and out of it when he left the doors open on peoples' drives: said he must have hidden in the old dust sheets, and gone hunting during the day. He's a painter and decorator, so when he goes out to work, he's usually at the same address all day.

'This morning he was unloading the paint pots from his last job to reload for the place he's working in all of next week, and this little chap just sauntered out through the back doors. Cheeky-looking ornament that he is, he just swanned in and stood by his empty food bowl with a look of disapproval on his face that it wasn't full and ready and waiting for him. He's a bit of a traveller, is his lordship; Oyibo Barnabas Joe, to give him his full name.'

'I'm sorry to have bothered you unnecessarily,' said Holmes, fighting down the tantrum he could feel coming on. He might as well have stayed in the office doing something useful, like putting a half-page ad in the local paper. Deciding that that was just what he would do when he got back, he returned to his car and drove off with an angry squeal of tyres.

The thought crossed his mind unbidden that the great Sherlock Holmes wouldn't have spent his time looking for pets, but he quickly pushed this away, not wanting to undermine his dream so early in the venture. Maybe the time would come when *he* would find a blue carbuncle ... maybe even in his Christmas goose!

Meanwhile, back at the ranch, Garden was glowing with triumph. He had phoned all the veterinary surgeries in the area, and all the animal sanctuaries here and nearby, and had hit pay dirt with two of them. Princess Leia was in a rescue centre just a few miles out of the town, and Prince Rupert had turned up at a rescue centre as far away as Farlington Market.

After informing both that he had located the owners, then informing their owners of their precious pets' whereabouts, Garden had been ready and waiting when a third client turned up, and he was able to deal with the gentleman his own. Again, it wasn't anything exciting, but it was a bit more of the bread and butter work they probably would be relying on, and with these small consultations, the word would spread about their service – especially if they delivered the goods.

The third client had come in about vegetables being stolen from his allotment. It wasn't just the odd parsnip or carrot; this was much larger in scale. Every time he visited his patch, more of his lovingly nurtured vegetables and flowers – for he grew these too, for display in the house – had been taken. He had no idea who was doing it, but he wanted the plot put under surveillance and the culprit or culprits brought to justice.

This tiny plot of land was his passion, and he couldn't bear the thought that someone felt they had the right to help themselves to the fruits – and vegetables – of his labours. Garden had diligently taken down the details, then received some photographs of the bare patches on the well-kept plot, and had assured its carer that he would discover who was 'at it' with his produce.

Apparently complaints to the council, from whom the allotment was rented, had proved fruitless. Complaints to the police had proved equally unsuccessful, as they claimed they simply didn't have the manpower to put an allotment under overnight watch on a long-term basis, and the man was incandescent with rage that nobody except himself cared. His plot was the most densely planted and most rigorously attended, and he felt that his heart would break if whoever was responsible was not apprehended and punished for their sheer brass-necked cheek.

He had been keeping watch as much as he could, but he had to sleep sometime, and nothing had been filched during daylight hours when other allotment renters were at work on their patches. Garden suggested that maybe, if this passionate gardener could watch alternate nights, the detectives would cover every other night, until they had a result.

This was agreed as a satisfactory arrangement, relieving the frustrated grower some sleep at least, and he went off, happy in the knowledge that Monday night, at least, he could go to bed and sleep, knowing that his patch of ground was under surveillance.

Holmes returned to the office with a face like thunder – fortunately for the piper's sake, he had gone on his own lunch break – and Garden sat back and listened to his partner blustering and swearing as he gave the account of how he had spent the majority of the rest of his morning. The redder Holmes's face got with fury, the more the voice of triumph in Garden's head sang. He, at least, had some good news: he had some bad news as well, but this should be tempered with the tidings that their first two cases had been solved without him setting foot outside the premises.

When Holmes had finally complained and sworn himself to a standstill, Garden gave him a beaming smile, and the glad tidings that he had located both Princess Leia and Prince Rupert, and passed on the good news to both the royal households which, at this very minute, were rejoicing in the news that their little darlings would within the hour be back at home where they belonged with their respective mummies.

Holmes did not seem as happy as Garden had hoped he would be, as he finished his tale of success with, 'and that's the first good news.'

'What's the second?'

'We have a third case.'

'Really?' The moustachioed partner had perked up at this statement. 'Tell me all.'

'A chap called Jimmy James called in …'

'I can hardly believe the lack of imagination some parents display when naming their offspring,' interrupted Holmes.

'He's an allotment holder just outside the town and, apparently, someone is stealing his fruit, veg, and flowers on quite a large scale. He's given me some photographs of the bare patches that have been left – here, look – and he does have a real problem.'

Holmes examined the photographs briefly. 'And what, exactly, does he expect us to do about it?'

'That's the not-so-good news. I promised him that we would put his allotment under surveillance every other night, if he fills in in between. I positively assured him that we would catch whoever was doing this and hand them over to the police.'

'You did *what*?'

'Promised him we would ... do alternate nights,' Garden finished in a hurry. 'But don't worry, we don't start until Monday night, and he may even catch who's at it himself before that.'

'Well, thank you *very* much, Garden, for planning to deprive me of fifty per cent of my normal sleeping hours over a few bits of greengrocery.'

'He said nothing is ever taken during daylight hours when there are other people working on their allotments. Surely we could split it into two shifts? After all, it doesn't get dark until quite late at this time of the year, and one of us could take the early shift until about two-thirty, and the other from two-thirty until seven.'

'Marvellous! Absolutely bloody marvellous. And if we get inundated with other cases in the meantime, how the devil are we supposed to stay awake to investigate them?'

'If I'd turned him away, he would have told all his friends and neighbours, he's in such a state about it, and we could have been ruined before we even got going.'

Holmes thought about this for a moment and had to grudgingly agree, but he wasn't at all happy about it. 'Had he been to the police?'

'Too busy, apparently.'

'Had he complained to the council? To my knowledge, they rent out these plots.'

'Equally unable to help. We were his last resort.'

'Bugger! Just like Bognor. Well, let's hope that our vigilance proves fruitful, eh?' This pun cheered him up a little, as did the noise of the outside door opening and closing once again, also proving that the piper was back at his post and puffing away like billy-o in his efforts to attract the public's attention to this brand new and novel service available on its very own doorstep.

It was barely a minute later when Shirley Garden knocked lightly on the door and ushered in a well-built woman in her middle to late thirties. Before Mrs G could utter a word, she made her problem known in a very bombastic way.

'My name is Lesley Markham, and I have reason to believe that someone is using my car during the day without my permission,' she stated boldly in a no-nonsense voice.

Both Holmes and Garden sprang to their feet, standing almost to attention at this unexpectedly bossy woman in their midst. 'Please take a seat, Ms Markham …'

'Mrs.' Holmes's political correctness had tripped him up this time.

'Er, Mrs … Markham, and let me take a few details,' offered Holmes, risking an avuncular smile.

'I won't be fobbed off,' she announced, flinging herself into the client's chair in front of Holmes' desk and making it creak alarmingly in protest.

'First, tell me why you think someone has been using your car,' Holmes began.

'I don't think. I *know* someone has been using it. I only work ten minutes' walk away from my home, so I always go in to work on foot. I leave my car in the garage – *locked* in the garage – and usually only use it evenings and weekends.' At this statement she nodded her head once,

17

briefly and decisively, in emphasis.

'I began to suspect, last week, that all wasn't as it should be when I found my seat in not quite the right position. That I could explain away by my maybe, suddenly, having required a slightly adjusted position. Later that week, however, I was surprised to notice that there was more fuel in the tank than I knew I had. The volume seemed to have gone up instead of down. That was definitely impossible, and I knew, instinctively, that there was something wrong, so I made a note of the mileage.

'I then left it alone for a couple of days, as I wasn't planning to go out anywhere, and when I checked it this morning – by sheer coincidence, I understand, your opening day – against my handy little notebook, and there had been over a hundred miles driven since I last looked. I also examined the fuel gauge to find that the fuel was a bit lower and, once again, my seat wasn't in exactly the right position. Hmph!'

'Very damning evidence, Mrs Markham,' Holmes concurred. 'Would you be so kind as to tell me who else lives at your address?'

'What's that got to do with anything?'

'Please, madam, allow me to do my job. Their names, please?'

'There's my husband, Edward. He, of course, has his own car and works in Farlington Market. There's also my daughter, Ailsa, who is still at school, just finishing the first year of her A-levels. She's at the grammar school in Market Farlington and has a bus pass, which is just as well, as my husband leaves so early for work. That's it.'

'We shall put your garage under surveillance and have your little mystery solved in a trice, if you would be so good as to give me your address and contact numbers,' tootled Holmes, ever helpful.

As the good ship Markham sailed out of their office, Garden rose and went over to Holmes's desk. 'You do know what you've done, don't you?'

'Um, taken on another client?' Holmes asked in an interrogative voice. Surely he had done the right thing? Whatever could Garden be concerned about?

'You've agreed to us doing daytime surveillance as well as all-night surveillance,' said Garden, crossly.

'Crumbs!'

'Come on, let's go for some lunch. We might be about to die of exhaustion; the least we can do is make sure we don't pass out from lack of nourishment.'

'What about Shirley?'

'Mummy dearest can take a break after we're well fed and watered,' replied Garden, with uncharacteristic *schadenfreude*. Prior to his association with Holmes, he had hated his mother like poison. It was only with the older man's intervention that he had discovered his negative perception of their mother-son relationship had been fomented and manufactured entirely in his own mind.

Being a secret cross-dresser, he had assumed that his mother would hate him for it, and so had not had the guts to confess to her. They were, in his opinion, at daggers drawn, and he wanted to get away from her, his sad life at home with his mummy, and to dump his grey and boring office job. Once Holmes had heard this sad tale and made him confront the dragon Garden saw his mother as, it turned out that John H. had taken it upon himself to regard every communication between them as hostile. A busy woman herself, she had often left notes for him, texted him and sent him e-mails, all with the best of intentions. Garden's guilt at his secret passion had made him read all these the wrong way, and he had avoided her whenever possible, keeping his room firmly padlocked against intrusions into his secret world.

Holmes had not only uncovered the hoard of misapprehensions and misunderstandings, but had taken a liking to Shirley and, much to Garden's horror, taken her on as secretary and receptionist to the business. Her son, fortunately, had had time to make some adjustments to his attitude, as the premises were prepared and kitted out for their occupation. As luck would have it, there was a flat upstairs which he could move into once it had been redecorated and re-carpeted, and he grabbed this opportunity to live independently so that he could get used to his mother not being a monster.

Still unable to shake off his false premise about how his mother felt about him, he had moved in with Holmes in his Farlington Market apartment for a while, then gleefully moved into his own home – his own space – to reassess his attitude towards his mother. Now, they existed, in Shirley Garden's mind, in perfect harmony, in his, in a state of truce but, in this sudden, unmissable chance to score a point against her, he had expressed himself in the old way.

Chapter Two

Holmes became quite jolly after a bellyful of steak and kidney pudding, and not even the thought of both night- and day-time surveillance could dampen his spirits about what he saw as the inevitable success of their new business venture. When they returned to the office, he sent Shirley off to get herself something to eat, mumbled something about sorting out official dinner breaks for the three of them, and asked Garden to take his mother's place on reception until she returned.

Garden, well aware of who held the purse-strings in this partnership, settled himself down with some empty files and began to type up the notes from their first morning for printing. Every case, no matter how small, needed to be recorded and filed. One never knew when information would be useful in the future, and the empty filing cabinets had been leering at him since they opened the outside door, mocking their lack of either experience or history.

About two o'clock, another of the inevitable old ladies tottered into the office and collapsed into the client's chair. 'Good afternoon, young man,' she greeted him, fanning herself with a copy of the local newspaper which she had just purchased. 'It's getting rather warm out there today.'

Garden saved his computer notes and looked up with a welcoming smile. 'Good afternoon, madam. My name is John Garden, one of the partners in this firm. How may I be of assistance to you?'

'I have a problem with a house, Mr Garden, and I really don't know what I should do about it. I saw your signage and thought that you might be just the person who could advise me as to what to do for the best.'

'Tell me more, Mrs ...?'

'Everton. Eileen Everton. Miss. Pleased to meet you,' she replied holding out a claw-like hand to be shaken. 'I have inherited a house from my great-aunt, who died recently.'

'I'm sorry for your loss,' interjected Garden, trying to be as sympathetic as possible.

'Oh, I never liked her; she was a cranky old biddy, and she was ninety-eight when she passed on, but I was her only surviving relative, as she never married, and she was the last of the sisters of that generation.'

'So, do you wish to sell or rent out the house for income? If that were the case, I'd suggest you consulted with one of the local estate agents.'

'I haven't made up my mind yet what I want to do with it. If you would let me tell you the whole story from the beginning, without any interruptions, then you might understand why I came here, young man.'

Garden felt chastened, as he had done as a child when one of his mother's aunts had told him off for some mischief or minor misdemeanour. 'A very sensible idea, if I may say so,' he replied, and put on a face of concerned concentration.

'I used to go there a lot when I was little and it was such a wonderful rambling old house for a child to run around in. My mother and her aunt fell out when I was in my twenties and, I must confess, that I have been neither near nor by the place in decades.

'To my knowledge, all her possessions of any value were auctioned off under the aegis of her solicitor when she went into a nursing home and the house has stood there ever since, the worthless items still in situ, but without either a tenant or a caretaker.'

Garden was furiously scribbling notes as she spoke, and

looked up at this juncture to nod sagely. She continued, taking his nod to indicate that she should continue. 'I am aware of these facts because she has left everything of which she died possessed to me, and one of the conditions of her will was that the thing be published in the local newspaper and *The Times*, the way things used to happen in her day. I can only presume that she was cocking a last snook to those of her acquaintances who might have outlived her, to let them know that they wouldn't get a penny piece from her – a last demonstration of her spiteful nature.

'The will duly appeared in those publications about three weeks ago, and ever since, I have been having calls from all sorts of people; some in person and some on the telephone, trying to purchase the property, lease it, or represent me in its sale. I must admit to feeling rather harried. A couple of days ago, however, I had a personal visit from one of the local estate agents telling me that it had come to his knowledge that someone had entered the property, as a light had been seen burning there on some evenings.

'I am most unhappy about this, and I would like the place checked out. I don't want it entered at the moment, but I would like someone to take a look at it during the evenings. If I can commission you to undertake this task, we can discuss later what should be the next step.

'Meanwhile, I will continue with my cogitation on what I should do – whether to have it renovated, converted into flats, or sell it and, if I sell it, what condition do I want it to be sold in. I have a lot to consider. I think that when we have worked out whether someone has trespassed on the property, we should proceed to get the keys from my great-aunt's solicitor as he is still in possession of them, then I should like you to accompany me on a tour of inspection.'

'Why not your solicitor or an estate agent?' asked

Garden, thinking that her request was most unusual.

'Because both of them would have something to gain from my decision, and I realise that you will have nothing to get out of it, except for your normal fee. You will give me a more impartial opinion than either of those gentlemen.'

'That is very perceptive of you, and I think it is a well-made decision.'

'It is also the reason that I am not seeking an opinion from any of my friends and acquaintances, as they might harbour thoughts of benefitting from its sale or the proceeds when I eventually die.'

Garden didn't know quite how to respond to this overt expression of mortality, and merely smiled at her again, then a question suddenly struck him. 'Do you think you could go home and make a written record of who called or contacted you about the house, and anything that you remember them saying about it?'

'I can certainly do that. I may be old in years, but my memory is as sharp as ever. Perhaps when you have seen and considered that, we can work out a date from which you will keep an eye on the place for me.'

'Let me just make a note of your contact details, and take down the address of the property in question for our records. I shall await your next visit with eager anticipation.' He wasn't laying it down a bit thick, was he? But there was something about this old woman that made him feel almost like a Victorian gentleman coming to the aid of a maiden in distress – and, from her title, she was certainly still a maiden.

'I have in my handbag a photograph of the house as it used to be when I was a child. I turned it out of my mother's things, for I was fairly certain that such a likeness existed.' Miss Everton had no need to scuffle and fumble in her handbag to locate the photograph. As was to be expected from such a precise lady, it was tucked inside a little internal pocket of the receptacle, and she handed the small black and white image across the desk to him.

He took it and glanced at it, before staring a little harder. 'It's a fair-sized property. It must be worth quite a tidy sum: even if it's just knocked down for redevelopment, the land must be valuable.'

'That's exactly what I thought, and this little old lady's not for diddling, Mr Garden.' Miss Everton was evidently nobody's fool. 'I shall go away now, check my diary, for I keep a record of all calls and communications should I have a sudden attack of memory loss – one never knows – and bring you in the written statement as soon as it's ready. Then, we could discuss terms and conditions.' Very business-like.

'Thank you very much for coming in to consult with me today, Miss Everton. I shall look forward to your next visit in the near future.'

'Thank you very much, young man, for your time and, dare I say, your old-fashioned courtesy. Both have been very much appreciated.'

Miss Everton positively swept from the office, her head held high, her stature regal. She had set wheels in motion which would sort out the unsettling mystery that had suddenly appeared in her life, and make her decision about what to do with the property in the relative peace and quiet that would follow this resolution.

Shortly after her departure, Shirley returned from the quite short break she had taken for lunch, and Garden went back into the rear office to re-join Holmes, thoroughly excited about this new case he – he, Garden – had just taken on. The old man would be so jealous that it was not he who had manned the desk in their receptionist's absence.

The piper had also taken another break – playing must be quite exhausting work – when Shirley left the office, and they could hear him now, resuming with a reel. As

Garden got behind his desk, he couldn't decide whether his brainwave about using a piper to bring custom, or at least curiosity, to their door had left him fond of the pipes, or whether he would be glad never to hear them again. They had certainly carved a place in his memory for the launch of this business venture, and today would live in his mind forever.

'Oh God! Not another surveillance case. We're going to need clones if we carry on like this,' moaned Holmes, his head in his hands.

'Don't worry about it. I'm sure we'll get a quick result on both of the other cases we have, and this one won't even start properly until after Miss Everton has come in with her information about the various parties who have been bothering her about disposing of her inheritance,' Garden assured him.

'We'll manage. After all, we don't need to start at the allotment until Monday night, and we can be on guard outside Lesley Markham's house first thing in the morning. I'll go over there and you can open up here, if you like. I don't mind an early start. Then you can take the early stint at the allotment, and I'll relieve you at half past two so that you can, at least, get a few hours' uninterrupted sleep.'

At this selfless suggestion, Holmes' good humour was restored. 'John H., you're an absolute brick. This is going marvellously well, but I can see how easy it would be to get swamped with work.'

'I've got a sneaking suspicion that we could be facing a famine or feast situation, where we get snowed under, only to find ourselves with nothing to do for a while. But at least that will give us a chance to keep the files up to date and in order.'

But Holmes wasn't listening. He had heard the wail of the pipes in a sudden crescendo – he would have thought of it as the skirl, first thing this morning, but by midafternoon, it had definitely degenerated in his opinion into a caterwaul – and the bell that announced that someone had entered the outer office from the street rang out. 'More business, my boy; more business, by the sounds of it,' he said, smiling and rubbing his hands together in anticipation.

It proved, however, to be a reporter from the local paper, come to interview them for the business section of the newspaper, along with a photographer to take a shot of the outside, and the two men in their office.

'So, you've already solved two cases, and this is only your opening day,' said David Remnant, chief (and only) reporter for the *Hamsley Black Cross Echo*, usually just known as *The Echo*.

'Pretty slick, isn't it?' asked Holmes with what he considered the appropriate pride.

'And there are just the three of you working here?'

Holmes gave a grin of triumph, and announced that they did have their secret weapon, a deep undercover agent, but Garden feigned a coughing fit, then, when Holmes came over to pat him on the back, hissed in his ear, 'Don't blow Joanne's cover before she's even had the chance to frock up.'

'Now, can you tell the *Echo*'s readers about your fourth member of staff.' Remnant was nothing if not persistent.

'Can't do that, old boy,' Holmes replied, now that he had been put on his guard.

'What use is a secret weapon that everyone knows about,' commented Garden, filled with relief that Holmes hadn't, like Mr Toad before him, let boastfulness get in the way of practicality. He also didn't want it broadcast that he was a cross-dresser. That was an intimate secret known by only the three of them in the office, and that was how he would like it to stay. Joanne had to be kept well under wraps if she was to do any good in this chancy business venture.

As the reporter left, Holmes blushed an unlovely red in his embarrassment at almost outing Garden. 'I'm so sorry, old chap. I just didn't think. I was so damned pleased about this wonderful start we've had that I suppose I just wanted to show off.'

'And just how long have you lived at Toad Hall, Mr Toad?' asked Garden, sarcastically. 'Just remember that wartime saying, "Be like Dad. Keep Mum", and we'll be all right. And remember that walls still have ears, and that loose lips might not sink ships any more, but they can sink businesses like ours.'

'I'm not that old,' Holmes blustered in reply.

'Neither am I, but the old sayings make a lot of sense,' returned Garden.

Changing the subject completely, Holmes asked, 'What did you do about payment from those two old biddies that came in this morning?'

'I tried telling them that it was on the house, as a first day only offer, but neither of them would have any of it, and they both said that they would put a tenner in the post which we could either treat as payment, or just have a drink on them. They were just so grateful to get back their pets that they wanted to say thank you in some way.'

'Good man. Open a new accounts book and enter the two sums of ten pounds, "in return for locating missing animals". We're up and off, John H! We're actually in business.'

'May I suggest that *you* open an accounts book while I create a computer file to record the same, then we have a back-up in the book, should we be unfortunate enough to be infected by a virus? I've already typed up the notes of how the animals were located and raised paper files. If you would be so good as to print them out, I have paper files ready and waiting to take the notes.'

'Umm ... not sure how to do that.' Holmes was a real

technophobe.

'Then I'll wait until we've finished this first task, and we can go to the printer together so that I can show you.'

'Shouldn't stuff like that be Shirley's job?' asked Holmes, with a note of hope in his voice.

'It will be, but you need to know how to do it should you be on your own in the offices, and need stuff printed out. OK?'

'OK,' agreed Holmes, whose face told a totally different story.

They had no more new clients that first afternoon but two solved and three more on the go wasn't bad for a first day. In recognition of this, at closing time, Holmes suggested that they went for a drink together to celebrate this flying start.

'Actually, do you mind if I don't,' asked Garden 'only I've got to wash Joanne's hair tonight and there are so many versions it will take me ages to get them all dried and styled. 'Oh, OK,' said Holmes, a little nonplussed, 'would you mind awfully if I asked your mother to accompany me? I had envisaged it as the three of us, but I don't see why she and I should miss out on a little celebration drink just because you're busy.'

How could Garden refuse, when it had been put so nicely, and if it meant that he wouldn't have to go out for a noggin or two with his mother then he wasn't bothered at all. He still found it difficult to think of her as an ally rather than an enemy, and he trotted off upstairs – leaving Holmes to lock up – to his little flat, now so snug and cosy and, most importantly, just his.

Meanwhile, Holmes and Shirley set off and walked down the road to the Fox and Hounds. Holmes had decided against the tiny Coach and Horses next door to their offices as too crowded, and he had noted, on previous short visits, that the clientele were just 'not his sort' – not that he was a snob, you understand, merely a bit choosy about with whom he spent his leisure time.

After the incidents that had brought him and Garden together at the Black Swan Hotel, he really didn't fancy going there, either; not just yet. No doubt he'd grow out of his antipathy towards it over time but, for now, he felt he'd rather avoid its memory-filled ambience.

As they walked together, he lit his pipe, having asked Shirley's permission first, and was delighted to be informed that she liked the smell of a pipe. Apparently her father had always smoked one, so she associated the aroma with happy memories. Marvellous, thought Holmes, puffing contentedly away, only to have to knock the bowl out on the wall of the pub before they entered, such delights as a quiet smoke no longer being on the menu, as it were, in today's public houses.

He ordered a gin and tonic and a pint of best bitter at the bar, leaving Shirley to choose a table, and when he joined her again, he was in a really benevolent mood. Nothing could be finer than being interviewed by the local paper – memo to self, contact local newspapers in Farlington Market – solving a couple of cases, then going out for a drink with an attractive woman. Just for a moment, he was glad Garden hadn't wanted to join them. This felt very daring, out with a woman in a public house, and he considered himself, to coin an innocent old phrase, quite the gay dog.

When he got back to his decidedly Edwardian apartment that night – his rooms, as he liked to refer to them, in honour of his favourite fictional detective – Colin the cat found his owner (slave!) in a very jolly mood, and benefitted in the best way, by being served an extra-large portion of his favourite food, and being played with, with his favourite toy, a tattered old clockwork mouse that he had chewed nearly into extinction.

Chapter Three

At six o'clock Monday morning, Garden became aware of a furious intermittent buzzing sound and a flashing light. Dragged unwillingly from a dream in which he was being awarded a special medal for bravery, he suddenly became consciously aware that this was the alarm clock that his mother had given him years ago, when he found it particularly difficult to get up for work, a first symptom of his disillusionment with office life. He had retired it after only a week, as it was a ferocious and startling wake-up call, but that he had sensibly re-instated for mornings when he would have to get up extra early for his work as a detective.

His befuddled mind soon grasped the fact that he was on surveillance that morning, watching Mrs Markham's house to discover who had been borrowing her car without permission, then making every effort to cover up their tracks. A quick icy blast followed by a stinging hot ten minutes under the shower soon brought his senses into line, and he dressed carefully in the few dull office clothes he had retained for just this sort of situation, congratulating himself on his foresight.

Sometimes it was important to look nondescript, something he had abandoned when he had sloughed off his skin as an office worker in an insurance company. Now he dressed in brightly coloured clothes and patterns, and had felt like a caterpillar that had metamorphosed inside its cocoon and emerged as a beautiful butterfly. Well, today he was back in moth's clothing, but it would do him a good turn. Who would ignore someone trying to watch them surreptitiously if they were wearing red trousers, a turquoise shirt, yellow tie, and green jacket?

Wearing his old uniform of grey suit and white shirt, he set off for the target property feeling determined to succeed, if a little tired. As usual, when one plans to go to sleep early, one's mind is plagued with interesting and diverting thoughts, and last night had been no different. His brain had constantly thrown up scenes that might occur in the course of his new career, and he had not managed to derail this interesting train of thoughts until one-thirty, or thereabouts.

Here he was, however, off on his first surveillance job in plain clothes, and he imagined himself as an agent deep undercover on a dangerous mission that would save the world, and gain him rewards and gratitude from the British government. Men are much better at this sort of thing than women in that they are all frustrated heroes.

Mrs Markham's house proved to be in an area where parking was allowed on the opposite side of the road, behind which was a small area of grass for local children to play on, and which sprouted a bench or two if one were too old to play on the swings and slide.

He had put a pack of sandwiches and a flask of tea in the car, cannily picking up a newspaper on his way out of town, taking advantage of the fact that newsagents have to open very early every day, and felt he was well prepared.

Parking his car in the one and a half car-lengths considerately left by two other vehicles, he unfolded his newspaper and began to scan the front page, his window slightly ajar so that he could hear if anyone left the house opposite. The road was a quiet one, especially at this time of the morning.

At seven thirty, the front door opened and a tall, slim man, the physical opposite of Mrs Markham, left the house, driving away in the car that had been parked on the drive. That must be Mr Markham, thought Garden, and assumed that the daughter of the house would be next.

At exactly eight o'clock, the front door opened again, and he saw Mrs Markham seeing off a teenage girl who looked like an exact, if smaller, model of her mother. Having waved off her beloved offspring to catch the school bus, the door closed again, and Garden became rather absorbed in his newspaper, waiting for the sound of the front door opening and closing again to announce that the mistress of the house was on her regular short walk to work.

After a while, Garden started on the crossword, having got fed up with the stories, and not being at all interested in the business or sports pages. When he next looked at his watch, it was a quarter to ten, and still he had heard and observed no movement from the house. What was going on? He'd give it half an hour more before going over to investigate. Maybe she left by the back door, and he had, therefore, not seen her leave.

At eleven fifteen, he folded his paper, put it down on the passenger seat and got out of the car, before approaching the house trying to look as if he were just a regular caller. He rang the doorbell just to make sure, whilst planning to gain access to the rear of the property to have a good look through the windows.

To his surprise, the door was opened almost immediately by Mrs Markham herself. Giving him a puzzled smile, she said 'Good morning, Mr Garden. How can I help you? Is there some information which you need, to further your enquiries?'

The only reply Garden could think of in his utter shock at finding the woman still in the house was, 'Why aren't you at work?'

'Did I forget to mention that today's my day off? I'm so sorry, Mr Garden. How very remiss of me. Have you been here long?'

'Only since seven o'clock,' replied the detective in a

voice full of self-pity.

'I'm so sorry. I don't know how to apologise enough for my omission. I hope I haven't inconvenienced you too much.'

She had, but he was loath to say so, as it would definitely not be good for business. He would do what anyone else with half a brain would do in the circumstances, and blustered that there was no harm done, he had almost cracked the crossword while he had been waiting, and that he would be back the next morning, on duty, as agreed.

He left the woman still on the doorstep apologising profusely for her oversight, got back into his car, and drove off with a screech of tyres to vent his ire. He had made the effort to get up at, what for him, was a totally unreasonable hour, he would be on surveillance again tonight, this time at Mr James's allotment, with the prospect of being woken up by that sadistic alarm clock at the same time tomorrow morning. So much for his daydreams of saving the world!

Holmes had arrived in the office early, at eight thirty, fifteen minutes ahead of Shirley, and he was walking on air. His drink on Saturday night with Garden's mother had turned into two drinks, followed by coffee and accompanied by a very long chat, and the alcohol had given him Dutch courage enough to ask her if she would like to go out to dinner with him. To his absolute delight and surprise, she had agreed, and said that she would look forward to it, next Saturday evening being set as the day of what Holmes thought of as their very first date.

Now he could bedevil himself with other questions about dating etiquette, having cleared the initial hurdle: whether to kiss or not on a first date, whether to invite her back for coffee after dinner, what to say if she invited *him* back for coffee, and did coffee *mean* coffee, or was it code for something else entirely?

To put it bluntly, he was in a right old lather, just with the thought that he supposed she was now his girlfriend. Did that mean that Garden was his almost-stepson? No! He was rushing much too far ahead in his mind: best just to try to banish the subject from his thoughts. Saturday would come quickly enough.

When Shirley Garden arrived, he gave her 'good morning' and blushed as she thanked him again for Saturday night, saying that he was a thoroughly fascinating man to talk to. He returned to his office, his heart aflutter, and began to wonder where good old Garden was, even going as far as mounting the staircase to the flat to knock on his door in case he had overslept.

It slowly dawned on him that Garden wasn't oversleeping the sleep of the just, but was out in his car keeping an eye on Mrs Markham's garage and her precious car, and he came back downstairs again with the feeling of embarrassment. His mind really wasn't on the ball this morning. How could he have forgotten the arrangements they had made on Saturday with that pushy woman? Then he remembered the surveillance that would have to be undertaken on Mr James's allotment, and began to worry that he would be too tired to be on his toes for Saturday night, if that turned into a protracted affair.

Affair. The very word made him shiver with excitement, and he thought back to the last girlfriend he had had. It was so long ago that his memories of her seemed to be in black and white. In his mind's eye he saw himself as a young new noise in the local government offices, and he had had the temerity to don a pair of extra-wide flares, a kipper tie, and a psychedelic shirt for their very first date, not realising that, as with so many things in his life, he was two steps behind trend.

Alison, her name was, a pretty, shy girl from the office. In those days, although he had already developed his bumptious side, underneath he was a shy, retiring soul, and they had never got further than a kiss and a bit of a cuddle. It must be thirty years, now, since he had ventured out on the town with a pretty girl on his arm.

Now he looked back on the scene, his hair must have been longer than hers, and all over his head. He was sure he had a photograph of the two of them together at one of the office dos; he must look it out when he got home, just for old times' sake, and to take his mind off what lay ahead in the near future. Elated, he certainly was, but terrified almost out of his wits at the same time.

Garden's arrival at the office was just as full of emotion, but he was less walking on air than ready to punch the living daylights out of it if it didn't get out of his way. He slammed open the outer door, startling Shirley, greeted her with a curt, ''Llo,' and exploded into the rear office as if he were a demon appearing on stage by the theatrical magic of a trapdoor.

Holmes, who was enjoying a cup of tea at the time, spilt quite a bit down his tie in surprise, as his younger partner stomped over to his desk, flung himself into his chair, and exploded with, 'Bloody woman,' then sat there in brooding silence.

'Whatever's the matter, old chap?' asked Holmes, rubbing at his tie with his handkerchief in the vain hope that the stain that had just arrived there would disappear as if by magic if he rubbed hard enough at it.

Garden was too furious to speak for a few moments, merely sitting bolt upright in his office chair, seething and mentally cursing the forgetful Mrs Markham with all the un-pleasantries his mind could conjure up. Eventually he took a few deep gulps of air, and began his sorry tale.

'First, I was awakened by the devil's own alarm clock at six o'bloody-clock, and parked opposite the Markhams' house by seven o'clock. I wore my drabbest clothes so that I wouldn't stick out like a sore thumb – just look at me! –

and I watched as, first Mr Markham left for work at seven thirty, then the daughter departing at eight, then nothing; a big, fat zero – no departure of Mrs Markham, and no signs of life inside the house at all.

'Eventually, at 11.15, I went over to the house and rang the bell whilst working out how to get to the rear of the property to get a peek through the windows to check that the woman hadn't collapsed or fallen. *Then*, she only goes and opens the door to me, and says how sorry she is, but she *hadn't mentioned* yesterday that today was her day off from work. How silly of her, et cetera, et cetera, while I stood there gaping like a goldfish, trying to clear my mind of scenes of having to call an ambulance for assistance. If I'd acted how I felt at that moment, calling an ambulance wouldn't have been an option, it would have been a necessity!'

'Hold your horses, Garden, old chap,' soothed Holmes, pressing a button on his desk and requesting that Shirley bring through a cup of strong coffee for her son, who had worked himself up into a state of fury over a simple misunderstanding.

A soft word often turns away wrath, but in this case, Garden felt like going over and beeping Holmes one on the nose, and only with his mother's swift arrival with a receptacle of liquid caffeine did he rein in his temper. 'It's a lovely day, Garden. Why don't you take that outside and have a nice long smoke, then we'll discuss what happened to you further,' the older man advised.

Seeing this as the wisest thing to do, Garden shed his jacket, undid the top button of his shirt, loosened his tie, and went off out of the back door to where there was a bench, placed especially for the smokers of the firm which, at this moment, numbered two. As Garden stewed on the bench he thought to himself, if only we could get something interesting to investigate, like a pair of ears in a cardboard box!

He returned to the office just in time to surprise Holmes, who was having a quiet chuckle to himself about his partner's labour-in-vain start to the day, when the smile was wiped off his face by Garden's reminder that they were both on allotment surveillance that night.

'Yes dammit! I remembered that this morning.'

At this exclamation, the phone on Garden's desk rang. It was a call from Jimmy James, who explained he was on early lunch break today, and he thought he'd better let them know that there had been no action at the allotment over the weekend. That definitely confirmed that they would have to be in attendance all evening and throughout the wee small hours.

The rest of the morning was spent scouring the Hamsley Black Cross and Farlington Market local papers' lost and found columns, to see if there was any business there to be drummed up. There were a couple of pleas from pet owners whose little darlings had gone missing, but a few telephone calls ascertained that both had returned home of their own accord, and that was that for the morning.

With Holmes's new lunchtime regime, Shirley was on first break from eleven thirty until twelve thirty, with Garden sitting in for her in the office. Garden was to take the twelve thirty to one thirty slot, and Holmes, the one-thirty to two-thirty break, thus ensuring that there were always two people on hand to deal with any business that came in.

These times were absolutely barren of custom, but at three o'clock, a woman came into the office with the news that the bank had not opened that morning. Efforts to contact the manager at home had raised no response, and eventually, one of the staff had called the police, who had gained entrance to the premises, only to discover that the safety deposit boxes and the cash machine had been emptied, as had the safe, of any cash that was stored inside it. This was news indeed.

'A bank robbery.' exclaimed Holmes. 'There's meat for our platter.'

'I'd rather you concentrated on my problem first,' stated the woman who had brought these serious tidings. 'I'm here to engage your services, not to sit and listen to you witter on about who might have done over the local bank.'

Holmes immediately put on his business face, and asked her to take a seat and tell him how he could help her. 'I'm sure my husband's having an affair, but I can't seem to catch him out. I want you to keep an eye on his movements for me and report back if you can secure any evidence of him playing away,' she stated baldly.

'Although we should be perfectly delighted to take on your commission, I must be honest with you and inform you that we could not commit ourselves to any surveillance just at the moment,' Holmes explained, for once thinking before he overloaded them with work that there were not enough of them to cover.

'That's alright. He's just gone up to Northumberland to stay with his mother for a week. That's why I've taken this opportunity to call in to speak to you,' she retorted.

'That couldn't suit us better,' Holmes assured her, and began to tease the details out of her. 'Your name, please?'

'Deirdre Matcham.'

'Your husband's name?'

'Stephen.'

'Your address?'

'68 River Road, Hamsley Black Cross.'

'Your husband's place of employment?'

'Glover and Pure, Estate Agents, just next door to the bank.'

'Do you have a recent photograph of him?'

'Here,' she said, removing a snapshot from her handbag. 'That was taken only last month when we went away for the weekend.'

Holmes took the proffered likeness and tried not to gape as he noticed that the man appeared considerably younger than his wife, whom he judged to be about forty-five. 'Can you tell me what first made you suspicious?'

'I was getting out the suits of his that needed to go to the dry cleaner's, and I found a partly used packet of condoms in one of the pockets.'

'And, you don't, um, er, use them yourselves?' Holmes was definitely embarrassed to be involved in a conversation concerning a means of birth control, with all its connotations of the act of having sex.

'No. Never have. I was sterilised years ago,' she replied in a direct manner, embarrassing him even further with the suggestion of women's bits and pieces that this statement carried with it.

'Er, anything else, Mrs, um, Matcham?' Holmes was definitely rattled.

'If you mean have I ever found lipstick on his collar, then the answer's no, but he's been getting a lot of phone calls on a mobile I've never seen before, and which he carries with him always, even sleeping with it under his pillow, and he has been disappearing off on little jaunts that he claims are for work.'

'Have you spoken to his employer?' asked Garden, deciding to give Holmes a little break to regain his composure.

'Have I heck as like. That office operates in complete chaos, most of the appointments being in the employees' heads rather than a formal diary, and nobody ever seems to know where anybody else is at any given time. If I made enquiries there, they'd all stick together. They're all men and probably used to covering for each other during the odd fling.'

'May we have the known mobile numbers you have for your husband and, of course, his office number?'

This dealt with, she gave her husband's working hours, as far as she knew them, and her own contact numbers, told them she would be in touch as soon he resumed his usual routine, and was about to leave when Garden asked, 'Have you tried calling his mobile when he says he's not in the office?'

'My husband seems to have no end of trouble with his mobile. It's either not in an area where he can get a signal or out of battery when I try to call him. Nobody can be that unlucky.'

'Ring us when you want us to proceed.'

'And I'd like a copy of your charges, terms and conditions, if you would be so kind.'

Dammit! Holmes knew he had omitted to order something when he organised the stationery, and this was the thing he had overlooked, now brought to his attention in very embarrassing circumstances. 'We're still awaiting delivery of those from the printers as we are such a new firm, but I promise I will deliver one personally as soon as they arrive,' he blustered, hoping that this excuse would suffice.

It did, and Mrs Matcham left the office a slightly happier woman than she had entered it.

Holmes gave her a five-minute start, and started urgent consultations with Garden about what they should charge per hour, and how much they should ask for up front. This agreed, he got straight on to the printer and gave his order while Shirley did a mock-up of the handout for him to send over by e-mail. On this particular piece of public information, their USP was free consultations but, if business picked up, this may be subject to change.

'Phew, Garden, that was a close-run thing.' Holmes mopped the perspiration from his forehead with a pristine white handkerchief, and looked over at Garden sheepishly.

'Jolly good improvisation though,' Garden batted back to him. 'Very quick thinking by you.' It was always better to butter up the man's ego and keep him sweet. 'And we have another new case, to boot.'

'We're on our way, my boy. I can just see us in a decade's time, with another ten branches.'

'Don't forget you get the early watch on allotment surveillance tonight,' added Garden, instantly bringing the man back down to earth in a sentence, and earning the expletive, 'Bum!'

On reflection, Garden silently agreed with him. He had just realised that he would have to take second watch at the allotments, and go straight on to watching Lesley Markham's garage in search of someone taking her car without consent during working hours – and he couldn't guarantee that they'd be nice and cooperative and take the vehicle early in the morning. He might be there for most of the day. He'd be destroyed from lack of sleep by the time the premises were locked up for the night. Not quite what he had in mind in the excitement of setting up this venture.

Before they closed the office for the day, there were three callers whose arrival caused great consternation for the two business partners. The first one came in about four o'clock. 'Good afternoon,' he greeted all three of them as they sat in the front office having afternoon tea together, this half of the day having been very quiet, but not wanting to leave the outer office unmanned.

'Good afternoon,' Holmes replied, standing and holding out a hand to greet their new prospective client. 'How can I help you?'

'I wondered where you kept the patio furniture. Is it out the back? Do you have anything in cast iron?' He smiled.

Three startled faces stared back at him, one of them with storm clouds gathering on its forehead. 'Are you mad, man?' asked Holmes, an edge of steel in his voice.

The man stopped smiling and replied, 'It says Homes and Gardens on the window.'

'It says *Holmes* – with an "l" – and Garden on the

window, and it also clearly states that we are private investigators. I am Sherman Holmes and this is my business partner, John H. Garden. We deal with matters that need investigating, not garden furniture. No, you are very much mistaken.'

'Sorry to have bothered you,' replied the now-puzzled man, walking out and looking hard at the window to ascertain that it was not the three inhabitants of the building who were hallucinating.

Half an hour later, a middle-aged woman came in and asked if they stocked any barbecues, and just before five o'clock, a middle-aged man came in in search of potting compost.

'Right, that's it!' barked Holmes. 'Garden, get on to the signwriter straight away and tell him to come back and re-do the lettering on the window with the emphasis on what we do. I will *not* be mistaken for a garden centre. It's outrageous.'

As soon as he had done that, Garden sloped off upstairs to his flat. If he had to be up ready for his shift at the allotment by half-past two, then he needed all the sleep he could get considering the time that he had risen this morning, and the fact that he would have to do back-to-back surveillances the next day.

He would spend an hour or so practising putting on false eyelashes, a skill that he hadn't yet perfected, eat a microwave dinner for two – the ones for one weren't big enough to keep a bird alive – then set his alarm clock so that he could get up to relieve Holmes.

Holmes met Jimmy James at the entrance to the allotments at just before ten o'clock. Having no idea what to dress in for this activity, and not owning anything as unobtrusive as a pair of jeans and an old sweatshirt, Holmes was as immaculate as ever in a light suit and a white shirt. For the sake of the informality of the situation, he had not worn a tie.

'Blimey, guv'nor, if he's using a torch you'll glow back at him like a lantern with that pale gear on,' commented the client.

Holmes blustered that it didn't do to lower standards just because a job didn't involve a desk and documents, to which James replied, 'You haven't done this sort of thing before, have you?'

Again, Holmes squirmed, and changed the subject to that of where he should position himself to get a good view of the relevant lot, but not be in clear view, and James directed him towards one of the last plots which had a small shed on it. 'If you wait just here in the shadow of the building, that should do you fine, and you can look down the plots, but not be seen by anyone approaching from the entrance.

Carefully hidden thus far behind his back, Holmes produced a folding fishing stool and prepared to take his place. 'So, you have got some common sense then,' the allotment-holder grunted, then added, 'I'll expect your partner to report in tomorrow morning first thing, so that I know whether there's been any action or not: nothing happened last night, so you're in with a chance,' before disappearing off into the darkness.

Holmes didn't like the sound of that possibility but nevertheless made himself as comfortable as possible on his tubular seat and began his long, boring wait.

Except it wasn't as boring or as long as he had expected. About midnight, he heard rustling noises coming from the entrance to the allotments plots, and chanced a peek round the small wooden structure. At the end of the enclosed area he could see a figure creeping furtively down towards the back, what looked like a holdall in one hand and a garden fork in the other. The only light was from the moon, but it was bright enough for him to duck back into his hiding place.

As the figure drew level with the shed, Holmes rushed out at it with his arms out in front of him, shouting, 'Aaaargh!' The unexpectedness of this took the figure off balance, and it dropped what it was carrying, gave a yell of fear, and lost its balance, rolling down on to the earth of the vegetable plot, crushing a few plants on his way. Holmes, similarly unbalanced, toppled down on top of him, and the two men began to grapple very gingerly, neither wanting to be hurt. Eventually the detective's opponent managed to regain his feet and ran off in the opposite direction.

Holmes tore off after the fleeing culprit who, before he left the allotments, turned and faced the good private detective, reaching out and landing a direct punch to the eye, then continued fleeing from this ghastly, pale apparition that had so startled him.

With one hand over his eye, Holmes tottered back to collect his stool then returned to his car where he immediately phoned Mr James, and then the police station, to report an attempted theft and several similar previous incidents, and a personal assault to boot.

Garden was terrified out of a deep sleep with the ringing of the telephone beside his bed in the early hours, and nearly jumped out of bed with surprise, adrenaline pumping through his system, his heart pounding. Who on earth could it be at this time of night?

It was with a feeling of great relief that he realised that he would not have to get up soon and go and sit in a deserted allotment waiting for someone who, in all probability, would not show up. 'So, you got him?' he asked Holmes.

'Not quite, but I got his holdall and garden fork, and I'm just about to take them into the police station. No doubt there will be fingerprints that can be matched to the owner, and earth that can be matched to that at the allotments. They'll have to take it seriously now. Mr

James is driving over to meet me there, and I shall come into the office a bit late tomorrow, to compensate for my very late night.'

Chapter Four

Garden was up bright and early the next morning, and down in the office at eight thirty to turn the phones off answerphone. He found that there had been one message the night before, at about ten o'clock. Replaying it, he heard the voice of Eileen Everton, but with a slight quaver in it, as if she were nervous about something.

'Um, this is a message for, um, Mr Garden. This is Miss Eileen Everton calling about that house I told you I'd inherited. My neighbour has just got back from a visit to her daughter, and she passed the old place on her journey home. She said there were lights moving about inside it – she thought they might be torches. I shall be in to see you later today, as I really think we ought to get the keys and have a look around inside.'

The main door pinged as his mother let herself in, and with this noise, something pinged in his mind. He was supposed to be on surveillance outside Mrs Markham's house right now! Grabbing a light jacket from the back of his chair, he hared out of the office without a goodbye, rushing into his car and squealing off towards the place where he had intended to be an hour ago, hoping his absence had not been noted.

He did not have time to stop for today's newspaper, but he would have to be content with using yesterday's to hide the brightness of the magenta shirt he had put on this morning with nary a thought for where he should have been headed. He had turned off his alarm after Holmes had rung him, almost as a reflex reaction, and his mind had been a blank when he woke at his usual time, without the help of artificial aids.

He drove slowly down the second half of the road in which the Markhams lived and parked as unobtrusively as he could. Five minutes after he had arrived, the formidable figure of Mrs Markham came out of the front door, checked to see that it was locked, then marched down the front path and turned right, on her way to the office. He had made it just in time, and she gave a little wave to him with her right hand as she disappeared up the road.

Turning back to yesterday's news, he was upset to find that he had finished both crosswords, and was left with only the minor puzzles to engage his mind. Only a few minutes later, however, he was alerted by a movement out of the corner of his eye, and spotted the head and shoulders of the youngest member of the household, Ailsa Markham, peering round the corner of the end of the terrace. She must have seen the diminishing figure of her mother hurrying off to her office, stayed stock still for the time it took for the now-distant figure to disappear round a corner, and allowed the rest of her body to follow her head and shoulders.

She slowly rounded the corner with a boy in tow, and they both headed for the locked garage. Slipping a hand into the pocket of her school uniform, she took out a small key and unlocked the garage door. That done, she extracted a set of car keys from her rucksack, and the two of them went into the garage and got into the car.

Ailsa backed the car on to the drive, got out and closed and locked the garage door, then reversed out into the road and drove away. Garden dutifully followed them. It might be job done for someone else, but he felt it was his duty also to report where the car was taken.

The girl drove first to the woods, where the two of them left the car and went into the remains of an old hut. Emerging forty minutes later looking a bit dishevelled, she then drove to a coffee bar in Farlington Market, leaving the car in a convenient space not far from her destination.

Garden took the opportunity to double-park and shoot into a coffee shop to emerge a couple of minutes later with the largest serving of Americano they offered, then looked for somewhere to park where he could still observe the coffee bar door.

The couple of youngsters emerged some thirty minutes later, and he followed them again, just to end up back at the Markham house, where they went inside, after locking the car and placing it neatly in the garage. The boy emerged at lunchtime and sauntered off down the road whistling. It sounded like he'd enjoyed his morning. Twice! Little madam; lucky boy!

He could now go back to the office to write up his report and submit it to his client, who would, no doubt, be most displeased. And, no doubt, her daughter would hate his guts forever. Hard luck, Ailsa! He was only doing his job, for which he would also issue an invoice. They were beginning to earn.

Just after they had all returned from their split-timed lunch breaks, Miss Everton entered the office and asked Shirley if Mr Garden were free to see her. Shirley duly buzzed through, confirmed Mr Garden's 'free' status, and ushered the old lady through to the inner office.

'Good afternoon to you, Miss Everton. I got the message you left on our answer-service. Take a seat and tell me everything you can about what your neighbour saw.' Holmes looked up in confusion. Garden never mentioned that there had been a message for the business, and he scowled across the room at his partner.

Garden smiled back innocently and turned to face his client with an expression of deep interest on his face. Holmes may have been the hero of the night, grappling with a would-be thief and having to face the wrath of the local police, whom he had pipped at the post, but Garden had wrapped up a case since the office had opened, and was dead chuffed with himself.

'It was the woman next door, who knocked on my door just as I was going up to bed last night. She'd just driven back from her daughter's house, and as she'd passed where the house is, she said she could see lights moving around inside it. Well, she knew that wasn't right, so she came straight round to tell me, and I said I'd talk to you about getting the keys and going out there one evening to keep watch. If nothing happens, we could go in the next day and see if we can work out what has been going on.'

'Why don't we get the keys this afternoon and have a look around it before it gets dark today, see if whoever it was has left any traces behind?' asked Garden, thinking that doing things this way round was a much better plan, as he could get an idea of the layout of the rooms so that he could identify where whoever the intruders were in the house, if they returned.

'Young man, you are quite right; just get on and do it, whatever it is. I shall trot round to my solicitor and collect the keys forthwith. I shall return here a little later.'

At this juncture, Holmes made a face of such longing across the room that Garden suggested, 'Why don't I and my partner pick you up from home, maybe about five thirty, then you could get yourself something to eat before we go out.'

'How very courteous of you, Mr Garden. I should be very grateful to get home and have a little rest before leaving the house again. I shall see you at five thirty.'

When Garden returned from seeing out the elderly lady, Holmes face was like that of a wistful child, looking forward to a treat. 'Thank you very much for including me in this expedition. I caught up with my sleep a bit this morning, and I didn't come in until eleven o'clock, so I feel as fresh as a daisy,' he said, stifling a huge yawn, which belied his words of bravado.

At five fifteen, a bleary-eyed Holmes and a better

rested Garden left the office leaving Shirley Garden to lock up, and headed off for the address that Miss Everton had given them. It proved to be a detached house in the style of the 1930s, with a small but immaculate front garden. Holmes rang the doorbell, and their client answered it fairly promptly, but looking as if she had just woken up from an afternoon nap. 'Good day to you again, gentlemen,' she greeted them, and went to fetch a light jacket, checking that she had the relevant keys for the empty property. Popping these in her old-fashioned handbag, she closed the door firmly, locking the deadlock, and followed them to their cars.

'I've never had one,' she announced, settling herself into the passenger seat of Garden's car.

'Never had one of what?' he asked, caught off guard.

'A car,' she replied. 'I just never seemed to get round to learning to drive.'

'Well, I should be grateful if you would act as navigator, because neither of us recognises the address you gave us.'

She directed him away from the town and to the north, where a fair acreage of woodland brooded. She then guided him down a small road through the trees to a position from which he could not immediately recognise a house, then pointed through the foliage to a property just visible, if one knew it was there.

'It's quite isolated, isn't it?' he remarked. 'I'm surprised your neighbour noticed that it had intruders.'

'It's so dark in here after twilight, with no street lighting, that any light looks like a beacon,' she replied. 'Here, turn left. There are no gates marking the entrance to the drive.'

Garden indicated, and Holmes followed suit behind him. Using two cars guaranteed that they could both head for their separate homes afterwards, with Garden taking Miss Everton, and Holmes free to head for Farlington

Market and his Edwardian-style apartment.

After about two hundred yards, a hideous Victorian pile loomed before them, giving the appearance that they were about to enter the realms of a Gothic novel. After parking, Miss Everton withdrew the keys from her handbag, and pulled out a huge key for the front door. It creaked open with all the enthusiasm of a door in a horror film, revealing a cavernous hall behind it. The sun had not set yet, so there was some natural light filtering through the dirty window panes.

'Just as I remember it,' the old lady sighed, in a nostalgic breath, 'only rather smaller. I suppose memories get more inflated in one's mind after a while. The staircase is still quite magnificent, though.'

Holmes looked around him and said, 'There's some disturbance of the dust on the floors. There must have been someone in here recently.'

'And someone's thrown cigarette butts in the fireplace,' Garden added, walking over to a vast stone edifice in which, once, a welcoming fire would have burnt. 'Are all the internal doors locked, do you know, or are we free to wander around, Miss Everton?'

'I have no idea, it's so long since I've been here,' she replied. 'I only have the keys to the external doors – front, kitchen, and French doors from the drawing room.'

Garden tried the first door to his right and found the kitchens and scullery, with dirty cups on a wooden draining board beside a double shallow stone sink, and the presence of an electric kettle. 'There's definitely been someone using this place for something, but whether it's kids or not, we have no idea, at the moment,' he opined.

Here, too, there was evidence of recent feet disturbing the years of dust that had accumulated whilst Miss Everton's aunt had been in a nursing home. A rusty range stood brooding in an old chimney breast, and a tap dripped monotonously over one of the sinks.

'I bet this place is eerie at night,' said Holmes, evidently affected by the atmosphere of neglect and abandonment, and looking over his shoulder covertly.

'It was a bit unsettling, in my opinion, when I used to visit it. I always felt as if I were being secretly watched,' cut in Miss Everton, with a shudder. 'There's no way I could live here. It's just a question of how to sell it: whether to someone who will demolish it and build something else, or someone who wants to convert it into something like a nursing home or flats.'

Holmes also gave a shudder, and thought that being left here when one was old and deprived of one's independence would be his worst nightmare. 'Shall we move on?' he asked.

'Not before I photograph the evidence,' replied Garden, who already had out his smartphone and was snapping away. 'Never know when a bit of photographic evidence will be useful,' he explained, as the other two looked at him in surprise. 'If you want to prosecute whoever has been using this place, it's as well to have evidence of their presence,' he finished.

They visited the drawing room next, which also showed signs of recent occupation, with a carelessly discarded whisky bottle in the fireplace along with another collection of cigarette butts. The dining room had a definite aroma, easily traced to the remains of a Chinese take-away meal on a card table.

'This is very sloppy,' commented Holmes. 'Whoever's been in here doesn't seem to think there's much likelihood of Miss Everton coming to check on her inheritance in the near future. Good, the other internal doors aren't locked.'

The morning room, study and library showed very little signs of disturbance, but the stairs showed the presence of some traffic. They moved upwards, discovering that pieces of furniture not in good enough condition to sell had been left to rot and fall to pieces. No one had cleared the place properly, although Miss Everton swore that a firm had been instructed – and paid – to empty it completely. Even a four-poster bed, in a state of great dilapidation, still sat, forlorn, in one of the large bedrooms.

Holmes had become even more susceptible to the air of decay, and jumped whenever one of the others spoke. 'Are there any attic rooms?' asked Garden, making his partner actually appear to levitate, for a fraction of a second.

'Of course there are, Mr Garden. You can hardly imagine that a place like this ran without servants,' she replied coolly.

'Where is the access, Miss Everton?' he asked politely.

'At the end of this corridor through that narrow door. That leads to the staircase to the servants' night-time quarters. There are several rooms up there, for this place took some running, with the sort of catering and entertaining the original owners would have done.'

Holmes certainly looked haunted as they climbed the dim, narrow staircase to the top of the house. As they progressed through the maze of small rooms, Holmes actually yelped at what turned out to be a dressmaker's dummy in the dark corner of one of the rooms, and Garden looked at him in surprise. He hadn't supposed his partner was that susceptible to atmosphere.

There was no disturbance to the accumulated dust and grime up here, indicating that this had not been an area whoever had trespassed had found of interest or use. When they left the old house, the sun was sinking in the west, and the outside of the building seemed to be brooding in its arboreal hideaway.

Holmes drove away with relief, and Garden loaded Miss Everton back into his passenger seat, intending to drop her at her own house, preparatory to returning to his flat and practising his make-up technique for the next time 'Joanne' would be needed. He had a new dress that he very much wanted to try on, but had not had the opportunity, so far, to admire in his full-length mirror.

Before she left the car, they discussed when they should return to the house in the woods and arranging, to meet after she had phoned and confirmed which evening she was next available, with the same transport arrangements as tonight but the next rendezvous, at nine thirty.

Arriving home Garden was now free to slap on as much war paint as his heart desired. He had put on his new dress, then, after admiring himself from every possible angle except that of standing on his head, he sat down at his dressing table to apply some make-up, being careful to don a protector for his clothes like that used by a hairdresser when cutting hair.

He was just finishing back-combing his hair when there was a ring at the front doorbell. Although it was very late to expect a caller, his professional instinct, newly minted just a few days ago, ripped off his clothes protector and raced down the stairs, with a dawning realisation that he wasn't at all himself at the moment and would have to be fairly inventive to whoever was disturbing his evening.

Arranging his face into a smile he opened the door to find Mr James outside. The client gave him a bemused look at the unexpectedness of a woman answering the door, and Garden remembered, just in time, that he should not know the man's name. 'Can I help you?' he asked, in his best Joanne voice.

'I was looking for either Mr Holmes or Mr Garden,' stated Mr James, trying to see behind Garden to see if either of these gentlemen was present.

'I'm afraid they're both out on a case at the moment. May I be of any help?' Garden asked, offering no explanation as to who he was, or who he was pretending to be.

James' eyes moved down the figure of the tall woman, finally resting on her feet, which were encased in tartan socks and stout Hush Puppies. Following his gaze with a sinking feeling, Garden improvised wildly. 'I have such a problem with my feet after a day spent in stilettos that I usually change into something more comfortable for the evenings,' he lied shamelessly.

Giving him/her a very old-fashioned look, James explained that he had just called round to offer his thanks for the help the new firm had given him in ridding him of his greengrocery thief. He had just left the police station after giving his statement – and being informed that the perpetrator had been picked up and was the purveyor of vegetables at a local market – and he had just called round on the off-chance to thank Mr Holmes. Would the lady mind passing this on to him when she saw him? Garden/Joanne wouldn't mind at all. Mr James walked away shaking his head in puzzlement. He had the feeling that he had been duped in some way, but could not work out how.

Garden ascended the stairs again with a feeling of great relief that he seemed to have got away with it, even though he had completely forgotten about his footwear. It was a careless mistake that he could not afford to repeat. The only thing that could have been worse, in his opinion was answering the door in his daytime garb, but in high heels. On looking in the mirror, he was horrified to see that his false eyelashes, applied with such care, had come away on his right eye, and he looked like he had a spider on his eyelid.

Chapter Five

Wednesday was a quiet day with no new clients and Holmes running around fretting about advertising. However Garden did get a call from Mrs Markham and he told her what had transpired the previous day.

'I can't believe it,' exclaimed the woman, in high dudgeon, 'Are you absolutely sure?'

'I have pictures,' said Garden, 'and if you give me your mobile number I can send them now.'

Having got her number, Garden was able to send the pictures whilst she was still on the line and he could hear her sharp intake of breath as she viewed them.

'That little madam,' she said, 'and that shifty Luke Armstrong, boy are they in trouble. I'm sorry I doubted you, Mr Garden. You have done a quick and efficient job. Just send me your invoice.'

'It's already prepared Mrs Markham,' said Garden, glowing with pride, 'thanks for your business and if you or your friends need anything else looking into, please contact us.'

'I will certainly recommend your services, goodbye.'

Garden put down the phone and turning smugly to Holmes, said, 'Another satisfied customer.'

It was Thursday afternoon before Miss Everton telephoned to say that she was finally free on that evening, and Garden agreed that tonight would be the night, passing this information on to Holmes, who was convinced, to the contrary, that Saturday was the night – the night that he would have a dinner *a deux* with Shirley.

He had become more and more jittery as the week wore on and had finally made a visit to a pharmacy out of the town to buy a little packet of 'life-savers' for his adventure into the romantic. He had also wimped out on the venue, plumping for familiar territory in his local, *The Sherlock*, Shirley turning down his offer of a lift, saying that she would make her own way there if he would give her directions. Was this a good sign that she did not want either of them to drive? The very thought sent cold shivers of anticipation down his spine.

Nine thirty was the time they had arranged with Miss Everton to pick her up, and they both went home first to get something to eat and to change into dark clothing in case they were seen creeping round the old Gothic pile.

When they arrived at her house, Miss Everton was dressed in black and looked very much as if she were in mourning for Prince Albert, an impression only enhanced by her wrinkled face and wispy hair. Her eyes were very lively, though, no doubt in anticipation of the adventure to come.

It was dark when they reached their destination. The car was left on the edge of the woods as they made their way through the first straggling saplings to get a glimpse of the house. They had already noticed, however, that there seemed to be a source of light ahead of them, as Miss Everton's neighbour must have done on her trip back from her daughter's.

There seemed to be a dull yellow glow from the front entrance, and a couple of moving lights, presumably torches, on the ground floor. There were definitely people in there, but there was no clue as to who they were. It was Garden who spotted the end of a car sticking out at the rear of the house, and they made their way as silently as possible to investigate.

There were two vehicles, and Garden used the torch on his mobile phone to see their number plates clearly enough to note the numbers down. There must have been somebody in the house who was on guard, however, because there was a shout from inside, and the two detectives had to hide themselves and pull Miss Everton with them behind a large shrub, as the back door opened.

They stayed there until the door had closed again, holding their breath as much as possible in case their breathing gave them away. Making their way back slowly and carefully to the car, it was only as they got back into it again that Holmes exclaimed in disgust.

'What is it? What's wrong?' enquired Garden, and Holmes pointed to the right sleeve of his jacket with a moue of distaste.

'When we dived for cover, I must have landed in some animal droppings,' he croaked, removing the offending article and getting out of the vehicle to put it in the boot of the car, where it would not be so obviously fragrant.

Taking no notice of either of them, Miss Everton suddenly shushed them and pointed towards the house, where the two cars that had been hidden behind it began to edge out from behind the building's bulk. 'It looks like they're going. Shall we give them a head start then go in?'

'Let's all crouch down out of sight, so that they don't spot our silhouettes as they leave,' suggested Garden, but they needn't have bothered, as there was obviously a way off the property from the rear, and the cars did not need to pass them. Ten long minutes later, the two men got out of the front of the car, then had to go back for their client, who had stretched out on the back seat and had dozed off.

'Come along, Miss Everton, they've driven away and we can go in to see if things are any different from the last time we came,' urged Holmes, in his best 'humouring little old ladies' voice.

'There's no need to patronise me, Mr Holmes. I'm just a bit tired as I had an aerobics class this afternoon.' That soon settled his hash: fitter than she looked, then.

As they entered the house, they noticed a couple of spades and shovels in the hallway, and a noxious smell assaulted their nostrils. All three extracted handkerchiefs from their clothing and covered their mouths and noses.

'Whatever's that ghastly aroma?' asked Holmes. 'Surely it can't be coming from under the floorboards?'

'Did we see absolutely all the house last time?' asked Garden, as a sudden thought struck him.

'We never went down to the cellar. Do you think that awful stink could be coming from there? It certainly wasn't noticeable last time we were here,' she replied, wrinkling her nose in distaste.

'Look, Garden, there's an old oil lamp on the mantelpiece,' Holmes alerted his partner, using his phone as a torch.

Garden approached the lamp and held out a hand. 'The glass is still warm,' he announced, getting out his lighter and applying it to the wick. 'There, that's better.'

'That's what we must have seen from outside. The lamplight has certainly got a yellowish tinge to it,' Holmes declared, with a self-satisfied smile. 'Come on, let's go and see what is making that revolting pong down there.'

Miss Everton pointed him to the door as Garden held the lamp. He applied his hand to the door knob and turned it, but nothing happened. He tried again, and it still refused to budge. Taking a few steps backwards and ignoring the little twitters of Miss Everett, he charged the wood with his shoulder, but the only result was a ricochet, and a pain of some sharpness for our unlikely hero.

'What is it, Miss Everett?' asked Garden, and she shuffled across to him and whispered in his ear. Without further ado, Garden went over to the recalcitrant door and opened it. 'It opens outwards, Holmes,' he informed his partner, who was holding his damaged shoulder and wincing.

As the door swung open, the smell got stronger, and

they realised they had been spot-on in identifying its source. Garden held aloft his beacon and went first down the rickety wooden staircase, Holmes following, with Miss Everton bringing up the rear. She had less need of light, for she had been down here many times in the past, and the details were all coming back to here now her memory had received this prompt.

The cellar wasn't as large as they thought it would be, and Garden started walking round the perimeter, holding aloft the oil lamp and almost choking on the foul air. He tracked it down to a dark corner, where the decaying body of a woman was laying. Getting a grip on his protesting stomach, he called to the others to keep away, and walked back the few paces, taking the light source with him. There was no need to expose their client to this visual horror. 'Dead body, over there,' he informed them, almost gagging.

Their client must not have had such a highly developed sense of smell, or was more used to such nasty niffs, for she ignored the atmosphere and merely pointed to a dilapidated table at the opposite end of the underground room. On its surface sat two coarse sacks and a smaller calico bag. 'I wonder what's in there?' she asked, eyes bright with excitement.

Holmes and Garden immediately took this opportunity to move away from the source of their nasal discomfort, and Garden carried on holding up the lamp while Holmes began to open the receptacles. The first sack contained nothing but papers and documents, and he soon shoved them back inside, perhaps to be examined later. The second's contents were much more exciting, consisting of a large amount of bank notes, and things were beginning to click into place.

Holmes picked up the calico bag and began to pull it open, to reveal a fine selection of very expensive jewellery and watches. 'Well, well, well,' he said, his voice like syrup. 'It looks like we've found the hoard from the bank.'

'We'd better alert the police immediately,' responded Garden, with a little smirk at what Inspector Streeter would say at their unexpected haul. 'Damn! Can't get a signal down here. I'll have to go back up, and you two had better follow as I've got the only reliable source of light that doesn't need a battery.'

Suddenly there was an unexpected scuffling noise back at the doorway down, Holmes shoved the jewellery back into its bag, Garden extinguished the lamp, and the three of them retreated behind a convenient wine rack, still full of dusty bottles from yesteryear, feeling their way in the complete darkness. A voice shouted, 'Well, you didn't leave the lamp in the hallway. I don't know what you've done with it, but we'll have to use our torches. Come on, and we'll get the sparklers, so that we can show them to that dodgy jeweller.'

Two sets of heavy footsteps trundled down the wooden stairs and, peeping out from just behind the wine rack, Garden could see two men checking out the contents of the calico bag, before one of them slung it over his shoulder, and the other one lit the way back to the ground floor. Garden thanked his lucky stars that the smell of the lamp would have been overwhelmed by the smell of the body. As they got to the top, the other one said, 'When are we going to get rid of her?' but they heard no more, as the door closed, and sinking hearts in the cellar heard the sound of a turning key.

As the sound of their footsteps above retreated, and they heard the bang of the front door, Holmes said hollowly, 'What are we going to do now? We've got no phone signal, and they've locked us in.'

There was a jangling in the darkness, and Miss Everton said, 'Just as well I have a key to the cellar on my little keyring, isn't it?' as Garden used his lighter to set the lamp going again.

Holmes handed out strong mints in the hope that the fumes would slightly dull the stench of the corpse, as they patiently waited another ten minutes before venturing back upstairs, after which Garden immediately tried his phone again. 'Nope, still no signal,' he declared, and they had to get back into the car and drive until he was able to make the call to the police station.

As he punched in the number, Miss Everton declared, 'I believe I know both of those voices, but being out of context, I can't identify them straight away. But, I'd know them again if I heard them.'

'Not much good to us,' grunted Holmes ungraciously, as he'd been thoroughly rattled by what they had found, and the visit from those responsible, and needed a bit of time to get back his customary good manners.

'Did they have gloves on?' asked Miss Everton, with a moment of perception that Holmes would have thought impossible.

'They did not!' replied Garden in triumph, as the phone rang. 'I peeped.'

It was DC Moriarty who was on duty that evening, and he took Garden's call, then followed that with the dubious honour of rousing DI Streeter, who was enjoying the unexpected luxury of an early night, from his bed. Taking the opportunity to spread the pain around somewhat, he, in turn, disturbed the quiet evening in front of the late film that was DS Port's way of unwinding, and then told Moriarty to stay where he was, as they would handle it.

Holmes and Garden, having had Streeter's spleen vented on them for interfering with police business again, were dismissed, as was Miss Everton, with the promise that statements would be taken the next day, and they'd better keep their noses out of anything else like this. Garden's explanation that Miss Everton had contacted them to find out who had been trespassing on her property cut no ice with the inspector, and he was still in high dudgeon when they left the scene.

Their statements were taken early the next morning, as soon as they had arrived at the office, and Miss Everton phoned to inform them that she, too, had had a visit from a very unpleasant and ill-mannered inspector, who needed a good spanking, in her opinion.

That afternoon, it was announced on local radio that two men had been arrested in connection with the bank robbery that had taken place in Hamsley Black Cross, although police would not release their names just at the moment, and Holmes sat straight down to make out an invoice for yet another satisfied client, asking if Garden had done the same for the woman whose car was being used without her consent.

'We're on to a good thing here, old boy,' Holmes crowed, without actually consulting the paltry amounts they had made; but then he didn't have to with his bank balance, which was bursting with so much health that it was almost obscene.

The rest of the day brought only a phone call from Deirdre Matcham, to inform them that she no longer needed them to keep an eye on her husband. He had been arrested at the bank manager's house in the early hours of the morning, accused of bank robbery and the murder of the manager's wife, and that she would be grateful if they would send her a bill for any hours they may have spent on her behalf. It seemed that her husband had 'crossed to the other side' and was having a fling with the bank manager. They had intended to run off together after robbing the bank but it seems they were rumbled by the wife whom they subsequently murdered!

'It seems that we helped solve a much more important case than we realised,' said Holmes to Garden, 'we really are on our way!' Holmes conveniently forgot that they had stumbled upon the result rather than deducing it.

'That leaves us a completely clean sheet at the end of our first week of operation,' Holmes commented. 'Let's hope we get more customers soon.'

But it was not to be, and all they had for the rest of Friday was a string of enquiries for wallpaper and gardening products, a situation that again left him in high dudgeon, as he announced that he would not be in in the morning, as he had a lot of personal things to catch up on.

That wasn't exactly the case, but he didn't think he could look Shirley in the eye on the day of their date, as he was bursting with embarrassment with what had been going on in his mind, and didn't want to see her again until it was across a dining table.

Holmes almost regretted his decision to take the day off, as he was in a state of high anxiety, and knocked over two cups of tea and fell over Colin four times, cursing the cat to hell and back every time it happened. Colin, suspecting that his slave was out of sorts, shot out through the cat flap and went and sulked under some bushes at the end of the garden.

As evening approached, Holmes became even more jittery, and scrubbed himself in the bath until his skin was pink and shiny, and splashed on a little aftershave, something he rarely did, thinking it unmanly to use scent, and only possessing it because someone had bought it for his Christmas present. He then spent a good two hours choosing what to wear, and had thrown three ties and two shirts across the room before he was satisfied with his appearance, having realised that he couldn't change his basic shape and age. Maybe he should get a toupee? But there wasn't time for fiddle-faddling like that, now.

Having fielded two cold calls before he could finally leave his apartment, he set out into the fine evening air, his mind in turmoil about what might happen later, and he eventually had to whistle an inane tune to keep his tousled thoughts at bay. He wouldn't take his car, so that he didn't have to drive, and he could always order a taxi later, as he thought Shirley might have done to get her to The Sherlock.

As he was on foot, he did not have to go round to the car park at the back, and he entered by the street door, blushing as he did so, at the thought of what might be ahead of him. He looked across the bar and saw his secretary/receptionist sitting at a table on the far side of the pub, and waved shyly to her, hoping that she could not read his thoughts which were all tangled up in bed-sheets and the like.

As he approached the table, he beamed a smile in her direction, only to have it wiped off his face as Garden came out of the gents'. What on earth was he doing here? This was *his* local, after all. As he turned his face towards his date again, ignoring the presence of his business partner, Garden approached their table and sat down as if he belonged there.

'I thought it would be all right,' explained Shirley innocently. 'Only, it's the end of our first week of business, and I thought you'd want to celebrate with all the staff. I'm sure you meant to mention it to Johnny, and just forgot, what with all that's been going on. It's been a good week, hasn't it? Perhaps you could do some more advertising when we all get back to the office, so that people can spread the word further afield?'

Holmes' face glowed a bright crimson, as he felt that the presence of the 'thingies' in his inside pocket was probably broadcasting on all wavelengths.

THE END

A MATTER OF HONOUR

Chapter One

'How did work go? Is there any news yet of the promotion?' The pretty young Indian woman greeted her husband, home for the evening, with a kiss on the cheek.

'Not yet, my little flower,' he replied, kissing her similarly, before hanging up his hat and light raincoat. 'We will all know in time who is to climb the ladder of promotion. We must just trust to the gods that the most worthy candidate gets chosen.'

'You are too fair. You must be more ambitious and hungry for success,' replied Mrs Chandra, then they lapsed into their native Urdu, having left behind the world outside their home.

This was a regular discussion when Mr Chandra came home from work. A promotion within the office had been on the cards for some time, and the vacancy had yet to be filled. There were, however, five possible candidates for the position, and Mr Chandra was only one of these. Thus, his wife asked every day if there were word of promotion yet. If her husband were not ambitious, she was certainly ambitious for him.

'The others are all fine men,' he told her. 'I must be proven to be more suitable than them before I am offered the position. And after all, they are younger men.'

'Pshaw!' was his wife's response to this regular claim of his. She knew who the best candidate was, and she couldn't see why they were so long in asking him to take the position.

In Hamsley Black Cross, on The High, the detective

agency of Holmes and Garden stood with its doors open, to let in some air to counter the summer heat of the office. It may not have been a hot summer, but the central heating had got stuck in the 'on' position, and they were waiting for an engineer to come and replace a part so that they had some choice in the matter of the temperature of their place of work.

In the front office, their receptionist, Shirley Garden, wore only a light cotton dress over her underwear, a cardigan drooping listlessly from the back of her chair. The welcoming flowers on her desk dropped defeated petals as the radiators continued to pump out heat, and even the merest puff of breeze from outside was a boon.

'Business is very slow at the moment,' commented a red-faced Sherman Holmes, his jacket and tie both hanging from the coatstand, his top button open and his shirtsleeves rolled as high as they would go.

'You should dress for the office temperature,' replied his partner, John H. Garden, who was attired in a sleeveless pink T-shirt and turquoise shorts. 'You'd be much more comfortable.'

'One of us has to be ready to speak to a prospective client without frightening them away. I'd never confide in someone dressed as you are.'

'And I wouldn't want to confide in someone who was so hot he was suffering from a very short fuse on his temper,' retorted Garden, knowing his Holmes, by now.

'Well, if someone does come in, you will have to nip upstairs to your flat and put on something a bit more respectable.'

'Deal. But for now I stay dressed like this.' Garden had won that one on points.

Chapter Two

Mrs Chandra did not have time to ask her dear Sanjay how the situation about the promotion was progressing at work as, when he arrived home, he was waving around his hands and obviously in a state of agitation. 'What is it, my dear? Has the position gone to someone else?' she asked, before holding her breath in anticipation of bad news.

'It is poor Mr Andrews. He was hit by a car whilst taking a lunchtime stroll down a lane to the river – you know how narrow those little roads are – and now he is in hospital fighting for his life.'

'What dreadful news, Sanjay, but we must look on the bright side: at least he will not be able to fulfil the more senior role, the right man for which they are searching.'

'That is true, my little flower; I must not be downhearted when the gods are, maybe, out to help me.'

'Another two missing dogs located safe and sound at the dog pound,' stated Sherman Holmes, wiping his overheated forehead with a large, dazzlingly white handkerchief.

'Another couple of minimal fees for the agency. I say, Holmes,' said Garden, this time in a violet T-shirt and puce shorts, 'I think it's about time we got our teeth into something more meaty, don't you?'

Ignoring this comment, Holmes said, 'I can't believe it's raining outside, and we're in here dying of heat-exhaustion. Thank the good God that the engineer is coming before closing time to restore our working conditions to something approaching acceptable.'

A light knock on the door brought in Shirley, Garden's mother and the receptionist of the business, with a tray holding a jug of iced water and two glasses on it. Her hair was wet with perspiration and straggled over her forehead, and her dress, once freshly pressed, hung in limp creases where she had been sitting. 'The heating engineer's just phoned,' she announced in a tired voice.

'*And?*' The interrogative came out in a shout, as Holmes had the feeling the man was going to slip out of their grasp, and they would be encased in this infernal pressure cooker for weeks to come.

'And he said he would be about half an hour late,' she concluded, then sighed from the sheer strain of working in such an atmosphere. 'No need to get your knickers in a twist. Sir.'

'Sorry, Shirley. It's just this damned heat. You get yourself off home and have a nice cool shower, and we'll finish up here,' replied Holmes with an apologetic smile at his own irascibility.

'I'll lock up, Holmes, then stand outside the front to have a cigarette when he's due, so that I can let him in. It'll save me having to stay in the office to unlock the door and be boiled to death.'

'Good man, Garden; good man. Well, we'll be off, then. Do you fancy a cup of tea in the nice, cool tearooms, Shirley?'

'Not meaning to be rude, but I'd rather get home and get changed out of my perspiration-soaked clothes and have a nice cool soak in a bath if you don't mind.'

'Some other time, then,' replied Holmes, chagrin in his voice. She really was a fine-looking woman but, after what had occurred when he thought they were going to have a romantic little tete-a-tete over dinner quite recently, he had realised that she'd be a harder nut to crack than he had anticipated.

Chapter Three

'Good evening, Sanjay. Whatever's wrong with you?' Mrs Chandra's husband had arrived home, not only silent this evening, but pale as well, with a worried frown creasing his forehead.

'It's Mr Davidson. He's been killed in a car crash. It was such a shock to me when I heard what had happened. It seems our office is cursed by the gods. First Andrews is the victim of a hit and run, from which he has since passed over, and then Davidson is killed in a traffic accident. Apparently he just left the road and crashed into a tree. And these things come in threes. Whatever will happen next?'

'I think the third thing has already happened. I went out shopping today and took the road through the woods, and a deer rushed out of the trees on one side of the road and landed on the bonnet of the car. It will need some work to repair the damage.'

'Well, I almost think, thank goodness for that. I will take it into the garage near the office tomorrow and get an estimate for the repair work. It will be a small price to pay if it takes the curse off my place of employment.'

Mrs Chandra adjusted her sari modestly and hurried off into the kitchen to see how the meal for her husband was progressing.

Chapter Four

The next morning, when Garden was in the office on his own, thankfully in cooler temperatures than they had endured of late, thanks to the work of the engineer who had called the previous evening, a serious-faced Asian man in a sober business suit entered the premises.

'Good morning, sir,' Garden greeted him.

'Good morning. Do I have the pleasure of addressing Mr Holmes or Mr Garden?'

'I'm Garden. And you are?'

'Mr Chandra.'

'How may I be of assistance, Mr Chandra?' Garden had caught the sober mood of the man and replied accordingly.

'I think my life might be in danger,' Mr Chandra told him, with a little frown of anxiety.

'Can you explain to me what makes you think this is so?' asked Garden.

'It is the situation at my place of employment, Mr Garden. I work at a firm of accountants in Farlington Market, and I am in a position to hope for a promotion to a step higher on the management ladder. There are another two candidates who may be chosen, but there were, last week, five of us available for consideration.'

'What happened to the other two?'

'One of them was sadly killed in a hit-and-run accident, and the other one had the brakes or something equally vital fail on his car, and, unfortunately, did not survive the ensuing accident.'

'And you think someone wants to kill you, too?'

'I fear that is so, Mr Garden. My dear wife Indraani thinks that these are not rational thoughts, but it seems such a sad coincidence that these two men should die so close together, leaving only three candidates for the promotion. Is there anything you can do to help me?'

'Have you informed the police of your fears, Mr Chandra?'

'You think I should do so?'

'Definitely. Maybe they already know that the two deaths were connected but, if not, they should be grateful to know what you have just told me.'

'I shall do so immediately. Thank you very much for your time and advice, Mr Garden.' Mr Chandra rose, bowed his head slightly in Garden's direction, and left the office.

When Holmes came in, Garden informed him of the early visitor's fears, but said he didn't think anything would come of it. 'Probably just a touch of paranoia on his part. Coincidences happen more often than we acknowledge them.'

'Maybe, Garden, but you never know.'

The morning brought only a case of a woman who thought she was being stalked, but she was so self-obsessed in the time she spent in their office that both men thought it was probably vanity on her part that had made her visit them. However, it would have to be investigated, and Garden said he would get straight on to keeping a watch on her after she had returned home late that afternoon, as she was on her way to the hairdressers and the beauty parlour after consulting with them, and she didn't think her stalker would follow her there, for some reason.

After the postman had been, Garden sat twitching and fidgeting in his chair. A small parcel had arrived with his name on it, and he was sure it was the black suspender belt with matching panties and padded bra he had ordered. It was an obsession of his to dress up as his alter ego Joanne, and he longed to put on the silken garments to see how they felt. While he was at it, he might as well put on an outfit as well, to see how the new items sat under clothing: he simply couldn't abide visible panty line.

When lunchtime arrived, he disappeared off upstairs without a word, so eager was he to try out his new delivery. If he hurried he could put the water on a Pot Noodle, and not waste too much time eating. He would pull on a wig as well, and select appropriate jewellery. He had not spent as much time as he would like to have done in Joanne's clothing of late, and he needed a fix.

Oh, yes, the new undergarments felt luxurious beneath his outer-clothes, and the part of him that was Joanne purred in appreciation, as he walked up and down his living room feeling the soft material against his skin. Good God, was that the time?

Pulling off his wig and throwing himself into his male attire, he wolfed down his meagre snack and rushed down to his desk again. He still had an hour or so before he set off for their new client's home to watch out for the man she said was stalking her, and he needed to show his face in case new business showed up; and he wouldn't want Holmes to think he was slacking because his flat was just up a staircase from their office quarters.

Garden had taken the early lunch break today, and Holmes the middle one, so it was to an empty office that he returned, but he made a point of going through to say he was back for the benefit of his mother, and to prove that he wasn't bunking off – even though he had been ten minutes or so late in returning, he had padded down the staircase as quietly as possible so as not to alert his mother to his return.

On Holmes' return, he put his head into the back office to let Garden know that he was back before taking her place at the receptionist's desk, as it was his turn to cover for their secretary. He had made an astonished face when Garden had looked up at his greeting, but Garden didn't take much notice, still being in the thrall of the silky undergarments that had just arrived into his possession. Maybe he could order a couple more sets in other colours? Thus preoccupied, he was surprised how quickly the time had passed when Holmes came back to his desk.

After a few minutes he was conscious of being watched, and looked up to see what was catching his partner's attention, only to have Holmes make a horrified face again and return his attention to his notes. Five minutes later it happened again, and this time he held Holmes' gaze.

'Whatever are you staring at?' he asked. He had run a comb – rather carelessly and without benefit of mirror - through his hair after he had taken off the wig, and he couldn't imagine what was causing Holmes to look at him so oddly.

'Earrings,' squawked Holmes, reddening with embarrassment.

Garden put up his hands and found that he hadn't taken off his clip-on earrings, snatched them from his lobes and placed them hurriedly in his desk drawer, but Holmes continued to stare at him.

'What?' he asked somewhat tetchily. 'What is it now?' He could not understand what was fascinating the other man so.

'Make-up,' squeaked Holmes, hurriedly looking back down at his desk and Garden, taking a small mirror out of his drawer, noticed, with some embarrassment that, in his overwhelming joy at Joanne's new underwear, he had forgotten to remove the make-up he had so hurriedly applied before checking his appearance in the mirror for that dreaded VPL – visible panty line.

'Quick trip upstairs,' muttered Holmes, as Garden hurriedly got to his feet. 'That's the way to sort the ladies out,' his partner concluded in a somewhat muddled fashion.

Chapter Five

'Good evening, Sanjay,' Indraani Chandra greeted her husband. 'You don't look at all well. Are you feeling a little off colour?'

'Good evening, my flower. No, I am not unwell; merely worried,' he replied.

'And what is it that is worrying you?' asked his wife.

'It is one of the other candidates for promotion: Peterson, this time,' he returned, his face paling further.

'What has happened to him?'

'He has fallen down an escalator in a department store at lunchtime and broken his arm.' Sanjay informed her.

'How tragic. Now, can I get you a cup of tea?'

'Indraani, you don't sound very sympathetic. The poor man could have broken his neck.

'What a pity he didn't, and that would make one less in the running for this senior position,' she replied; rather cold-heartedly, he thought.

'But it is his right arm, and he won't be in work for a long time. He cannot write and will have a job even using his computer. Apparently it was a very bad break.'

'Then the gods are smiling on you, Sanjay. Do not complain about this accident.'

'But I feel I may be next in this cursed situation.'

'Don't be so silly, Sanjay. Nothing will happen to you. This is just silly superstition on your part. Now, drink your tea while I see to your meal.'

Chapter Six

In the police station in Farlington Market the next morning, a woman sat in Detective Inspector Streeter's office dressed in a floor-length flowing kaftan, her long hair crimped into a retro frizz, a plethora of beads round her neck and rings on her long, tapered fingers. It was a long time since he had seen a hippy, but the sight brought back many memories to the inspector of trouble the police had had in the late sixties and early seventies, not that he had even been born in the sixties, let alone on the force.

'How can I help you, madam?' he asked politely, although he hated the non-conformist members of society and just hoped she wasn't a traveller. He had had enough run-ins with travellers to last him a lifetime, and they had turned him into somewhat of a bigot. She certainly wasn't old enough to have been around in the swinging sixties – the summer of love and all that - but she was no spring chicken either, he thought, somewhat waspishly.

'I am Mystic Carla, and I am afraid that I have caused the death of two men and the injury of another,' she announced, without preamble, and taking the inspector rather by surprise.

'What?' he spluttered. 'You've committed two murders and had an attempt at a third?' He'd certainly caught her drift, if not the specifics of it.

'I have cursed them, Inspector, and two of them have passed over, the other suffering only mortal injury. I wish to hand myself in before I cause further damage to human life,' she explained, a smug smile curling at the corners of her mouth.

'Would you like to explain how you have caused these unfortunate events, and to whom they have happened?' asked Streeter, completely nonplussed. 'And may I have your full name, please?'

'I am Carla Rothwell, also known as Mystic Carla, tarot card reader and psychic, Inspector,' she replied, with a little preen. 'At the moment, my husband is being considered for promotion at the firm of accountants situated a few doors down from this police station. He is hoping to become head of a team of accountants to work with international clients, and there are – or rather, were – four other prospective candidates.

'I'm afraid that I am so anxious for him to get the promotion that I put a curse on the other four men. So far, two are dead, and a third has been injured. 'How did these men die or get injured?' asked Streeter, sure that he would have details of a couple of murders.

'Harry Andrews was involved in a hit-and-run and died of his injuries, Dale Davidson was killed when his brakes malfunctioned, I believe, and Rex Peterson fell down a department store's escalator and broke his right arm rather badly. I fear that my curse has worked only too well. The company is the loser, however, for whoever got the promotion was to lead a team made up of the other men, and I'm afraid they will have to recruit more staff before they can implement their new section.'

'Who is the other man?'

'Sanjay Chandra, who is almost middle-aged. I don't think he will give my husband, Peter, too much competition.' She smiled smugly again, and then had her breath taken away when Streeter had *her* taken away to the custody suite, to be retained until he had made his own investigations. He didn't like his time being wasted, and he wasn't going to stand for it without wreaking revenge.

To his amazement, the two men named had died during the last few days and, even more surprisingly, a call to the named accountancy firm had produced the news that, not only had they lost two staff in tragic circumstances, but that a third had had a very bad fall, would have to take some time off work, and would then return decidedly under par because he had broken his right arm.

While he sat in his office recovering from this surprising and disturbing news, a phone call was put through to him from a man, Sanjay Chandra by name, informing him that he thought his life was in danger. Maybe he should read his horoscope more often. Maybe there was something in this after all.

Reassuring Mr Chandra that he was perfectly safe – he had a self-confessed murderer in custody, after all: he just needed to find out how she had committed the crimes physically. All this mumbo-jumbo was ridiculous, wasn't it? – he ended the call, his mind racing as he worked out how he was going to prove that the so-called Mystic Carla had killed two people, and just why she had confessed.

In the offices of Holmes and Garden, Garden decided that he would have to discuss with Holmes whether they should report the visit from Mr Chandra the day before. He might need police protection if what he believed was correct, and his life was, indeed, in danger.

At first, Holmes pooh-poohed the whole idea, as he was not at all keen to speak to Inspector Streeter, but eventually Garden persuaded him that it would be best to do so just in case anything happened to that worried accountant. It was with trepidation that he listened to the phone ring at the other end of the connection and, when he heard Streeter's voice, he came over all blustery; like autumn weather.

'Well, I didn't exactly meet him, myself, but Garden didn't seem to think the man was out of his tree,' he spluttered in self-defence, then listened carefully.

'What? You've got someone who what? And you

believe them? Extraordinary!'

Putting down the handset, he stared at Garden in disbelief. 'The man says he's had someone come into his station and confess to the murders of Harry Andrews in a hit-and-run, Dale Davidson, whose brake pipes were cut, and also claimed responsibility for the fall that was apparently suffered by another member of the accountancy firm's staff.'

'How odd, but then Mr Chandra did seem to think there was something sinister behind the events. Did he say who exactly was in custody?'

'Said he wasn't able to give out that sort of information to non-police personnel – non-disclosure, that sort of thing.' Holmes harrumphed in disgust at such secretive behaviour. 'So, I suppose that means we don't need to waste any more time worrying about Mr Chandra. He should be fine now somebody has 'fessed up.'

'Sounds like it,' replied Garden. 'Pity. I thought it might turn into quite an interesting case.'

'Apropos of nothing, old chap, I think the three of us need to get together and see how we can boost business – maybe expand the advertising for our little venture – and I just had the idea that the office is not the most peaceful atmosphere in which to do this. Why don't you two come round tonight for a bite of supper and we can chew more than the fat. I know an excellent source of ready-prepared meals that are of first-rate quality, and we could have a good old session over one of these. What do you think?'

'Well, I've got to go out again today to keep an eye on that delusional woman who thinks – or hopes – she's got a stalker, so it would be quite convenient not to have to cook a meal afterwards. If my dearest mother says yes, then I'll come along.'

As Garden went out of the office to keep an eye on the environs of Miss Patman, thirty-five years ago a Miss Hamsley Black Cross and still missing the limelight,

Holmes trod determinedly into the outer office to put his supper proposal to his receptionist-cum-secretary. It may not be as good as a tete-a-tete, but an evening spent in her company, even if her son were in attendance, was better than nothing. It wouldn't be out of the way to put candles on the table, considering that he was going to be paying for a top-notch meal for their consumption.

Chapter Seven

That evening, Sanjay Chandra came home with a smile on his face. 'You look very happy tonight, my Sanjay,' Indraani greeted him. 'Did you have a good day at the office? Have you been given the promotion?'

'Not yet, my little flower, the firm will have to advertise for new members of staff before anything is decided. But, I did hear that someone has confessed to the murders and the injury that have haunted the company. It would appear that I am safe at last.'

'Hire more staff members? How can this be so? They had a solid list of candidates, and you and Peterson are the only ones left. Surely you're a much better candidate than him?' Indraani stamped her petite foot and pouted at her husband.

'Are you not pleased that my life is no longer in danger, my dear wife?'

'Of course I am, but they should have appointed you straight away.'

'It's not quite so straightforward, Indraani but, of course, you don't understand business. Leave this to me.'

Indraani pouted at her husband again, then stalked off into the kitchen.

Chapter Eight

Inspector Streeter was getting very frustrated indeed. He had been questioning Carla Rothwell for hours, but she still insisted that the deaths were caused by magic that she had conjured up from the mystic ether. She denied point-blank that she had driven the car that hit Mr Andrews, that she had cut Mr Davidson's brake pipes, or that she had pushed Mr Peterson down the escalator of a well-known department store.

Suddenly he didn't know what to do. It was all very well detaining a citizen who had confessed to two murders and an attempt at a third, but if she would only talk about this mumbo-jumbo, he had no solid evidence. Maybe he would have to let her go until his men had turned up something from the clothes of the first victim, the car of the second, and the witnesses of the third. He had never been in this situation before, and felt all at sea, although Mystic Carla still seemed as cool as a cucumber and as self-satisfied as a cat that had got at the cream.

He couldn't hold her for much longer with no evidence other than her own word that she was responsible, and he had even told that amateur Holmes that he had someone for all the incidents that had occurred. He would look an absolute incompetent if he had no physical evidence, and had to own up that he had let his self-confessed murderer go.

DS Port and DC Moriarty would have to get things sorted out for forensic examination, while he sent a couple of PCs to the sites of all three incidents and see if they could summon up any witnesses. He, Streeter, would be making a radio appeal and inserting a plea in the local paper for witnesses to come forward. He would not be thwarted on this.

He would keep her in custody until later that evening, as she had already left a message on her home phone and her husband's mobile about her whereabouts. He'd then send her home in a police car, just to further put the wind up her.

Chapter Nine

Garden had had a fairly fruitless and exhausting day, following Miss Patman from shop to shop, and from bistro to tea shop, as she made her rounds of the local retail and catering establishments. There was no sign of anyone following her, but they had been engaged to watch her. Fleetingly, he wondered if she had only engaged their services so that she could be sure of at least one set of male eyes upon her throughout the day. She was sixty if she was a day, and she looked like she had had quite a hard life since she had swanned around in a swimsuit. However, as Sherlock Holmes would undoubtedly have said, "There is danger to him who snatches a delusion from a woman".

Doggedly, he trailed on, now quite looking forward to a civilised evening in Holmes' apartment in convivial company, instead of having to eat a microwave meal in his own flat. It might prove quite entertaining, and most relaxing, to lounge on one of his partner's Chesterfields with a glass of wine in his hand, rather than sitting on his rather hard futon with a ready meal on his lap, for he didn't boast a dining table yet. He would certainly not have the energy to put on Joanne's clothes again, to re-experience the luxurious feeling of her new underwear, so he might as well go out.

Picking up his mother on his way, Garden rang the bell of Holmes' apartment, quite looking forward to an evening in familiar company. He was beginning to come to terms with his crossed maternal wires with his mother when he had lived in the family home, and was getting to know her anew.

Holmes opened the door, peering with appreciation at Shirley's fashionable dress and her attractively made-up face. At Garden, he looked with trepidation, pleased that the man didn't prove to be wearing earrings and warpaint. He had had no idea what his partner had been doing during his lunch break, but was rather worried that wearing make-up may be his new fashion for the office. Thankfully, he was wrong, and Garden was a little startled by the sigh of relief that Holmes gave when they shook hands.

'Come on in,' he invited them, standing aside to admit them, and settled them in his comfortably Edwardian-style sitting room. 'Let me get you a pre-prandial drink and we shall discuss how to move the business forward.'

Shirley looked around her at the period furnishings. There was an over-mantel mirror that had an elaborately carved frame above the fireplace, and the sideboard was also a confection of the carver's art. The Chesterfield sofas on which they perched were reproduction, more for the comfort than because Holmes couldn't source originals. He was not a fan of horse-hair and was glad of modern furniture-making techniques when his evening and weekend comfort were at stake.

The heavy maroon velvet drapes were drawn soon after they arrived to give a cosy atmosphere of times past, and Holmes handed round glasses of a delightfully dry sherry to his guests.

'What do you think about going on local radio?' asked Garden, as the idea suddenly popped into his head. It would be a good means of publicising their services for those who did not know of their existence.

'That's a topping idea, old chap,' replied Holmes. 'Me or you? I suppose it should be me, as head of the firm,' he added, immediately becoming media conscious, and the thought of his own voice filling people's living space was suddenly very appealing.

'I don't think I should like to do it,' replied Garden. 'I

hate to hear my own voice recorded, so I think your tones would be more acceptable.'

Holmes smirked at this praise, proposed a toast to future business, then set the three of them talking about flyers and business cards in various shops on the counter. This latter seemed to him to be a remarkably discreet way of advertising, where only those who may have need of their investigations would pick up one. 'What about an appearance on regional television?' he asked, at once seeing his face on the area's TV screens.

'You can count me out,' Garden replied immediately. I don't want people to see me in case they recognise me as Joanne. The more I can keep out of the limelight the better. I don't mind the investigation side of things, but I want to stay in the working background, if that's all right with you, Holmes?'

'Perfectly, John H. Have you any ideas, dear Shirley?'

Surprised at being thus addressed, John H's mother turned bright crimson, and looked into her lap in confusion. 'Sponsoring local events?' she offered, more in desperation than in hope.

'Splendid idea, my dear. It's not as if the coffers are inadequately filled. That sort of thing should certainly spread the word admirably. We'll make a publicity pundit of you yet, Shirley.'

Fortunately, as she fought to recover from this charm onslaught, something beeped in the kitchen, and Holmes sprang up to attend to the food and serve the first course, while Garden hosted her to her chair at the dining table.

The crab bisque disposed of, Holmes served a *boeuf bourguignon* for the main course, and Garden was setting to, to attack his plateful, when a missile shot through the air, and landed mouth first on his plate. Colin, Holmes' spoilt and beloved cat, had managed to get on to a high book shelf and aim straight for Garden's portion of tender beef.

Gravy splashed all over his shirt and tie and on to the table cloth and his wine glass landed on its side, while Holmes sat there in bemusement, and Shirley gave a little squeal of surprise. 'Colin, get out to the kitchen. I've left you some in your bowl, you naughty boy,' declared Holmes in indulgent tones, then turned his eye to Garden. 'I'm awfully sorry, old chap. Let me get you a damp cloth with which to clean yourself up.'

'Do you have any more of this no doubt excellent stew?' asked the besplattered Garden.

'Terribly sorry, but no. Why?'

'I can hardly eat food that a cat has landed in, now, can I?' Garden was totally bemused that Holmes had not fathomed this one out.

'Sorry. I put the last of it into the cat's bowl. I'll have to fetch you some bread and cheese to be going on with, but I can assure you that you'll enjoy dessert.'

'If I can get first go at it,' mumbled Garden under his breath for, if it involved cream at all, no doubt Colin would be back on the prowl for his share of the course.

As Garden toyed with a piece of mousetrap, Shirley picked at her food uncomfortably. She would be glad to get home. In her experience, it never did to socialise with colleagues from the office, and tonight she was breaking her golden rule simply because she couldn't think of any way of avoiding it.

Dessert proved to be good old spotted dick and custard, the heat of which deterred even a cat of Colin's determination. As Garden spooned the heavy confection into his mouth, he decided that Holmes cat was the only one with psychopathic tendencies he had ever met, and with his sights set on only one human target – himself. The animal acted like a huge furry angel with his owner, and had left his mother alone, except for a few minutes when he had deigned to allow her to stroke his muscular back, but whenever Garden visited, he always came off worst.

Chapter Ten

Time had run out for Streeter, and Habeas Corpus was waving a stern finger at him with regard to Mystic Carla, aka Mrs Rothwell. A self-confessed murderer in the hand was worth two in the bush, in his opinion, and it was with great reluctance, that he had to let his quarry go. Having the final say in the matter, though, he sent her home in a police car with two uniformed officers in it to keep her company, as a hint to her that she was still not off the hook.

The officer from the passenger seat of the vehicle accompanied her to the door, and waited while she called into her husband. He wanted to see her into her other half's custody before he returned to the station, to make sure she didn't float off anywhere else with murderous intent.

There came no answer, so he followed her into the house, she clicked on the lights, then screamed for all she was worth. At the foot of the staircase which, in this abode, rose from the sitting room, lay the body of her husband, crumpled into a heap.

The constable caught her as she passed out, and then requested, via his police personal radio, that his partner in the car contact the police station about another possible murder; or, at the very least, a possible suspicious death, for when he had looked at the body, he noticed a large amount of blood behind the head.

On closer examination, this turned out to be a hefty blow from a blunt instrument, and not one that could have been caused accidentally by the fall. There was a definite indentation of the skull, and the local area had now clocked up its third murder as well as a possible attempted one, in a very short space of time. Rex Peterson was absolutely positive that he had been pushed down the escalator, and there was obviously a dangerous person at large which, now, could not be Carla Rothwell.

Later that evening, Inspector Streeter felt like pulling out his hair in frustration. If Mrs Rothwell couldn't have committed this latest murder, who on earth could have, for they must all be connected? She was definitely in the clear, and he had no suspects. It was true that the modus operandi had been different in all four cases, but the deaths so close together, not to mention the attempted murder, could not, surely, have been coincidence? He didn't believe in coincidences, not where murder was concerned.

Chapter Eleven

The next morning, Garden went back to keeping an eye on Miss Helena Patman, a task he considered to be a complete waste of time but, as long as she paid her bill at the end of the surveillance, who was he to judge her?

Sitting outside her house in his car, he read his current library book, the corner of his eye on the entrance to her front garden. Only the postman had called so far, and he did not think she would receive any more visitors this morning; he could feel it in his water. She was not at work today, as she was at the end of a few days' off, and he expected her to stay in the house for the duration.

It might be a different case tomorrow when he had to follow her to a small art gallery in Farlington Market, which made him think that maybe they had opened their offices in the wrong town. A little deeper consideration of this drove him to decide that that would not have been a good idea, as people wouldn't like to consult a detective agency on their own doorstep. They would prefer to disguise their consultation with a trip to one of the other local establishments, and then slip in quietly where none of their neighbours would be likely to notice them.

Happy in this conclusion, he let his attention slip a little and was, therefore, bemused to hear the sound of shrill screams coming from the open kitchen window of the house in which their client dwelt. Dropping his book without heed to which page he had reached, he exited the car with all alacrity, and headed towards the house.

Meanwhile, Inspector Streeter, finally accepting that Mystic Carla Rothwell couldn't be his murderer if the same person were responsible for all, had paid a call to what he had discovered was the employer of the three dead men and the one only injured.

Messrs Carlton, Piccadilly and Mayfair, Chartered Accountants, were only a few streets away from the police station, and he asked to see the senior partner immediately, being straight away led to the office of a Mr Sandiford. Expressing his surprise at the surname, Mr Sandiford smiled at him, and informed him that the firm's name was a complete fiction from earlier times. The company had been set up by three men with much more prosaic names, but they had adopted the fancy-sounding components of the firm's title by deed poll, thinking that it would bring them more business from the local business snobs, and they had been right, at the time.

'It hasn't done too badly for us, since then, either,' he concluded his little historical anecdote, before expressing his chagrin at the loss of so many employees at a time that they were expanding.

'Did you not think it odd?' asked Streeter, giving the man a cod's eye stare.

'Don't really look at anything other than figures,' he replied, oblivious to the real world around him. 'Odd thing, though. They were all up for a promotion,' he commented. 'There's only one candidate left, so we shall have to advertise for extra staff before we make the decision about who shall head up our new international department.

'We're in expansion, you know. At a time like this, globally, there's even more need for good accountants to make the most of the firm's figures,' he informed Streeter, who had stood there with his mouth open at the thought of a firm doing so well in today's financial climate. Fiddling the books, more like, he thought, but did not vocalise.

'Who is left to consider for this promotion?' Streeter considered this a cunning question, and was rewarded by an answer in the affirmative.

'There's still Sanjay Chandra: very good head for figures, and very creative,' replied Mr Sandiford, colouring up as he let slip the last phrase of this information.

'I'd like to have a word with him, if I may?' requested the sturdy inspector with a gleam in his eye, then thought to check the employee's attendance at work which had been excellent.

'Good day to you, Mr Chandra. I'm Inspector Streeter of the Farlington Market CID, and I would like a few words with you about your unfortunate colleagues.'

Chapter Twelve

Garden could get no answer to his pummelling on the front door, and the screeching continued unabated. Thus, he went round to the back of the house where he found the patio door into the living room unlocked, and let himself in that way. The screaming was much louder inside, and he covered his ears as he headed to the front of the house.

In the kitchen, he found Miss Patman with the hands of another woman round her neck, trying her best to strangle the ex-beauty queen. '*Stop*! At once!' he commanded them in a very loud voice, and the two women fell apart. 'What the hell's going on here?' he shouted, thoroughly discombobulated by the presence of another woman in what he thought was a case about a male stalker.

Miss Patman put her hands to her throat, rubbing at it where it had been crushed, swallowed somewhat ostentatiously then, in a rather hoarse voice, thanked Garden for his timely appearance.

'And this is?' he asked, feeling his temper rise at the lack of information that had been given to him at their original consultation.

'My apologies, Mr Garden. This is Sherelle Lavelle, who has hated me ever since I pipped her at the post for Miss Hamsley Black Cross. She attacked me three times in my year of duty to the town, and I eventually moved to another area to get away from her. I returned here only because my mother is getting rather frail and forgetful, and I honestly thought this woman would be over it by now.

'I only caught glimpses of my stalker out of the corner of my eye, and I'm afraid I don't often wear my glasses,' she explained, patting at her mussed up hair and proving that this habit was out of vanity rather than prudence.

'Shall I phone the police?' asked Garden, still somewhat bemused.

'I never wanted to kill her,' stated Sherelle Lavelle. 'I just wanted to get back at her for what she did to me all those years ago. She was sleeping with one of the judges, you know.'

'This is true,' confirmed Miss Patman with a shameful smile.

'How could you,' added Ms Lavelle.

'I know. He was rather awful, and terribly old,' continued Helena Patman. 'We used to be best friends, you know,' she informed her knight in shining armour, indicating the woman who had but a few short minutes ago had her hands round her throat.

'Did you really?' Garden was now definitely mystified by the working of women's minds. Dress like one he might, but fathoming out the mental processes of one was a completely different matter.

'Shall we call it a day?' asked Sherelle, with a tear in her eye.

'Why not. What happened to that awful boyfriend of yours?'

'I married him, more's the pity. He left me five years ago, and I'm still on my own.'

'How about you and me going out on the town, then, just like the old days?'

'But, Miss Patman, she's just tried to kill you, and she's been stalking you.' Garden was now aghast.

'It may not be Friends Re-united, but it works for me,' replied his erstwhile client. 'Send me your bill at your convenience. You may go off duty now, Mr Garden.'

Garden walked back to his car his mind in a whirl. Could their relationship really have gone from murderous enemies to best friends in the blink of an eye? Women! Who could work out how they thought?

Chapter Thirteen

At the offices of Messrs Carlton, Piccadilly and Mayfair, Inspector Streeter was interviewing Sanjay Chandra about his movements at the time of the deaths, or the events that led up to them, and the accident.

He explained that, at the time of the death of Mr Andrews, he had been working late at the office. It had been impossible to work out exactly when Mr Davidson's car had been tampered with, but there seemed to have been no opportunity, as Mr Chandra seemed to have spent all his time between the incidents either working late or at home with his wife.

For the incident with the escalator, he had a cast iron alibi, as he had brought a packed lunch that day, and he and a junior colleague had been rushing to get out the annual accounts of a local firm, and neither of them had left the office during the time that this unfortunate accident had taken place. 'Had samosas and a little leftover lamb jalfrezi,' he offered, 'and delicious they were, too. My Indraani is a superb cook.'

An examination by the appointed doctor – and the evidence of the rectal temperature – had confirmed that Mr Rothwell was murdered as soon as he had got home from the office, and Mr Chandra had an alibi in the form of Mr Sandiford himself, who had been explaining that the firm would wait until they had appointed replacement staff before appointing a head of department.

He was, of course, very shocked to hear news of Mr Rothwell's death from the inspector, but he couldn't be of any help in their enquiries. Indraani would, no doubt, be very distressed when he got home and told her.

That evening, his wife greeted him with her customary smile, and listened while he told her that Mr Rothwell had been murdered the previous day. Her first reaction was one of happiness as she said, 'And now you will be promoted while they get new underlings to work for you?'

'No, I told you yesterday that there were to be new staff. I thought I'd made it clear that the promotion would not be given until after the new members of staff were in place.'

'You never said exactly that, Sanjay. How could Mr Sandiford be so unfair as not to recommend you after all your years of devoted service and unpaid overtime?'

'I might still be appointed, my dear. But that is for the gods to know, at the moment, and not for us mere mortals.'

Indraani huffed off into the kitchen to attend to her pots of food, whilst an anxious frown adorned her husband's face.

Chapter Fourteen

The next morning, Sanjay rang in from his office to see if he could come in to visit Garden again in his lunch break, as he would never dream of doing something like that during the firm's time.

After the phone call, he discussed the details of what was happening at the firm of accountants with Holmes, who sat for a moment, lost in thought. 'Seems to me to be a very clever murderer,' he pontificated. 'It must be the man himself doing it just to secure promotion.'

'Can't be,' replied Garden curtly. 'He says the firm is going to replace the men who were killed with new employees before they come to a decision about the promotion.'

'Then, he must think he's odds-on favourite. He must be guilty, otherwise why has no one tried to attack him? Stands to reason that he's responsible. He'll have wangled his alibi for when the man was pushed down the escalator. Maybe he had the chance to alter the man's watch so that he didn't know what time it really happened.'

'That's far too airy fairy, Holmes. The ambulance crew and the department store must have a note of the actual time it occurred, for their records.'

'That's splitting hairs, isn't it, old chap? And what about this boss man? What's his name again?'

'Sandiford,' supplied Garden.

'Why can't it be him having a purge of staff so that he doesn't have to pay redundancy money? It's quite feasible.'

'It seems too far-fetched for me, Holmes. There must

be some other explanation.'

'What about that chap Rothwell's wife getting someone else in on the act to "do" her husband, who was the intended victim after all? It could all be an elaborate plot to get rid of hubby and strengthen her reputation as a psychic.'

'Holmes, you really do have a fertile imagination.'

'And you say this Indian feller's coming in here in his lunch hour? He's the last man standing. Don't tell me that doesn't mean something, because I won't believe you.'

'Make your mind up. You seem to be suspecting everybody.'

'Par for the course, in this job. You have to look at every situation from every angle,' replied Holmes smugly.

'I wouldn't like to be inside your head. It must be like being at the eye of a hurricane, with everything whirling around madly in your mind.'

'Merely logic in there, Garden. Can't solve things without it; take my word for it.'

Sanjay Chandra turned up at about a quarter past one, his packed lunch with him in a small shoulder bag, and asked permission to eat it while they talked. Permission received, Holmes began to fire his theories at him, confusing the client so much that he dipped his onion bhaji into his tea instead of into the raita.

'Please,' he exhorted the moustachioed older man, 'just let me think about all these ideas. They have not occurred to me before and you are making my head spin.'

'Got to look at all the possibilities, Mr Chandra. Can't let someone get away with all these murders and the attempted one as well; just not cricket.'

This mention of his beloved cricket confused the client even more, and he wondered if Holmes had, in fact, escaped from a lunatic asylum, and Garden was, maybe, harbouring a fugitive. 'Mr Garden, I don't understand.'

'Never you mind, Mr Chandra,' chipped in Holmes, his

voice an unwelcome sound in their client's ears. 'We will come back to the office with you this afternoon and we will have a word with this Mr Sandiford.'

'But you will lose me my job,' wailed Sanjay, trying to drink from his little container of lime pickle instead of from his teacup.

'Nonsense. We'll just drop in for a little chat.'

'And we won't come straight after lunch,' Garden reassured him.

'We won't?' asked Holmes, now confused.

'No. We'll drop in just before you finish work, so that Mr Sandiford's day won't be too disordered,' declared Garden decisively. If they were going to go a-visiting at all, it would be at a time when the poor man had a chance of easy escape through his wife expecting him home, or a business dinner to attend: allegedly. He knew he would have had something similar if Holmes had just turned up in his office, a perfect stranger, and started asking him odd questions that implied he was a murderer. Still, Holmes was the boss, ultimately. It was his business, and he must run it however he wished.

Chapter Fifteen

Holmes and Garden arrived in the car park of Messrs Carlton, Piccadilly and Mayfair at a quarter past five, having shut their own office a little early, as they had no clients in for consultation. For this reason, they had also taken separate cars, so that Holmes did not have to take Garden home, nor Holmes return for his own motor.

Sanjay Chandra saw them enter the reception area, and immediately went out to greet them and apprise the receptionist of the reason for their visit, or as respectable a version as he could think of on short notice. If Mr Sandiford got wind of the fact that Holmes thought him a multiple murderer, he might get very irate, then Sanjay would be looking for another positon elsewhere, and Mrs Chandra would be very unhappy.

Mr Sandiford greeted his two uninvited guests with a little puzzlement, but with perfect manners. Such was the innocence which shone through his comments and opinions that even Holmes could not raise the enthusiasm to point the finger and proclaim him to be a murderer who was too mean to pay redundancy money.

He seemed genuinely distressed about what was happening to his staff, and likened it to the Agatha Christie novel the name of which was now unmentionable. 'They seemed to be being wiped out, one by one,' he summed up, 'and I wonder if this is the macabre work of an unscrupulous and psychopathic business rival. Certainly I don't think any of my staff would be able to locate a brake pipe – which I believe was cut on Davidson's car – let alone have the murderous intent to cut one.'

'That's an angle we haven't thought of,' said Holmes, looking thoughtful, and even Garden seemed to find this an interesting proposition. 'Could you give me the names of any of your business rivals who seem at all aggressive in their approach to acquiring new clients, and such?' Holmes didn't really know what he was talking about, but it seemed as good a question as any at the time.

'Let me think on it, gentlemen. Let me mull it over overnight, and see if I can come up with anything,' Sandiford declared in an attempt to bring this unscheduled interview to an end.

'Thank you very much for your time,' Garden said in reply, thus aiding and abetting the man's aims, then tactfully escorted Holmes back to the reception area. Before Holmes could protest that his questioning had been cut short, Mr Chandra appeared as if by magic and now stood before them with his hands clasped together in a beseeching manner. He bowed his head slightly at them and asked,

'I wonder if you would do me the honour of returning with me to my marital home to take a cup of chai with my wife and me. You are both being so helpful that I would like my Indraani to meet both of you, who are so diligently engaged in protecting me from harm.'

'That's very kind of you, Mr Chandra,' Garden accepted for the both of them, leaving Holmes with his mouth hanging open, and no say in the matter.

Chapter Sixteen

Three cars drew up at the modest terraced townhouse, and Mr Chandra ushered them up to the first floor, calling out, 'Indraani, my little flower, we have important visitors. Where are you?'

A woman appeared at the door of what the two visitors assumed was the kitchen, as delicious smells were issuing from it. Her face set a little rigidly as she realised that her husband was not alone, but she managed to turn the grimace into a smile of welcome after only a fraction of a second, and held out her hand to both of them in turn.

'I see your car is back from the garage,' commented Sanjay conversationally, as she bowed politely to each of her guests in turn.

'It has needed some work doing on it,' she replied.

'That is life, my flower. Now, come into the sitting room while Indraani makes us chai.'

Garden took a seat with a rather preoccupied expression, and seemed to be lost in thought as Holmes and Mr Chandra made polite conversation. '... eh, Garden?' The junior partner of the firm suddenly became aware that he had, indeed, been lost in his own thoughts and conjectures, and that he didn't have the slightest idea of what Holmes had just asked him.

'Sorry, Holmes. I didn't quite catch what you said,' he replied, a little shamefacedly.

'Didn't quite catch it? Why, you were in a world of your own. Penny for 'em, old man, and we were just saying how worrying it must have been for Mr Chandra here, hearing of all his colleagues being bumped off.'

'Quite so,' Garden replied, still not really up with the conversation.

'Come along, old man, pay attention,' Holmes exhorted him, as Indraani entered with a loaded tray, immediately capturing the full attention of the man's partner. 'What are you staring at, Garden. It's rude to stare.'

'Sorry, Holmes, Mrs Chandra,' he apologised. 'Will you excuse me a minute while I go outside to make a phone call.'

'You don't have to go outside,' Sanjay explained politely.

'It's a rather personal matter,' Garden explained, leaving the room and trotting down the stairs to the outside.

All four of them were sitting sipping sweet, milky chai in the Chandra's living room when there was a ring on the doorbell and Sanjay, as the head of the household, went down to answer it.

When he re-entered the room, he had the figure of Inspector Streeter in tow, much to Holmes' utter surprise. Was the man out to quash their investigation? With a glint of triumph in his eye, the Inspector recited the familiar caution to Indraani, arrested her, and took her away in handcuffs.

Chapter Seventeen

'How on earth did you fathom that one out?' asked Holmes in an aggrieved voice, when they had retired to the nearest public house to discuss what had just happened.

'There was simply nobody else left who could have done it, except for her. When we arrived, I noticed that she had an oil stain on her sari that looked as if it were part of the pattern, at first. Mrs Chandra wasn't the sort of person who messed with the workings of a car, so I wondered if she'd been under one recently.

'Then Mr Chandra mentioned that her car was back and she said she'd had some work done on it. It wasn't a million miles away from a dirty great sign that she had been trying to ensure that her husband received any promotion that was going.

'I phoned Streeter when I went outside, and he got a couple of his men phoning round the garages in Farlington market to see if a Mrs Chandra had dropped a vehicle in for repair recently, and one of them discovered that she'd had some work done to the front end and had had the bonnet replaced.

'It probably won't be a long time before a witness near the Rothwell house remembers seeing an Indian woman in the street on the day of Mr Rothwell's murder. She must have slipped into the house via an unlocked door when he was home for lunch, which she would have known if she'd phoned Sanjay and he'd happened to mention it. He said he phones her every day to make sure that everything at home is running smoothly. And she could just have waited until he returned, as Mr Chandra was liable to be late, as always – all that unpaid overtime.

'It was what she said as she was arrested that got to me, though: the reason she did it all.'

'"A matter of honour," repeated Holmes, bemusedly. 'It was a matter of honour due to his long service that her husband be awarded the promotion. Whatever next?'

THE END

THE HAUNTING OF SHERMAN HOLMES

Chapter One

'I won't have any of those rubbishy decorations in an office of mine. I simply don't understand this mumbo-jumbo of paganism, and American, to boot – and why do they have to call it Holloween instead of Hallowe'en?'

Garden could hear the absence of an apostrophe in the first rendition of the word.

'I find it absolutely beyond the pale and positively sinister. It always used to be All Hallows Eve, when I was a boy; or at least, I think it did. And now we have all this airy-fairy nonsense of decorations and pumpkins – foul vegetables that they are – and wearing masks and disguises, with gangs going round and terrorising respectable folk in their own homes,' snarled Holmes.

'You've had a party of early trick-or-treaters round, haven't you?' Garden asked, with a sigh. 'Whatever can you have against an excuse for innocent children to dress up and call on the neighbours? They're usually accompanied by a parent or another grown-up.'

'These weren't. They were about six feet tall and had cigarettes, acne, and attitude.'

'What? But you can hardly hold them responsible for an innocent childhood pastime at the end of October,' Garden replied, quite reasonably.

'It's socially acceptable begging in the best light.'

'Holmes, you old grump. Where's your inner child?'

'I am, fortunately, without issue, and am harbouring no such being.'

'Then you need to get one. It's half the fun of life, being able to look at certain things from a child's point of view.'

'You'll be asking me to start believing in Santa Claus again.'

Garden gave another heavy sigh. When Holmes was in this mood, there was no point in arguing with him.

'Sherman, can't we at least have a pumpkin with a candle in it in the window?' This question was from Shirley Garden, John H.'s mother and secretary/receptionist of the Holmes and Garden private investigations business, for whom her boss had a very soft spot.

After a short silence, Holmes capitulated and agreed, but on the condition that he didn't have anything to do with buying or carving it. Shirley did a little dance of glee, then fled from the office to purchase a pumpkin rather than draw any unwanted attention to herself. She needed, at all costs, to avoid Holmes' admiring glance.

Later that afternoon the smell of recently carved gourd pervaded the offices, and Sherman Holmes wrinkled his nose. 'Can we also get a can of air freshener?' he pleaded.

'Do you really dislike pumpkins that much?' asked Garden. 'I love the soup, and have you ever eaten pumpkin pie?'

'I have actually tried the latter. We had a chap in the office for a short time who was American, and he insisted on making a huge one for everyone to try, at what he referred to as Thanksgiving. I thought I was going to do what is known in the vernacular as "blow my guts".'

'Sherman!' Shirley was disgusted by the very thought.

'Was it really that bad?' asked Garden, now interested.

'Absolutely foul.'

'Maybe the man was just a bad cook,' he offered.

'Bad cook be damned. He was wolfing it down as if there was no tomorrow and making all sorts of horrible little squeaks of delight and appreciation.'

'We are, indeed, two nations divided by a common

language and fractured culture.'

'Johnny, stop being a smart arse.' ordered his mother imperiously.

'If either of you wants to take the blasted thing home when it's served its purpose, that's fine by me, otherwise it goes in the dustbin.'

'Recycling of vegetable matter bin.' Garden had now become pedantic.

Thus was the mood in the office of the detective agency on the day that Mr Harry Twister entered its portals, the bell pinging to announce his arrival and putting a stop to the petty squabbling that had been taking place therein.

'Good afternoon, sir. How may we help you?' asked Shirley, retaking her seat behind the reception desk and immediately looking demure. Holmes and Garden stood as still as statues, trying to look benevolent and caring. 'Do take a seat.'

Mr Twister introduced himself, inspiring introductions all round and seated himself opposite Shirley. 'I have a problem which I am unable to solve,' he began.

'Come on through to the back office,' Holmes invited, and led the way as all three men disappeared and Shirley sulked. She never got to hear any of the good stuff.

Harry Twister began his strange tale from a chair placed between the two desks. 'It's like this. There is a house in the possession of my family which has not been occupied for some time, because the stories go that it is haunted.'

'It's what, sir?' Holmes looked startled, and Garden sat up straighter with interest.

'It is said to be occupied by a number of ghosts and spirits who only manifest themselves on Hallowe'en. Now, this is a difficult problem to get to grips with. I've had a word with the police and they are, of course, unable to help me, but Detective Inspector Streeter said that this might be right up your alley.'

'Have you ever consulted a psychic or ghost-hunter?' queried Garden, feeling a little foolish at such a question.

'There is no point in talking to such people. Not only are most of them charlatans, but I'm convinced that they would "find" all sort of presences there just for the publicity. No, what I need is a couple of rational heads that wouldn't be swayed by such thoughts.'

Holmes took a moment to preen himself. 'I think you've come to exactly the right people. Nobody more level-headed than us, eh, Garden?'

Garden nodded his agreement, then wondered what Mr Twister would think of his alter ego, Joanne. Would he consider her existence level-headed or just plain potty? 'I think we could investigate with complete integrity,' he added, without a hint of a blush. Joanne was private, and what a man did in his private life was no one's business but his own.

'Of course,' Mr Twister continued, 'I realise now that common trespass is a civil matter, and not something that can be attributed to spirits or ghosts and, therefore, not able to be investigated by the police. Thus, I find myself here, invoking your help.'

'What precisely would you like us to do?' Holmes was definitely intrigued.

'I wonder if you would allow me to employ you to visit the place with me, perhaps this afternoon or tomorrow, and then return to it on the thirty-first at dusk, to spend the night there. There are tales of other people attempting to do so and going mad in the process. I have no idea of the veracity of these tales, but the family would very much like to sell the property, and the scurrilous stories are currently hindering our attempts to market it. I know it's an esoteric undertaking, but I should be very grateful to retain your services in this matter.'

Holmes was hooked, his face a mask of anticipation, and he accepted with alacrity, arranging for them to meet at the offices the next morning for a viewing. Before their new client left, he told Holmes that, if that individual didn't mind him saying so, he was the absolute spit and image of Sir Arthur Conan Doyle, and Garden thought his partner would burst with pride. 'But you're Sherman, nor Sherlock,' he concluded.

'I rather think my mother must have been scared by a tank during the War,' Holmes added; a somewhat outré statement. 'Did you know that Conan Doyle went to school with two brothers Moriarty, and that there was also at his school a student called Sherlock?'

'Would ten-thirty tomorrow morning suit you, sir, outside this office?' enquired Garden and, having set their rendezvous, Mr Twister took his leave of them, but not before commenting,

'Goodness me. His fellow students must have been an inspiration to him.'

When Mr Twister had left, Garden expressed his concern for what they had taken on but, as Holmes said with complete logic, if it was a load of old wives' tales, then it was easy money, and something that would further their reputation in the investigating field.

Chapter Two

Holmes came in in a terrible state of anxiety the next morning and, on enquiring what the matter was, he told Garden that when he had got home the previous evening, he had found his beloved cat, Colin, limping very badly on his left front paw. When he had inspected it, he found a swelling of some considerable size.

Delaying only to apply a couple of sticking plasters to his injured hand, he took the animal immediately to the late-evening surgery at the vet's, only to discover that the trouble was caused by an infection, probably from a bite inflicted in a fight with another feline. The vet had said that he would have to lance the infection and, that he would keep him in overnight to keep an eye on things, as he didn't have time to do anything until the morrow.

'I can't pick him up until two o'clock this afternoon, and I have a dental appointment which I can't cancel as I have been suffering, for the last couple of days, with toothache,' he explained then looked at Garden piteously but with hope.

Garden stared back at him, mute, until his partner steeled himself to ask the favour, as no obvious offer of help was forthcoming. 'I don't suppose you could possibly pick him up for me and take him back to my apartment, could you? He'll have had a general anaesthetic, and should be very dopey.'

Garden heaved a great sigh of defeat, and found that he was unable to refuse this small service, as Holmes was in pain, and the cat couldn't stay indefinitely at the veterinary surgery. 'I suppose so. Give me your keys before you go off for your appointment. Which vet's is it?'

'The one on the outskirts near the old church. Thanks, old boy. I'm pretty sure I'll need at least a filling, if not an extraction, and I simply don't know how long I'll be.'

Harry Twister turned up promptly, and the three of them set off, Holmes and Garden in Holmes' car, Mr Twister leading the way. It was quite some distance to the property in question and in some ways reminded them of a property they had visited on a previous case.

It was very large, isolated, and enclosed by a tall walled garden. It was also in a state of some disrepair, and loured there forlornly like a neglected dog that is ever hopeful of some kindness.

When they were out of the vehicles and standing before it, Twister remarked, 'It's a bit of a pile, isn't it?'

'It hasn't the most welcoming of aspects,' replied Holmes, staring at the place thoughtfully. 'I can quite see why it's got rather a reputation.'

'The family would really like to offload it, as we cannot afford either to redevelop it into something else, or demolish it for new building.'

'That would certainly be one pile spent on another.' Holmes was being witty.

'Just so,' replied Twister having, evidently, no sense of humour. 'Shall we go inside?'

The interior was so gloomy from the general accumulated grime on the window panes that it rather gave the effect of being underwater.

'Can we put on some lights?' asked Garden, looking about him dubiously.

'Only if there were an electricity supply, Mr Garden. I fear the supply has been cut off these many a long year.' Great!

In some internal hallways and corridors it was necessary for them to put a hand to one of the walls to feel their way along, so dark was it. 'Is it possible to get the supply restored for the thirty-first?' asked Holmes, a note of hope in his voice.

'I fear not. The wires are in too distressed a state for that to be safe. I'm afraid you will have to manage with torches or camping lanterns.'

'I'm sure we shall manage it,' said Garden with a confidence he didn't feel. The atmosphere was damp and choked with disturbed dust, and he felt that this truly was a house that deserved its reputation as a place haunted. Curtains hung in rags from the windows, carpets were moth-eaten and full of holes, cobwebs hung down as traps for the unobservant, and every door creaked.

Holmes, who brought up the rear, suddenly squealed and uttered, 'Oh, dear God!'

'What is it? Unexpected cobweb?' asked Garden with a grin.

'Ruddy spider: actually landed on my face. Ugh! Get off, you foul thing.' Holmes was slapping furiously at his person, trying to ascertain whether the creature had actually gone, or was lurking somewhere else about his clothing.

'You're surely not frightened by insects, Mr Holmes?' asked Twister.

'Only of the eight-legged arachnid variety,' he replied, his face a mask of horror as he looked up to check whether anything else octoped lurked there.

It seemed like days had passed during their tour round the rambling maze of the house, and it was with great relief that they emerged into daylight again after about thirty minutes. 'How many bedrooms does that place have?' asked Holmes, desperately trying to look interested rather than whey-faced and thoroughly unsettled.

'Don't actually know,' admitted Twister. 'I've always stopped counting at twenty on the first floor, then there are all those attic rooms that used to house the staff.'

'It's bloody enormous,' was Garden's first verbal

reaction. 'How are we supposed to know where to ghost-hunt?'

'I should station yourselves in the first floor bedrooms on the east side,' suggested their client.

'But ...'

'It's alright, Holmes, I've always got a compass in the car, but perhaps Mr Twister could indicate the side of the house where we should station ourselves, by pointing.'

'Up there.' Mr Twister did so.

'So, now we know. We shall be here at dusk on the thirty-first. Thank you for your business,' Garden ended the visit, and they went their separate ways, Mr Twister having handed over the keys of the property.

Chapter Three

Holmes made an early lunch of soup and a soft bread roll in a nearby café, then returned to the office to brush his teeth, producing a toothbrush and a tube of paste from his briefcase. 'Here are the keys to the apartment, Garden. I'm depending on you to get Colin comfortably settled after his surgical ordeal this morning.'

'I'm sure he'll be suitably sleepy when I've let him out of his cat-box,' replied Garden, quite nonchalant about his coming good deed. He left his mother in sole charge of the business when he left the office, saying that he shouldn't be too long, and she could always contact him on his mobile if anything important came up.

Colin was waiting for him, absolutely zonko in his plastic conveyance when Garden turned up to collect him. 'I have a word of caution,' the vet said before he could leave the practice. 'Some animals can be quite disorientated when they come round from a general anaesthetic, and he's now loaded with painkillers and antibiotics. You really ought to stay with him until he is fully conscious again, so that he doesn't get too anxious.

This declaration left Garden feeling anxious himself but he dutifully carried the rather heavy cat-box out and put it on the back seat of his car before driving towards Holmes' apartment.

On entering, he put the plastic box on the floor and opened the end so that Colin could exit it on waking. He then went to the kitchen to make himself some coffee, knowing that Holmes always had some nice Columbian in his kitchen. A little rummaging even produced a mug, instead of one of the dainty cups and saucers the owner usually used.

Walking back into the living room, he noticed that Colin was stirring, and trying to stand up. The cat got his front legs out of the cat-box and promptly fell over. Garden chuckled quietly to himself. The cat made another attempt to get out of his temporary sleeping quarters, and this time made it to the hearthrug where he promptly collapsed again.

'Not such a big boy now, are you?' said Garden, with a smile.

Colin looked around, being for the first time conscious of the fact that he had company, and he glared. Garden slowly approached one of the Chesterfield sofas, with the object of settling himself down with his coffee until Colin had completely recovered, then high-tailing it out of here.

Colin wobbled uncertainly to his feet again and turned in Garden's direction, commencing to hiss. Garden held his nerve, as the vet had said, he might be quite groggy when he woke up.

Colin started to growl deep in his throat, something which Garden didn't realise a cat could do. The cat, looking inebriated, staggered a few steps towards the figure of Garden, who was not quite at the sofa yet, but frozen to the spot with trepidation.

'There's a nice kitty, Colin. It's only your Uncle John come to visit you,' declared Garden in soothing tones. The sound of his voice was like a red rag to a bull, and Colin showed his teeth, then hissed ferociously. With a howl of indignation at the presence of such a person in his territory, the feline launched himself at his cat-sitter.

Still being slightly under the influence of the anaesthetic, the cat missed, but Garden, considering that cowardice was the better part of self-preservation, dropped his mug of coffee in fright and fled from the room, slamming the door behind him.

Hastily scribbling a note which he left on the hall table, informing the owner of the property that he had spilled a cup of coffee in his living room, Garden fled to his car, his legs shaking. If Colin had really still been affected, all it had done was to make him more vociferous in his true feelings for his owner's business partner. The last thing he heard was a howl of fury and the sound of the cat hurling himself against the firmly closed door.

He hadn't really registered it until now, but the vet had had a few sticking plasters on his hands, and he would bet good money that his injuries were down to Holmes' beloved Colin. And he wouldn't go back into that room for all the tea in China. Holmes was a truly deluded man if he thought Colin was such a cuddle-bunny.

Chapter Four

The next morning, Holmes bustled in, very bristly about the coffee that had been spilled on his floorboards and precious rug. 'Took me ages to get it out, and I can still see where it was, if I look carefully,' he moaned at Garden. 'And you got a mug out of my kitchen cupboard. I thought I'd got that well hidden away. I usually only use it for cocoa. Whatever came over you, man?'

'How is Colin?' asked Garden, trying to change the subject.

'I found him soundly asleep on the chair. I checked his dressing, and he hadn't been chewing it: in the main, he just ignores it, which is good news as his stitches will need time to heal.' Suddenly becoming aware that he had been bamboozled, Holmes returned to the previous subject.

'You left me a note that you had spilled some coffee, but why the dickens didn't you clear it up before you left? Most unmannerly.'

'You don't know what that animal was like when he woke up,' Garden said in his own defence.

'*That animal*? That's my Colin that you're talking about. He's a very friendly cat.'

'Look here, Holmes; the vet said he might act strangely when he came round, and when he did wake up, he was absolutely wild.'

'I can hardly believe it. What did he do?'

'Well, he fell over a few times trying to find all four of his legs at the same time.'

'My poor baby!'

'Then, he started hissing and growling, then he just

flew at me. Fortunately, as he wasn't quite himself, he missed, I dropped my coffee, and ran out of the room, shutting the door behind me. He even threw himself at the door after I shut it.'

'Garden, you obviously don't understand that cat. And I truly believe you suffer from hallucinations. Hrmph!'

Garden let this go and went off to put on the kettle; normally his mother's job, but he didn't fancy an argument with his partner so early in the day. When he had distributed the cups of coffee, he went to his desk and asked in a conciliatory way how Holmes' tooth was.

'Just a filling, fortunately.' Holmes was still feeling a bit tetchy.

'How about we both try to draw a plan of that house from memory? I know it's a long shot, but if we get the general run of the rooms, it might help us on our mission.'

Holmes brightened up at this suggestion, and they both set to, to reproduce as much as they could of floor plans for the property in which they would be spending the night on the thirty-first. As they were about this task, they heard someone enter the front office and ask if they stocked Hallowe'en decorations, and Shirley's patient explanation that they were not in the business of selling such fripperies. 'That's the third one this week,' declared Holmes. 'Why can't they read the sign on the window properly? I've had the thing re-done.'

'Maybe we should have some cards from an optician's on our counter. We could have a reciprocal agreement. Anyone who moans whilst having their eyes tested about some niggling problem that needs looking into, the optician could give them one of our cards, and when someone comes in here for decorating or garden materials, we could give them one of his.'

'Sort of, cross-seed, you mean?'

'Exactly.'

'Not a bad idea.' Holmes contentedly returned to his

plan, his tongue sticking out of the corner of his mouth in concentration.

At the end of this mapping task, they both felt pretty pleased with their efforts but, on comparison, their plans were totally different to each other's. 'Holmes, you've got the morning room opening off the drawing room, and it's off the hall.'

'No it isn't. I distinctly remember walking through the drawing room to get to the morning room,' replied Holmes indignantly.

'You did, but there are adjoining doors from one to the other, apart from the entrance from the hall. And you've got the stairs coming up in the wrong place and have missed out two or three bedrooms on the first floor. And both of the bathrooms.'

'I didn't actually see any bathrooms.'

'That's because you were too busy disentangling yourself from that spider and looking to see if there were any more lurking in the vicinity.'

'Truce. Truth to tell, I'm not very good at maps and plans and things like that. Let me look at yours more closely.' Taking Garden's plan, Holmes perused it earnestly and finally sighed. 'This looks very like what we walked round. I suggest we use this one.'

'It won't be long before we're back there and actually using this to help us navigate. Now, what do we need in the way of equipment?

'Compass, just in case,' suggested Holmes.

'For indoors?' queried Garden.

'I get very easily lost with twisty, turny staircases, and I remember, as a child, I had to be led out of the maze at Hampton court, in tears. I missed the best of the trip because I couldn't get out of the dratted thing, then, when they counted heads to get back in the coach, they realised I was missing and sent out a search party.'

'Compass. Check,' intoned Garden.

'We'll need a good supply of lamps. I've got a couple of Gaz lamps.'

'So has Mother. And we could bring plenty of candles and torches. I expect we'll need sandwiches and flasks as well, if we're going to be there all night.'

'Good idea. And a book.'

'And toilet paper,' added Garden firmly, for he had been caught out on this one in several locations. 'The facilities might be available, but the necessary paper wasn't.'

'Why?'

'I'd rather not say but, believe you me, we'll need it.'

Holmes suddenly twigged to what Garden was suggesting, and coughed to cover his embarrassment.

'Now, what will we need in the way of technical equipment? We'll need a means of recording anything that we hear. We'll need torches to shine on anything dodgy, and we'll need cameras, and telephones,' said Garden.

'Won't that all be a bit bulky?'

'Not at all. We've got them all-in-one in our mobile phones.'

'Good thinking, John H. Good thinking.'

'What about a duvet or eiderdown to keep warm? The evenings are getting a little chilly, and the nights even more so.'

'Good grief, we shall need a removal van if you think of anything else. We must just dress properly for the occasion: woolly hats, gloves, scarves and a decent wool overcoat.'

'Appropriate clothing,' droned Garden. 'Check.'

'I hope you're making a list.'

'Of course I am.'

Shirley Garden, their receptionist/secretary waltzed in as they were about their listing activity and declared that she had completed the window decorations to her satisfaction, and she urged them to come with her to see what she had done. 'I took the money out of petty cash,' she informed them as they went into the front office.

Holmes took one look at the black cut-out witches on their broomsticks, the black cats, the bats and the pumpkin head glowing eerily behind a curtain that Shirley had stood on a chair to pin up, turned purple, and walked off without a word. He was too cross to talk.

'We had to make some sort of an effort, not just to attract people to the window, but because you actually have a case connected with Hallowe'en,' she explained.

'And just how many more people are we going to have coming here in search of similar decorations now that you've done that. As Ebenezer Scrooge once said, "I shall retire to Bedlam".' Evidently, Holmes had recovered his ability to speak.

Chapter Five

They left the office closed during the day of the thirty-first at Holmes' behest, as he didn't want them to be bedevilled by children in horror fancy-dress coming round begging for rewards, not for doing something, but for not doing anything.

All three of them met in the rear office about an hour before dusk, the men to gather together all their equipment, Shirley to provide them both with a feast of sandwiches and cake. 'I'm going to take my sturdy old cassette recorder,' announced Holmes. 'I stocked up on blank cassettes before they became unavailable, and I've got four new ones here. We could leave it running in the hall to catch any sound that emanates from down there, if we're going up to those bedrooms.'

'How long are they?' asked Garden in concern.

'They're C120s.'

'So we'll have to keep coming downstairs to change them over, or put in a new one.'

'I must admit. I hadn't thought of that; but I don't see that it'll be a bother,' countered Holmes.

'It will be if there's something afoot down there. Would you fancy going on your own if there's wailing and the clanking of chains?'

'We'd go together.'

'Then I'll just fetch my baseball bat from upstairs: an unwanted gift that I knew would come in handy someday.'

'You've got a baseball bat?'

'Yep.'

'Good luck, my brave ghost-hunters,' Shirley bade

them, as they loaded all the things they needed into their cars.

Garden was the last to leave the office, determinedly clutching his precious toilet roll in one hand and his baseball bat in the other.

The light was definitely failing as they reached the house, and it looked even more menacing than it had done on their last visit. Some of the windows seemed to be eyes, watching their every movement, as they unloaded their equipment. After all, an uninhabited house during the hours of darkness has almost a duty to emanate a sinister and malign ambience. Its very existence hints at threats and danger, and chills ordinary mortal blood to the marrow.

With a deep breath to summon courage, Holmes said, 'We'll put everything in the hall, then we'll take it upstairs from there, after I've set my cassette to record. And we'll stick together. If anything happens, it will need more than one witness for it to have a chance of being believed.' Garden smiled in the gloom, sensing that this was more a mild act of cowardice than an attempt at efficiency.

It took them two trips upstairs carrying lamps, candles, duvets, sandwiches, and flasks, but eventually Holmes declared that they would 'bivvy' in the middle bedroom on the east side. It was a large room in which there still existed a musty old double bed and two stout armchairs. 'At least we can take our ease while we watch and wait,' he said.

They opted for first choice to use the armchairs, both of them thinking that it would be rather improper for both of them to stretch out on the bed together, but Garden had the feeling that, in the middle of the night, they may have to amalgamate their bedcovers into one space for maximum warmth. For now, he kept his mouth shut. Necessity is the mother not only of invention, but also of un-convention.

As Holmes lit the camping lamps, Garden made so bold

as to point out that the morning room did, indeed, have an entrance from the vestibule, but Holmes only grunted in reply, obviously not about to dignify this undoubtedly true statement with a reply. Instead, he said, 'Shall we grab a bite to eat? Shirley has labelled the sandwiches, and we've got cheese and pickle and ham and tomato. She's also done a flask of tea and one of coffee.'

'We mustn't eat anything just yet, otherwise we'll be starving by three o'clock. We might, however, have a cup of tea just to warm up.'

'How very sensible of you, Garden.' Holmes sounded most disappointed and was rather thinking of this as a school trip, where packed lunches were always consumed directly after exiting the school gates.

Taking their covers, they both settled into the armchairs with books by the rather less than adequate light of the camping lights until, at about eleven o'clock, there came the definite sound of footsteps from above in the attic rooms. Both figures froze, their eyes swivelling upwards. 'What's that?' whispered Holmes in alarm.

'Probably our imaginations getting the better of us,' replied Garden, also in a whisper.

'What, both of us?'

'Should we go up and take a look?' asked Garden.

'No. Entirely unnecessary if we just imagined it. If you want to go up there to take a look round, be my guest.' Holmes definitely sounded jittery.

'Not just at the moment, I think.' Garden was also spooked, and tried, without much success, to concentrate on his book again.

Just before midnight there was again the definite creaking of floorboards followed by the sound of a door slamming. 'What in the name of God was that?' Holmes' voice was now high-pitched with alarm.

'That couldn't have been us imagining it. We really ought to go for a bit of a scout around. After all, that's what we're here for.'

'What, up in those low-ceilinged attics?'

'We're being paid for this. It would be dishonourable of us not to at least take a look around up there.'

'Suppose so. Look, if we each take a torch, you can take the baseball bat as well, just in case.'

'Just in case of what?'

'Just in case, you know?' Holmes wasn't going to take any chances, and if they happened on something or someone, he wanted Garden to be the one swinging the weapon while he made good his escape.

'You go first,' ordered Garden, collecting what he needed.

'Why me?'

'Because I've got something in both my hands. I can't open any doors carrying these two things.'

'Hell! Well, better get on with it, I suppose.' Holmes' voice was full of false bravado as he made this statement.

As they slowly mounted the narrow, uncarpeted staircase, their hearts in their mouths, there came the sound of whispering voices back on the first floor, and this stopped them in their tracks. Holmes was so startled that he dropped his torch, which bounced back down the stairs and promptly went out. 'Heaven help us,' he muttered, catching hold of Garden's sleeve as he did so.

'Let's just go back down, shall we?' Garden asked.

'What, back down there where that whispering came from?' asked Holmes, noting how almost impenetrable the gloom was in this confined space and with only one torch now to light their way. Motes of disturbed dust danced in its rays, threatening to take shape and haunt them.

'Look, we either go up or down. If we go back down, we'll be nearer the front door than we'll be up in the attics. Here, you take my torch, and I'll bring up the rear with the baseball bat.'

When they plucked up the courage to return to the

bedroom in which they had been encamped, Holmes put both of the vacuum flasks hard up against the closed door. 'If anyone tries to get in, should we ever be relaxed enough to doze off, that'll wake us, when they get knocked over.'

'Just before we get settled, I think I'll pour us a cup of coffee – before replacing it, of course – and maybe that will keep us awake,'

'Good thinking, old chap.'

Chapter Six

Both the men, despite their misgivings, did succumb to sleep, and it was some time later that they were woken again, but neither was sure just what had disturbed them. A few seconds after they awoke, there came the sound of a definite evil cackle, and they jumped out of their chairs, both wondering where they were.

'What in the name of all that's holy was that?' Holmes sounded terrified.

'Night bird!' declared Garden, with more confidence than he felt. That had been no bird he knew. 'And, by the way, your cassette will have run out by now, and we really ought to go down and turn it over, or change it, I can't remember what one does with those things it's so long since I used them.'

'Do we have to?'

'Yes. We have to do the right thing, or we can't give a full report to Mr Twister.'

The stairs creaked on the way down, something they had not taken note of when they ascended, and the noise that the treads issued made them even more uneasy. All went well until the recorder was turned on once more, when there was a tapping at one of the hall windows, and a ghastly face looked in at them.

Neither noticed the creaking of the stairs on their flight back up them. As they fled, an owl hooted in a sinister fashion, and the moon, smudged and misshapen, glowed through a large, begrimed window pane.

The thermos flasks were, thankfully, unbroken after their incontinent flight from the hall and when they reached the sanctuary of the bedroom, they sat down with coffee again to bolster their nerves. 'I wish I'd brought a hip flask with me,' said Holmes between gulps.

'We couldn't have used it,' opined Garden. 'We have to drive away from here. I wouldn't fancy fleeing into the overgrown jungle of the garden, and this is a well out of the way place, and at this hour too, we could become lost for the rest of the night.'

Everything was peaceful again until about two o'clock, when there was some noise from the landing, and they went out to investigate only to be confronted by a ghostly figure at the head of the stairs. It seemed to be floating a few inches from the ground, and was of a lady in Victorian dress. With a yell, they both retreated back into their sanctuary, where they climbed on to the tattered remains of the bed and put their covers over their heads.

After a few minutes, Holmes asked, 'Would you mind most awfully going to see if that thing is gone?'

Garden, having a very great desire for the use of the sanitary facilities, which he knew were a few doors along on the opposite side of the corridor, obliged more out of desperation than courage. At the sight of the out-of-time woman, his bowels had turned to liquid, and it had been only by a great muscular effort that he had contained himself.

Fortunately, there was no ghostly figure at the top of the stairs, and he retired to the privacy of one of the water closets to relieve himself of a very pressing problem. 'Where the hell have you been?' asked Holmes, when he finally got back to him.

'I had to go to the, um, loo,' he replied, 'and fortunately, there was some paper in there, for I forgot to put ours in it.'

'And that, er, thing has gone, has it?'

'It has.'

'Should we, possibly, make an honourable retreat now?

We have enough witness evidence, I'm sure. Let's just leave our stuff until tomorrow.'

'We can surely take the sandwiches. I'm damned hungry now.' Garden was surprised that he had enough wits left to discern the feeling of emptiness in his stomach.

They made their cautious way down the staircase with the aid of only one torch. Now, the stairs were the sort that started in the middle of the hall, then bifurcated into east and west flights and, when they got to the bottom, there was a sort of groaning noise behind them on the west side and, turning, they saw the outline, in the torch that Holmes held, of a hooded figure.

Holmes yelped like a dog, and made for the escape of the front door. Garden stood his ground for a moment longer, taking the opportunity to whip out his mobile and snap a photograph, as they had not done this with the figure on the landing, before joining Holmes in his headlong flight to his car.

Chapter Seven

Both Holmes and Garden headed for their separate homes, having no more conversational intercourse that night. The next morning, Holmes came into the office looking grey with lack of sleep, only to find that Garden was in a similar state. 'Have you tried phoning Mr Twister yet to tell him what happened to us last night?'

'We've only got a mobile number for him, for some reason, and it's going nowhere.'

'You mean it goes straight to voice mail?'

'It does. But surely he'd have told us if he wouldn't be available, considering how important this job was to the house being able to be sold.'

'I don't think anything we could tell him would give him much comfort,' said Holmes, still not recovered from his fright just a few short hours ago.

Garden tried the number again every thirty minutes for the rest of the morning, and they related their tale of a haunting to Shirley, who was duly impressed with their courage – poor, deluded woman. 'And now we can't seem to get hold of our Mr Twister,' concluded Holmes.

'Why didn't you get a landline number and an address when he first asked you to carry out this commission?' she asked.

'I suppose we both forgot in the excitement of what seemed rather a fun adventure, but turned out to be one of the most frightening nights of my entire life,' offered Garden, and Holmes nodded sagely in agreement.

'Just so. It must've been "The Boy's Own" comic-paper coming out in our characters.'

'And who recommended him to us?' she asked, lifting an eyebrow.

'Of course! He said he had been to see Inspector Streeter. He'll know where to find him.' Holmes was very satisfied with this deduction. 'We'll pop over and visit him after lunch. You can cope, can't you Shirley?'

'I'm sure I can. If I could deal with the hordes of children I had calling round last night, I'm sure I can cope with a minor flood of people coming in to enquire if we stock fireworks.'

'Eh?'

'"Remember, remember the fifth of November". You know some people still mistake us for a homes and garden store, rather than a private detection agency.'

'I wonder why Streeter recommended us? He doesn't approve of what we do.' Garden was a little too late verbalising this question.

'We'll just go to his office and report what happened in that ghastly old house, and see if he has any way we could contact our client, if only for billing purposes.' Holmes was back in business mode. 'We did complete our mission.'

'We left halfway through the night.'

'He only asked for independent corroboration. By the way, did that photo you took on your phone come out OK?'

'Here, let me show you. There's the definite shape of a hooded figure at the back of the hall depicted.'

'And I have my recordings. Twister shouldn't need any more evidence than that, and if he wants to call in someone to exorcise it, he should be able to offload it on some insensitive developer who doesn't believe in all that bally-hooey: not that I did until last night.'

'Me neither.' Garden was in full agreement with this last statement.

To their irritation, Inspector Streeter kept them waiting

forty minutes before they were ushered into his presence. To their complete surprise, he had a triumphant grin from ear to ear. 'What's tickled your funny bone, eh?' asked Holmes.

'Oh, nothing important. What can I do for you gentlemen?' he asked, still unaccountably cheerful.

'We understand you sent a man to us by the name of Twister. Is that correct? He certainly intimated that that was so.'

'It is true that I sent him to you.'

'And you couldn't help him?'

'Not at all.' Streeter was playing his cards very close to his chest, for some reason.

'Well, we have carried out the task which he requested us to, but we can't get hold of him to report back.'

'Odd,' replied Streeter, monosyllabically, and still grinning like the Cheshire cat.

'Do you have any contact details for him?' asked Garden. 'Address or a landline number? He doesn't seem to be answering his mobile.'

'No.' Again, Streeter's grin shone across the office at them.

'Why not?' Both private detectives were now intrigued at the policeman's hesitance in providing them with information.

'Because, *he doesn't exist!*'

'What? What are you talking about?' Holmes was furious.

'He came to our offices and talked to us, dammit,' roared Garden.

'I'll grant you that you talked to a man who stated that his name was Twister, but he was actually an old friend of mine who used to work for a television company's special effects department. Did his name not give the game away?'

'He used to what? What game?'

'So what about last night?' Holmes and Garden were dumbfounded by this last statement.

'All just a bit of flim-flam. Now, let me tell you something, I'm just about sick and tired of you two sticking your noses into things that are nothing to do with you and should be dealt with by the police. Last night was just my little message that I won't put up with it any more, and your intrusion into official investigations will be looked on very harshly.'

'You mean, you set all that up? And the bloke was bogus?' Holmes could hardly believe his ears.

'Just so, and it tickled me no end to think of you with what hair you've got left sticking up on end in fright.' This remark was definitely aimed at Holmes.

'But Garden has a photograph.'

'Of a hooded figure? Another friend from the AmDram Society.'

'But what about the ghost that we stood and looked at?'

'Ever heard of Pepper's ghost? Merely an illusion. Look it up if you want to.' And now, if you don't mind, I'll relieve you of the keys to what has been used as a location for a television series about the supernatural. Everything was in place, you see. How could I resist?'

'You can't have back the keys until we've collected our possessions from last night. You haven't heard the last of this, Streeter!'

'Did you run away without collecting up all your stuff?'

'How dare you!' This accurate but highly embarrassing accusation of cowardice had really got Holmes' goat.

'What are you going to do about it, come back and haunt me when you're dead?'

'There's no answer to that,' replied Garden, as the two men stalked out of the inspector's office.

On their way back to Holmes' car, its owner said, 'You know what this means, don't you, Garden?'

'Eh? No.'

'It means *war*! I'll out-detect that man if it's the last thing I do! I won't stand for being duped like that and made to look a fool.'

'Oh dear,' sighed Garden. There could be trouble ahead.

THE END

The Adventure of
THE DEAD WILD BORE

Members of the Quaker Street Irregulars
– a Sherlock Holmes appreciation society:

Antony, Cyril
Cave, Christopher
Connor, Ludovic
Crompton, Stephen
Dibley, Aaron
Jordan, Elliot
Lampard, Peter
Mitchell, Rupert
Warwick, Dave
Wiltshire, Bob
Wood, Kevin
– and Sherman Holmes

Chapter One

Sherman Holmes put down the telephone handset and stared around him with satisfaction. He was at his desk in the dining room of his apartment, which was furnished and decorated in homage to his fictional hero, the consulting detective Sherlock Holmes.

He gazed fondly at the violin mounted on the wall above the fireplace and the row of meerschaum pipes displayed on the mantelpiece. He smiled at his slightly battered leather Chesterfields facing each other across the pathway of the fire's welcome heat, and he thought about his new, cloaked overcoat, which hung out on the hallstand, a deerstalker hanging above it. He was very pleased indeed with his late Edwardian time-warp apartment at 21B Quaker Street, in the relatively quiet town of Farlington Market.

Holmes was in his mid-fifties, fairly short and plump, and with a fine moustache that was definitely 'of the era', and he spent a lot of his time reading Victorian or Edwardian novels and re-reading the fascinating tales that Conan Doyle had related about his genius detective.

As he smugly contemplated his cosy residence, his cat, Colin – he of the mercurial temper – strolled in and began to rub his face on the leg of Holmes' trousers. 'Hello there, old boy,' he greeted his pet, not particularly acknowledging what a fine mood the animal was in, as, in his eyes, Colin never suffered from a bad temper and could do no wrong, no matter what house guests told him to the contrary.

He did not have a busy social life or many visitors, but

even his new friend Garden had complained of being ill-treated by this feline, and Holmes believed, contrary to the evidence of his own eyes, that this was merely playfulness on Colin's part, and that the cat meant no real harm – even when he'd decorated the inside of one of Garden's shoes in a most unpleasant way.

'He was just putting his mark on it, to show that he likes you,' Holmes had told Garden, but his partner knew better, and avoided Colin as much as good manners allowed. If it was possible for a feline to look malevolently at a person, then Colin certainly did so with Garden, and Garden wisely kept his distance.

John H. Garden had received Holmes' call on a cold, misty, damp November afternoon in his bijou flat above their offices in Hamsley Black Cross, and had been delighted to receive an invitation to accompany him that very evening to a meeting of a local branch of a Sherlock Holmes appreciation society.

He was as big a fan of Conan Doyle's detective as his colleague, and was grateful for the opportunity of something to do and some company, for he did not get out much either.

The threads of fate had drawn them together, then threw murder in their pathway, and in the light of this, they had made an unlikely alliance. At the time they had met, John H. was thirty and still living with his mother, with whom he did not get on. He had a very unhappy working life with an insurance company, and a huge secret life locked in his bedroom and wardrobes, consisting of frocks, skirts, blouses, ladies' shoes, wigs, make-up, and costume jewellery, and yet only his mirror had seen his alter ego, Joanne.

Physically, he was slim and on the tallish side, with wavy brown hair and a predilection to brightly coloured clothing, mostly due to his experience with women's clothes. Although he always dressed smartly, now he dressed brightly as well, and had been delighted when the office premises they'd leased proved to have a small flat above it, where he now lived a fairly contented existence, especially as Joanne had made her debut public appearance during their first case together.

The business had been trading for months now – not always busily, but steadily – but today was a Sunday, and they didn't open on Sundays as a matter of principle. Not only did they not expect anyone to be able to get away from family on that particular day of the week to consult them in confidence, but Holmes dictated that they have one day a week free just to pursue other interests. Wednesdays was half-day closing in the sleepy town of Hamsley Black Cross, so they took it in turns to man the office on this afternoon.

The only thing the younger man had difficulty in coming to terms with in his new life as a private investigator was his mother, but for different reasons to those from which his negative attitude had arisen in the past. He had considered her a dragon when he first met Holmes, and was simply terrified of her. It was only on taking Holmes to his old family home to give him courage to tell his mother the truth about his cross-dressing that had opened his eyes to who she really was – a warm and completely understanding woman, although he still found the truth hard to believe, and his previous impression of her almost impossible to erase from his memory.

Holmes had merely seen an attractive and fashionably dressed woman of about fifty, who seemed to have lovely manners, and who seemed to harbour no malice or resentment towards her son at all. Garden realised that the only reason he had felt why he did was because his mother was so busy, and their timetables rarely coincided. He had taken the fact that they had communicated mainly in e-mails, notes, and texts for something far more sinister, and believed his mother hated him.

He had been horrified when Holmes had engaged her as their receptionist in the office, but was gradually coming round to the idea of seeing so much of her, although he still found their relationship difficult.

Privately flattered that Holmes should invite him to the meeting in his local pub – it was another little entrée into the man's private world, although he had been there once before in very different circumstances – he felt rather bewildered that his partner should want to spend some of his precious free time with him.

His flat was now decorated to his rainbow-bright taste, and he walked through the plethora of brightly coloured pictures, ornaments, and throws into his bedroom to select something to wear suitable for the occasion.

Flopping down on to his cerise and lilac striped bedcover, he surveyed the contents of his male wardrobe, suppressing the thought that it might be a bit of a wag to turn up as Joanne. Deciding, however, that this would not be taken in good part, he decided that he really ought to wear quite dull clothing, almost akin to that which he used to wear in the office. After all, they were going to Holmes' local, and he didn't want to embarrass the poor man, and make him a figure of fun right on his own doorstep.

By the time he left the flat, he was clad in a pair of dove-grey trousers and a lemon shirt, with a bottle green tie – didn't want to show the old boy up – with a natty navy overcoat over the top. In Quaker Street he parked neatly behind Holmes' car and rang the doorbell.

It took some time for his summons to be answered, and when it was, it was by a very flustered Holmes. 'Come away in, old chap. I'm afraid I'm in a bit of a tizzy, and I'm not quite ready. Thing is, I was just getting changed when I heard this awful noise, and when I went into the sitting room, I found poor old Colin had been rather ill in my slippers. Been eating mice again by the looks of it, and he knows they don't agree with him.'

Garden was of the opinion that Colin had done this on purpose, either because he wasn't getting as much attention as he thought he deserved, or, more likely because he knew Garden was coming round. He wouldn't put it past the sneaky feline to be aware that he was on his way over.

Following Holmes into the main living room, he became aware of the sound of the washing machine chugging rhythmically from the kitchen, and the cat sitting on one of the sofas, glaring balefully at him. It looked like it was still war between them. He took a tentative seat on the free sofa, all the while with one eye cocked for any movement from his nemesis, and asked, 'So, what exactly do you do at these meetings, and who goes?'

'Oh, it's just a bunch of local aficionados. We meet once a month and discuss our favourite stories, and also give our opinions of various film versions that have been made of the great detective's exploits. Sometimes one of us reads a little essay written as a fictional exploit that never graced Watson's pen.'

'How long do these meetings last?'

'A couple of hours. We've always got plenty to discuss, as we include television series in our debates, and the pub provides refreshments for us. Have you eaten?'

'Actually, no,' replied Garden, suddenly concerned for his stomach.

'That's the ticket. There are always plates of hearty sandwiches, and soft drinks if someone is driving. If you fancy something a bit harder, we have a waitress take our orders. I shall pay tonight's subscription for both of us. We usually pay a fiver a head to cover the food and squash.' Holmes beamed at Garden and rubbed his hands together in anticipation of sharing one of his pastimes with his new friend.

'That's very civil of you, Holmes, but I can pay my own way,' he retorted.

'Wouldn't hear of it, John H. Wouldn't hear of it. Now, I'll just slip my coat on' – he smirked as he removed his very Holmesian new garment from its hook – 'I've taken the liberty of booking us a taxi as it's so inclement out, and I believe I've just heard it pull up outside.'

Holmes had stopped making mention of the fact that the local police inspector had pulled a fast one on them a few weeks before, but Garden knew that it still rankled, and was careful never to bring up the subject of them being duped by this individual – Streeter, by name.

Garden was glad of not having to drive, because the mist had become a fog in Farlington Market – probably more of a smog, he thought, as there were quite a few industrial units on the periphery of the town – and he wasn't the most confident or gifted of drivers. He got around alright in his rather elderly Fiat Panda, but it wasn't his preferred mode of transport, being stuck behind a steering wheel and responsible not only for his own life, but possibly for someone else's as well.

Within ten minutes, they were dropped outside a corner building, the windows of which glowed murkily through the fog, and Holmes opened the door of the pub, releasing the sounds of quite a crowd of people letting off steam prior to returning to the daily grind of work in the morning. 'How many people normally attend these meetings?' Garden asked with some trepidation.

'Oh, only about a dozen of us. We're in the meeting room upstairs, so we won't be bothered by this rowdy lot,' replied Holmes, waving cheerily at a couple of acquaintances. This was a part of the pub that Garden had not visited on his previous call there for a work dinner.

He led Garden through a door into a small snug from which two other doors led, one to the ladies' – the gents' being entered from the public bar or by an odd little outside door – and the other on to a narrow and quite steep staircase leading to the first floor. 'Up we go, then,' announced Holmes, his good cheer sounding in the tone of his voice, and Garden followed him upwards.

At the top of the stairs, a swing door led into a small meeting room measuring about fifteen feet by fifteen, in the middle of which stood a long table surrounded by chairs. On the tabletop were plates of doorstep sandwiches which purported to be either ham and mustard or cheese and pickle, and several jugs holding a choice of either orange or lemon squash.

They were five minutes late, due to Holmes having had to clear up Colin's mess before he booked the cab, and five or six people were already sitting round the table chatting quietly. They had just taken seats at the far side of the table when another four entered, passing on apologies from Dave Warwick, whose wife had gone into labour a couple of hours ago.

'That'll be his fifth, won't it?' asked a red-headed man from the end of the table nearest the window, and there was a small titter of laughter accompanied by a few lewd comments on the man's fertility.

A small, elderly, white-haired man at the other end of the table called the meeting to order, and they were off. As this month's subject was given as the portrayal of the immortal detective on television, Garden suddenly flushed. There were no women present, and he had a vision of how daft he would have looked if he'd come as Joanne. Now, what did he know about Holmes on television?

Trying his best to remember who was who, Garden merely listened as they set off on the most recent portrayal of their hero as a modern young man, working with computers and smartphones – a phenomenon that he had greatly enjoyed, but which seemed to be frowned upon by these enthusiasts, with the exception of one man, whom Garden learnt was Peter Lampard, and he had seriously enjoyed these excursions into the twenty-first century and all its technological gadgets. One fellow present seemed insistent on getting over his own take on things, however, much to the disapproval of the other men.

As the discussion launched itself, Holmes muttered the names of the speakers to Garden to help him with identification of the members. They entered the subject in hand with a discussion of the most recent portrayal of 'the master' as a young gentleman in modern times, with an ex-army man from Afghanistan as his side-kick.

There was a fair amount of disapproval at this updating of the classic stories, but one member in particular struggled to insert his opinion, over-riding the contributions of other members in order to put forward his own viewpoint, even quenching Lampard's obvious enthusiasm for this series.

'I think it's very telling that Holmes and Watson were taken to be in a gay relationship in several episodes,' said the man identified to Garden as Cyril Antony, a big man with a very pompous and overbearing nature, who was determined to be heard.

Other members, amongst them Stephen Crompton, the white-haired man who was the chair of the meeting, tried to shout him down, but he persisted on this theme.

'It was obvious they had a close relationship,' he boomed, ignoring protests to the contrary. 'They had rooms together, they worked together, and Watson returned to live with Holmes after he married. I am of the opinion that the plot for the film *Brokeback Mountain* was based on their physical but compelling gay relationship.'

'What absolute tosh and rubbish,' shouted Ludovic Connor, a bank clerk. 'Theirs was a simple friendship. How could you possibly think anything different?'

'What a sewer of a mind you must have, Cyril, to even suggest such a thing,' contributed Aaron Dibley, identified to Garden as a probation officer. 'Take that back.'

'You filthy swine. How dare you even suggest such a

thing?' shouted Peter Lampard, a gas fitter, who was particularly hurt at this attitude because of a secret in his own life.

'Getting a bit heated,' muttered Holmes behind his hand to his partner. 'Don't get involved. They can be like wild dogs when someone gets under their skin.'

'Not only do I believe this to be the case, but I back it up by the extremely camp acting of the principal actor in the previous series made for television. Sometimes he actually resembled Kenneth Williams in his indignation and superiority.'

Cries of 'Shame! Shame!' greeted this accusation, but he rode roughshod over them all.

'I should now like to read you a short story I have penned to seek your opinion,' yelled Antony above the furore. 'Its title is "A Study in Cerise", and I lay it before you all now for your opinions.'

'Order, order!' roared Stephen Crompton, for all the world like the Speaker of the House of Commons. 'Let Mr Antony have his say before you condemn him.' He was at least fair, if a little misguided at this juncture.

Cyril Antony ruffled a sheaf of papers which he had extracted from a slim briefcase, and began to read in a high, hectoring voice. 'Holmes, the greatest consulting detective ever, and his partner, Dr Watson, sat up in their double bed, Holmes with his embroidery, Watson with his more mundane crochet, and mulled over the interesting problem they had been left with earlier in the day.

'Both of them wore lace caps and bed-jackets against the cold of the season and, as they worked away at their pieces of needlework, Watson risked a fond glance at his beloved ...'

The shouting was loud and abusive, and Crompton took some time to call the meeting to order. 'Gentlemen, let Mr Antony have his say!'

'Get him out of here!'

'I want him expelled!'

'He should be horse-whipped and run out of town!'

'How dare he dirty the name of the world's greatest and only consulting detective!'

These and many other comments were made in loud voices, until Mr Crompton suggested that maybe now was not the time to read them the story, and begged Antony to, perhaps, leave it until another time.

Cyril Antony, as could only be expected, took this suggestion and the vociferous reaction badly, as his story was dear to his heart, almost like one of his children, and he had thought long and hard before he wrote it, and thought this alternative explanation to the unlikely friendship should see light of day.

He straightened his sheaf of papers on the table top, returned them to his briefcase, and stormed out of the meeting, slamming the door loudly behind him.

'Bloody cheek!'

'Damned upstart!'

'I'll smash his face in!'

Such was the mutiny that the chairman now had to quell, that he genuinely regretted his decision to let Antony carry on after the initial outburst of disapproval. Still, as his rather coarse (and now sadly deceased) wife had always said, one couldn't un-fuck. He'd just have to get this lot calmed down again and get the discussion back on track.

Christopher Cave, a cab driver, proposed that Nigel Bruce was perhaps the best Watson of all time in visual media, and was seconded by Elliot Jordan, a local librarian. Television abandoned, Kevin Wood, a teacher, proposed Basil Rathbone the best Holmes, seconded by Bob Wiltshire, a social worker, and supported by Rupert Mitchell, a local undertaker. The meeting then broke up in a much more harmonious mood.

Afterwards, all the members went downstairs to the bar

for a well-earned, in their opinions, alcoholic drink, after the skirmish that a meeting always engendered. Holmes had taken no part in the discussion, and Garden followed him downstairs a bit bemused. 'What was that all about?' he asked in hushed tones, when Holmes had ordered a Campari and soda and a pint of bitter.

'Do you remember me saying that I might set up a Holmes discussion group, if we didn't set up as detectives?' asked the older man.

'I believe I do. But you already belonged to this,' replied Garden, with a slightly interrogative edge to his voice.

'I did. And I was instrumental in setting it up. That's why it's named the Quaker Street Irregulars: in my honour. A few of us used to bump into each other in here, and the conversation invariably ended up being about Sherlock. But something has gone wrong in the mix, and look at the parlous state things are in now. I'm surprised that the discussion about whose were the best portrayals didn't descend into anarchy!'

'What in particular?' asked Garden.

'The idea that Holmes and Watson were gay, and the shouting and insults. It just wasn't supposed to be like this. It was supposed to be a civilised discussion group, and it has degenerated into something resembling a zoo.'

'You certainly do need to implement some sort of code of manners, but I think your main problem is that man who tried to read his story.' Garden broke off with a shudder that such a slur should be brought on to their heroes. Being rather 'different' himself, he didn't have a homophobic bone in his body, but Holmes and Watson had definitely never been intended to be thought to have any sort of physical relationship, and he thought that Conan Doyle himself would have found the idea repugnant.

'He's had a bee in his bonnet over that particular slant on things since he joined us a few months ago. I can't remember who brought him along, but he's been getting more and more of a bore on the subject, and nothing will deflect him.'

'Perhaps you could remember who proposed him and have a word with them.'

'I really can't for the life of me remember, but I suppose I could ring the others and find out who it was. If things go on like this, there won't be a Quaker Street Irregulars meeting to go to soon. It'll all implode.'

Garden drained his glass and asked if Holmes would like another. 'Actually, I feel a bit rattled by tonight's events. If you don't mind, I think I'd rather go home. Why don't you come back with me and we'll have a nightcap? You can always stay in the spare room if you wish.'

Garden could think of a thousand reasons why he shouldn't go home with Holmes, one of them being that he was very fond of his own bed, the other nine hundred and ninety-nine being Colin, Holmes' cat, but he didn't dare say so, and gave in with a good grace because he didn't like to see the man so upset. Things had been bad enough after that prank that Streeter had subjected them to, and he would, at the moment, do anything to preserve the uneasy peace that Holmes seemed to possess.

He had been given a little more insight into what made Holmes tick tonight, however, and he smiled at the thought. He was only going to have a cup of coffee and he would be sleeping in his own bed later.

The mist had cleared. The night was fine and clear. The walk back was exhilarating. Colin was on the hat shelf on the hallstand. And suddenly all was not well with Garden's world anymore, as he found himself wearing an unusually heavy fur scarf with claws and the spiteful addition of teeth.

As these needle-sharp weapons bit into his ear, he gave a yell and fell to the floor, Holmes returning from the kitchen to see what on earth was wrong with his guest.

Shooing the cat out of the hall, Holmes helped Garden to his feet and chuckled, as Garden raised a handkerchief to his bloodied ear and cheek. 'What a playful thing he is. He wanted to welcome us home,' declared Holmes, almost overcome with mirth.

'Is that what you call it?' retorted Garden bitterly. 'Look, if you don't mind, I'd better be getting back. I promised I'd phone Mummy tonight, and I'd better not be late or she'll skin me alive tomorrow in the office.'

'Why don't you just call round to see her?' asked Holmes, with complete rationality, as Shirley Garden only lived a couple of streets away.

'Because she said she might be out, so I'm going to ring her mobile.' This seemed as good an excuse as any.

'Why don't you call her from here?' asked Holmes, again with perfect common sense.

'Because she said she might drop round to see me on her way home, and I'd better not be out,' lied Garden, extemporising furiously, and hoping Holmes didn't think about it long enough to see the gaping holes in his excuses.

'Never mind, old chap,' Holmes said wistfully, 'But you could have asked her to call in here.'

'Least said, soonest mended,' improvised Garden meaninglessly, and made as quick an exit as he could without arousing any suspicion.

Chapter Two

It was that time of the month again, although a Friday this time, and Holmes had asked Garden if he would accompany him to the next Quaker Street Irregulars meeting. It seemed churlish to refuse, although Garden didn't relish the thought after the verbal punch-up of the last meeting, but gave in gracefully.

'If you grab what you need from upstairs at closing time, you can come straight over to my place, and we can go to The Sherlock early and grab a drink and something a bit more substantial than those sandwiches we had last time before things kick off. The catering's on the wane, in my opinion. When the group started we used to get much better value for money – chicken drumsticks, bowls of coleslaw, cold sausages. Maybe we'll have to discuss paying more.'

Just hoping that things did not 'kick off' again, Garden did as he was asked, and got his wallet and a coat from his flat above the offices as Holmes locked up for the day.

On the drive over, Holmes went into some detail about the members of the group, so that Garden didn't feel quite so much at sea this time with all the strange faces.

'Our chairman, Stephen Crompton – you know, the one who kept trying to call the meeting to order? – he's a retired doctor, so his interest in the detecting duo is quite obvious. He fancies himself in the role of Watson, only with a bit more brains. He was one of the first people that I started to talk to in there. He's a widower and lives alone, so it's one of his only interests: that, and going into The Sherlock and engaging people in conversation about the books.

'Elliot Jordan, the librarian, has read the books so many times that he can quote from all of them, and he's also a bit of a film buff, always putting down all the ghastly films that were made in black and white which weren't based on original Conan Doyle stories. He's divorced, and I remember he said that if his wife could have cited Sherlock Holmes in their divorce as co-respondent, she would have done, because she said he spent more time with the detective than he did with her.' At this, Holmes took a moment for a polite little laugh, as if anything could be more ridiculous.

'Kevin Wood, the teacher, has, as his specialist interest, the last series-but-one on television, and has every episode on DVD. He doesn't care for the films, especially the American ones. He is married, but his wife is somewhat the same about the Harry Potter books. In fact, they're thinking of applying to appear on the BBC's *Mastermind*, so they both live in their own little worlds.

'Now, Bob Wiltshire, who's a social worker, is a bit of a generalist, and is happy to read all these modern books that have been written, trying to recreate Conan Doyle's original London, and setting his hero in all sort of other scenarios as well. He doesn't mind what it is, provided it's a story that has Holmes and Watson in it. He's not over-critical.

'On the contrary, Aaron Dibley, the one who's a probation officer, is only for the original books. He doesn't care for any visual portrayal or modern stories trying to emulate the creator. He's quite rabid about his belief that Holmes' world should be all in the reader's head, and that no one could play him satisfactorily, not even Basil Rathbone. He likes to think that he can see the characters that he works with in Conan Doyle's criminal underworld.

'Now, who else is a member? Ah, yes, Christopher Cave the cabbie. He's a bit of an oddball. He seems to prefer offbeat portrayals like the American interpretations. There's the film, *Young Sherlock*, of which he is a fan, and one particular Hound of the Baskervilles that stars William Shatner which he's wild about. Dartmoor, in this particular version, seems beset with great boulders, and looks like it's actually set on the edge of a desert.

'Personally, I'd say it was a sound stage, but he's convinced it was filmed on the edge of a desert. The answer's probably in the credits somewhere, but I can't be bothered to look, and he simply doesn't care. He thinks it's the bee's knees.

'Oh yes, and there's Rupert Mitchell, a new member. All I know about him is that he's an undertaker from Farlington Market. A little dour in his manner.

'Let's see, we've covered Stephen Crompton, haven't we?' Garden answered that they had, and Holmes continued, 'That leaves – ah, yes, Peter Lampard, a very useful man if your central heating is playing up or on the blink. He's a registered gas engineer. He's been raving about the newest television series starring Benedict Cumberbatch and is absolutely delighted that someone's actually updated old Sherlock's brilliant mind to encompass the twenty-first century. Gets frowned on a lot for that opinion, which is not universally shared, I can tell you, but nothing shakes his admiration for the writers.

'Now, who haven't I mentioned? Ludovic Connor I don't know very well. All I know is that he's a bank clerk, and that he's really into the longer works like "A Study in Scarlet" and "The Sign of Four", that's he's not long had his fortieth birthday bash, and that he's single.

'That leaves us with Dave Warwick, an electrician, who's only recently read the books for the first time, and was instantly hooked. He came to us about three or four months ago; a refreshing breath of fresh air for us older codgers who've known the stories for decades. And he probably needs an escape from everyday life more than any of us. His wife's just given birth to their fifth child. He wasn't at the last meeting because she'd gone into labour, if you remember.'

'You haven't told me anything about that bloke that got up everyone's nose at the last meeting with his scandalous short story – "A Study in Cerise", wasn't it called?' interjected Garden.

'How remiss of me, old boy, but I try not to think about him whenever possible. He's really got a bee up his bum – if you'll pardon the expression – about the relationship between Holmes and Watson. You witnessed that for yourself at the last meeting, but he brings it up at every gathering. We usually manage to shut him up, but that short story was just beyond the pale. I hope you don't think that he's representative of us as a group. He's definitely out on a limb, as far as that's concerned.'

'He did rather stick out like a sore thumb. What's his motive, do you think, in antagonising all the other members about the relationship?' asked Garden.

'I, personally, think he has delusions of grandeur of getting into print and causing a bit of an uproar: as if we could help him with that – but he's certainly going out of his way to make his mark. I'm definitely going to put in a proposal tonight about him being black-balled: I've made my decision. He adds no value to the meetings and just causes trouble.'

'Won't that cause a bit of trouble if he attends the meeting?' Garden was curious to know how his partner would go about this.

'Not at all. I shall propose in the written form – in fact I have the letter in my inside jacket pocket. I just wasn't sure until just now whether I should hand it to our chairman or not, but I shall. The members can be polled before our next meeting and, if they're in favour of ejecting him, out he goes, and we won't have to see him again after tonight. At least we've got a bit of a cushion against the outside world for our little discussions, up there on the first floor.'

At this point, which had been mostly an informative monologue on Holmes' part, he drew up outside The Sherlock. They had travelled in the same car because Holmes said he had got hold of a copy of a film not much televised, that Garden had never seen before, and they planned to watch it together later after the meeting, and critique it. Garden was to stay in the guest bedroom, with promises that Colin would be banned from their presence while he was in the apartment.

The pub seemed very crowded to Holmes, but then, as Garden pointed out to him, it was Friday night this time round, and he probably came in a bit later when he usually visited, when other folk had gone on to other venues. Finding a table just vacated by three giggling young women, Holmes grabbed a bar menu for them, and they set to choosing their meal.

Deciding that Italian was not appropriate, and that good old-fashioned English fare was what was called for, they both selected chicken tikka masala and chips, and Garden placed their food order when he got the drinks, Holmes having purchased them last time they were here for a Sherlockian-themed evening.

As they were finishing their food, a particularly unruly group of young men sited themselves near their table, and one of them jostled Holmes' elbow as he lifted his pint glass to his lips, slopping bitter all over one of his trouserlegs. He shouted out in disapproval.

'What yer gonna do abaht it, granddad?' one of them jeered, and the others made threatening faces as they crowded round the table.

'Nothing whatsoever,' replied Holmes with dignity, and rose, adding, 'We were just leaving.' Nodding to Garden, he led the way to the door upstairs, the route to relative sanity.

'Why are we going up now?' asked Garden. 'It's twenty-five minutes before we're supposed to meet.'

'The last thing I need tonight is a pub punch-up. It may still be early, but they looked like they'd been there since lunchtime, and I'm not used to it being this crowded and rowdy. I normally drop in mid-week, when it's relatively quiet.' Garden noticed a slight flicker of fear in Holmes' eyes, and wisely kept his mouth shut. If Holmes had been a local government officer before, he was hardly likely to be the sort of person who would welcome a ruck, with fists and feet and foul language.

They climbed the narrow flight of stairs in silence. At the top, Holmes threw open the door almost as a gesture of defiance to those bullies downstairs, then stopped dead in his tracks and allowing Garden, who was miles away, mentally considering a new pair of stilettos, to cannon into his back.

'What the heck?' he exclaimed, but Holmes was as frozen in position as an ice-statue, for which it had seemed cold enough outside. 'Holmes, what is it?'

Holmes' body slumped, and he stood aside so that Garden could see into the room. In the chair usually occupied by the chairman was the figure of Cyril Antony, obviously dead, but he was only identifiable because of his rotundity. A sheet of A4 was stuffed into the top of his waistcoat. They approached his body, both on tiptoes, as if they could in some way disturb his slumbers, and looked down on the earthly shell of this one-time troublemaker.

There was a deerstalker on his head, but back-to-front, so that the back concealed his features from view. On his actual body, there were no signs of deadly assault. Reaching out one leather-gloved hand – quick thinking, mused Garden silently – Holmes moved up the deerstalker to reveal a restriction cutting into the victim's neck, its ends sticking out on either side, a small coloured-cotton circle on one end.

'By George! That's a violin string, if I'm not mistaken,' uttered Holmes in hushed tones. 'The man's been garrotted.'

Garden looked warily around the room, but with the exception of a couple of full jugs and plates of food, there was nothing untoward about the place. 'But we're the first to arrive – apart from him, of course. What was his name again?'

'Cyril Antony,' replied Holmes automatically, then added, 'And we can't have been the first to arrive after him, unless he garrotted himself, which I think is doubtful, given all the difficulties that that would present.'

Garden flushed, and bent his head to hide his embarrassment at this unconsidered remark. 'I suppose we ought to raise the alarm: call the police – or at least get the landlord to do so.'

'Not until we've had a good prowl around here first,' replied Holmes, and Garden almost expected him to get out a magnifying glass. 'And I'm going to start with this sheet of paper shoved, apparently carelessly, into his clothing.'

'But, surely you shouldn't disturb the crime scene,' advised Garden, slightly too late.

'I'm wearing gloves, and I can always shove it back later. I'm sure it wasn't inserted in an easily identifiable origami-style way. Who's to know, if we don't tell 'em?'

Realising the common sense of this remark, Garden looked over the shorter Holmes' shoulder as the older man smoothed out the sheet of paper, to reveal the title page of 'A Study in Cerise', the short story that the victim had tried to read to them at the last meeting.

'Well, I'll be blowed!' said Holmes with a strange harrumphing noise. 'Somebody took even less kindly to his little venture into Holmesian literature than we did.'

'Put it back, and let's get downstairs and alert someone to call the police. It won't look good if we don't. They'll think we're somehow involved if we call them on my mobile,' this last a possession he hadn't mentioned when he had cited phoning his mother as an excuse to go home after the last meeting, and which Holmes had forgotten about, as he wasn't yet used to such up-to-date technology.

The older man may have bought state-of-the-art computers for their offices, but he still wasn't comfortable with a smart-phone, and Garden reckoned he would have been happier with the really old-fashioned candlestick version of a landline. That was, somehow, more his style, as he managed to have about him a vaguely Edwardian atmosphere, completely in keeping with his apartment. Even his kitchen white goods were housed behind solid wood cupboard doors, away from prying twenty-first century eyes.

The mention of the police didn't infuriate Holmes as Garden thought it might do, and he supposed that it was his own way of dealing with the shock of sudden death, to keep his lip zipped about meeting DI Streeter again.

After a quick look round the room where nothing seemed out of place, not even the dust on the window ledges, Holmes followed Garden back down to the ground floor, and Holmes sought out the landlord, Greg Wordsworth, and his wife, Tilly. 'A literary-named landlord for a literary-themed pub,' he quipped, while they waited at the bar hatch in the saloon bar, the pub still retaining both saloon and public bars, along with the snug, instead of the open-plan layout of many pubs nowadays.

Wordsworth had said that Sherlock Holmes would turn in his grave if he threw the pub into one big open bar, and, at the time, *Sherman* Holmes actually wondered if he realised that their Sherlock was only a fictional character.

The two of them were in the back, where they were enjoying a bite to eat after the initial Friday rush, and joined them on the other side of the bar in less than a minute, Holmes having assured the barman that the matter was urgent.

Holmes beckoned towards the big, bluff man to lean over so he could whisper in his ear. 'What's this, Holmes?' the landlord asked in his ringing public school tones – God knew what he was doing running a place like this with the implied background of his accent – 'a naughty joke not for the ladies' ears, eh?'

Holmes, caught off-guard, began to bluster, and it was Garden who took positive action, lifting the bar flap and propelling Holmes through it, and all four of them through the door into the back parlour. Wordsworth began to protest, but Garden cut him off with, 'There's a dead man upstairs, and you need to call the police as soon as possible and stop anyone else from going up there so that the crime scene is preserved.' This did embarrass him a bit when he thought how Holmes had interfered with it, but he managed to swallow that, and stare the man in the eye with grim determination.

Holmes kept his calm visibly at the thought of tangling with the police so soon after what he was now beginning to think of as 'the ghastly incident'.

Wordsworth visibly gulped and his ruddy face went pale. He was a tall man with a haystack of naturally blond hair, pale blue eyes, and a burgeoning belly, grown from his occupation as a pub landlord. His wife was an incongruous sight beside him, a tiny woman with the build of a sparrow, and unnaturally bright red hair, her face plastered with far too much make-up. How those two had ever got together was one of life's mysteries.

It was his wife who recovered her power of speech first. 'Who the bloody hell is it, and what the hell are they doin' upstairs, dead, in my pub? I want answers.' She was certainly fiery.

'I have no idea, madam, but I suggest you call the police' – he nearly choked on the word – 'without further ado, and we can discuss the whys and the wherefores later.

You need to get someone on the door at the bottom of the stairs without delay, or the police might not be very impressed with your attitude to what is, evidently, a murder,' stated Holmes.

'Murder?' queried her husband. 'I just thought you meant that someone had had a heart attack or something – and that could be bad enough for business – but a murder …' His voice trailed away into silence, and they all looked at each other for a few seconds, before Tilly darted away, and they could hear her speaking into a phone in the hall behind the back parlour.

She returned in just a couple of minutes and informed them that there was an Inspector Streeter who would attend as soon as he could get there, and an ambulance on its way, just in case. Both parts of this statement raised a sigh from the two private investigators. The ambulance was going to be a total waste of time, and they had had a recent run in with Streeter that still made Holmes blush at how easily he and Garden had been taken in by his cruel subterfuge.

'How did he die?' Greg Wordsworth had suddenly recovered his voice, and it boomed out now to a level where Holmes put his fingers to his lips, in case the words themselves carried out into the bar, which was nowhere near as noisy as it had been when they'd first arrived. 'Shhh!' he said. 'Loose lips sink ships.' Three puzzled faces looked at him as he uttered this anachronism, which he had heard from his parents, and his partner was the first one to pull himself together.

'He was garrotted,' stated Garden curtly, trying to erase the picture from his mind of the face that had been revealed when Holmes moved the back of the deerstalker away from it.

'My Gawd!' squawked Tilly. 'Is there much mess to clear up?'

'Not at all, my dear,' Holmes reassured her, but her

look of relief was cut short as Garden added.

'Can't say the same for after the police have been up there and dusted every surface for fingerprints.'

'Saints alive!' she exclaimed, looking pained. 'I'll be cleaning for a month of Sundays. Me good meeting room. It was spotless when I left it this afternoon. I suppose we'd better get back to that bar while we've still got customers left.'

The Wordsworths escorted Holmes and Garden back to their proper place on the other side of the bar, and resumed their temporarily interrupted roles as mine host and his 'lady' wife. The barman, Dick Brownlow, was dispatched to guard the door to the staircase up to the meeting room and, within fifteen minutes, a tall, hawk-like man entered the pub by the doors to the saloon bar, accompanied by a younger, round-faced man dressed in a rather casual manner.

The taller, gaunt, immaculately dressed individual introduced them as DI Streeter and DS Port, then cast a baleful glance at the two private investigators, who shuffled their feet in embarrassment. 'You two again!' he spluttered. 'How do you do it?'

'Do what?' asked Holmes, adopting an innocent expression.

'Be on the scene of just about every murder that's committed in my manor? I thought I'd warned you off for good.'

'Just a happy knack,' replied Garden, and gave a little titter of amusement that wasn't appreciated by the inspector, but which made the sergeant's lips twitch with amusement. Garden was embarrassed too about meeting their nemesis again, and blushed as he tittered. They had looked such fools.

'Right, lead me to this body, if it is one. I caught the ambulance outside and told them to wait for my say-so.'

'I think Mr Holmes ought to go up with you,' ventured

Greg Wordsworth, with a catch in his voice. 'I'm very squeamish about death, and I'm liable to pass out. I don't think my wife should go up, either, and it was Mr Holmes who found the man.'

'Dear God! I don't suppose it matters who shows me, as long as I get to see it,' retorted Streeter, glaring at Holmes. He was not a happy bunny at all. Port found his boss's animosity towards the amateurs rather amusing, especially the way he had played such an intricate trick on them just a short while ago, and trotted off behind, grinning merrily now that his face couldn't be seen by authority.

Holmes mounted the stairs once more and could hear the exasperated sighing of the inspector, who was on his heels. He didn't enjoy this any more than Streeter, but it wasn't fair to blame him and Garden just for being somewhere when something happened. It was just fate, and not a personal attack on the DI. His sergeant seemed rather more relaxed, and Holmes hoped it would be he who took their statements in due course.

At the head of the stairs, he stood aside to let the policemen enter, then started to descend the flight again. 'Not so fast, Sherlock!' yelled Streeter over his shoulder. 'I want you in here. I want a word with you about just what happened when you found the body.'

'We just came up here prior to our monthly meeting, a bit early, actually, and this is how we found him,' Holmes blandly informed the detective, keeping his face as straight as possible.

'What meeting? And who the hell is he? That'll do for starters,' retorted Streeter roughly.

Attempting to stop grinding his teeth, Holmes, as calmly as he could, informed him, 'There is a meeting of the Quaker Street Irregulars in this room once a month, and this man is ... was ... one of its members. His name is ... was ... still is, I suppose, Cyril Antony.'

'And what, in the name of God and all his angels, is, or are, the Quaker Street Irregulars?' Streeter's face was beginning to redden with impatience at what he saw as not a very straightforward answer. He thought he had taught this upstart not to meddle, and here he was, again, at the scene of a murder.

'We're a club of like-minded people who get together regularly to discuss Sherlock Holmes: the books, televisual representations, and films.'

'A bunch of fantasists, then,' stated Streeter, somewhat rudely.

'If you wish to describe us as such.' With difficulty, Holmes maintained his temper and poker face.

'I do. And you and your so-called business partner were first up here?'

'After the victim and his murderer, yes.'

'Don't be a smart-arse. Just answer the questions.' Streeter's temper had now well and truly risen, and Holmes managed the ghost – how ironic - of a smile in recognition of this last request. 'What happened when you got up here?'

'I just opened the door, saw what was inside, and stopped. Then Garden and I checked to see that life was extinct' – Holmes was rather proud of this expression and smirked just a tiny bit – 'Then, we went downstairs and alerted the landlord and his wife to what had happened, and asked him to put someone on duty at the bottom of the stairs to stop anyone coming up and messing with the crime scene.' He felt he had acquitted himself well here, but Streeter was not quite so easily mollified.

'And what exactly did you do? Did you touch anything: interfere with the scene at all, or did you just go back downstairs like good little citizens?'

'We went back downstairs.'

'Without touching anything?'

'That is correct.' Holmes was not happy with untruths,

but he deemed it necessary, in these circumstances, not to inform Streeter of their inspection of the piece of paper tucked into Antony's waistcoat. He justified this by the thought that he was just saving the man from having a stroke due to the level of his blood pressure, induced by absolute fury.

The answer seemed to be enough, however, and the only other question he asked before dismissing the private investigator was, 'Are you sure your partner touched nothing either?'

'Absolutely sure,' was his answer, and this time it was truthful.

He was peremptorily dismissed while the inspector, an official of the services of law and order and not a rank amateur, got on with his very important job before summoning a SOCO team. As a parting shot, he ordered Holmes to give his and his business partner's details to the uniformed officer – which he knew very well - who should have arrived by now, and go home, where he would catch up with them later. Summarily dismissed, Holmes stomped off to do as he was bidden.

Chapter Three

Streeter started by sealing the crime scene and the door to the stairs and requesting that the door through to the snug be locked. There was no access from outside to this particular small room in the pub, so everything should be secure.

Next, he asked for the landlord to be brought to him at one of the tables in the saloon bar, got the uniformed constable to take names and contact details of all those still present – oops! – and set up his base with DS Port, demanding that the pub be closed for the remainder of the evening.

Greg Wordsworth came to the table with Tilly, only to have her sent away, as Streeter wanted to question them separately. The landlord was still shaken, and had a large brandy in one hand. 'Sit down!' the inspector ordered in an authoritarian manner. 'Just what's been going on in your establishment, Mr Wordsworth?'

'I really have no idea what's happened,' returned Wordsworth, to this abrupt question, his plummy voice filling the vacant space round them. 'The first the wife and I knew about it was when Mr Holmes and his associate called us to the bar – not the *legal* bar, you understand, ha ha – and we all went through to the back parlour for him to break the news to us.'

Streeter had not reacted to this weak witticism, but was surprised by the refinement of the voice. Accents like that automatically got under his skin and made him feel inferior, so Wordsworth's surmised upbringing immediately nettled him.

'There's no cause to treat this situation so flippantly, Mr Wordsworth. A man has lost his life upstairs in your meeting room.'

'I do realise that, Inspector, but the wife and I were having a bite of supper when the body was found. Do you know how long he'd been …? At what time he was …?' Wordsworth really seemed to have a phobia about death. '… When it happened?' he concluded lamely.

'We'll not have an accurate idea of the time of death until after the medical examiner has seen him, and possibly not until after the post-mortem, but I shall need to confirm your whereabouts, and those of your wife, from, say, lunchtime onwards.'

'But, my wife was there only this afternoon giving it a good polishing and vacuuming. There was nothing amiss when she was up there, to my knowledge,' Wordsworth replied defensively.

'I'm not implying there was, but I shall need her word for confirmation, and that of anybody else who could confirm that the body wasn't up there much earlier than it was found.' His voice had risen in volume, and Tilly had scurried over to the table to see what was going on.

'I 'ope you're not bullying my 'usband,' she shrilled at him. 'I fink 'e ought to consult 'is solicitor if you're goin' to go accusin' 'im of anyfink.'

Streeter's temper had been tried almost beyond endurance since he'd got here, and he was very close to losing it, what with those two private investigators being on the spot – again – Holmes' look of debatable innocence when asked if he'd touched anything at the scene, this upper class twit's silver spoon accent, and now this little bird of a woman having a go at him and threatening him with their solicitor.

'I shall require both of you to attend the police station to make statements tomorrow – no protests. I'm sure you've got enough staff to cover for your absence. I shall require the names and contact details of all your staff, and my sergeant and the uniformed constable will then take their statements. Now, who works here?'

Wordsworth cleared his throat and took up the reins of the conversation. 'We have four members of staff. Dick Brownlow – whom I dispatched to guard the staircase.' The word 'whom' immediately got up the inspector's nose, as he didn't know when to use it and when to leave it well alone. 'We've got Micki – short for Michaela – Shields, who's our barmaid, Suzie Peake in the kitchen doing the food orders, and Tony Richardson is waiter and glass collector.'

'Not short for Antonia, I suppose?' asked Streeter sarcastically.

'No, Tony's a chap,' replied Wordsworth, perplexed at this question, and not realising it was just Streeter's entrenched inferiority complex flexing its muscles in public.

'I shall need all their addresses and phone numbers, landline and mobile, but I'll leave this in the very capable hands of my DS, and the constable. Good evening to you both. I shall now dismiss the ambulance.'

As he rose, Port gave him a quizzical look. Whatever was wrong with the old man, saying his hands were very capable ones in which to leave anything – before now, he wouldn't have trusted him with so much as a chocolate bar, though that was for a very good reason – he'd have eaten it without a second thought.

By the end of the evening, Port left The Sherlock with a long list of customers for uniform to check out, and the statements of all the employed workers at the pub that evening, all of whom denied having been up to the meeting room since they had come on shift at lunchtime. The pub did have other staff, but some were casual, only called on when there were members of staff off sick, and others, who worked different days to the ones who were on duty that Friday.

When Holmes and Garden got back to Holmes's apartment, the host immediately opened a bottle of very acceptable wine – he wouldn't countenance drinking plonk, unlike Garden, who would drink anything if he was in a mood to – and went into the guest room to switch on the electric blanket.

He did have an advantage over Streeter in that he was familiar with some of the staff of the pub, and felt it unlikely that one of them could have killed Cyril Antony; although he could not be certain. As he went back to his sitting room, collecting two crystal glasses on his way, he said to Garden, 'So, what do you think of our new little puzzle? We seem to have fallen right into this case. That'll stick right in Streeter's craw. He can't do anything about serendipity.'

Garden thought quite a lot, actually. Firstly, he didn't consider that murder was at all a little puzzle and, as for having fallen right into it, he didn't really know whether he wanted to get involved or not. They had their own business to consider, and investigating this wouldn't pay any bills, as well as the fact that Holmes had declared war on the inspector, and he didn't know how his partner would react in the circumstances.

Giving himself a mental nudge, however, he remembered that it didn't matter how well or how badly the business did; Holmes was a millionaire who didn't need to rely on paltry little cases of divorce or lost doggies and moggies. He could do exactly as he pleased with no financial consequences, and Garden would still receive his monthly salary. Maybe he needed to lighten up a little bit. And Streeter was a nightmare when it came to uncovering the truth; he should carry some sort of written warning about his general incompetence.

With hardly a breath between Holmes' input, Garden

replied, 'I couldn't agree with you more. I presume, with the wine, we're going to sit up and discuss the matter.'

'Hardly sit up, old chap. It's only half past eight, but I feel we should look at the thing from an investigative point of view before we watch that film. After all, we were the ones who found the body. We owe the slandering scoundrel something, even if it's only justice. And, in fact, he was libellous as well, but let's put that to one side in the interests of finding out who did him to death.'

Only Holmes could use a phrase like 'did him to death' in all seriousness, and Garden tried to arrange his thoughts. 'Could it have been one of the staff?' he asked, going for the obvious, as the meeting had not yet convened.

'Unlikely,' relied Holmes. 'I think it's much more possible it was one of the members of the Quaker Street Irregulars.' He began to tick off the points on the fingers of his right hand. 'One: nobody outside the club really knew about the meetings.' The forefinger of his left hand held down the forefinger of his right hand, but then he fell silent.

'Two?' prompted Garden.

'Do you know, for the life of me, I can't think of any other reason. We don't really know anything about him, other than that he had that bee in his bum – excuse my language – about the relationship between Holmes and Watson, and that he'd written that dashed shameful story which he tried to read to us at the last meeting, before he was shouted down and left in a huff.'

'But you were going to get him black-balled?'

'Too right, I was. I wasn't going to let him get away with a thing like that, and I'm sure all the other members would have been in agreement.' Holmes' fine moustache was bristling with indignation, as he remembered last month's meeting.

Garden clapped his hands together loudly, prompting a sudden clatter from the cat flap in the kitchen. 'That's it!

There's your motive. If hardly anybody knew about the club and its meetings, the only people that would have been positive that he would be going there were members of the Quaker Street Irregulars.'

'But their families would have known where they were, and their friends,' countered Holmes.

'And do you think many of those really cared? I don't wish to belittle your creation, but it was only a dozen men getting together once a month to waffle on about Conan Doyle's books. Please don't take this personally, but it's not as if it were a government think-tank or anything, is it?'

Although Holmes' face fell, he took it on the chin and had to, however reluctantly, agree that the Irregulars were, in the great scheme of things, pretty small potatoes.

'What do we actually know about the murderer?' asked Garden, and as Holmes had nothing forthcoming, began to tick points off on his own fingers. 'One, he had access to violin strings – nothing to say these were recently purchased, but the presence of one makes me think this was a pre-meditated act. Nobody but a professional strings player would walk about with something like that in his pocket without evil intent, and you didn't mention that any of them played in an orchestra.

'Two, we can take it as read, I think, that it was a member of your little society or club, or whatever it is.' He moved down a second finger, then went on, 'Thirdly, as there was the title page of his short story manuscript shoved into the waistcoat of his suit, that whoever killed him has, or had, the manuscript itself.'

'And fourthly?' asked Holmes, watching Garden's smallest right finger slowly descend towards its neighbour.

'There isn't a fourthly. That only went down because it wanted to follow the third finger, and there was nothing I could do to stop it,' replied a now slightly embarrassed Garden. Maybe that action would have been easier if he'd been a pianist, or something else that encouraged him to use his fingers independently.

Ignoring his partner's apology, Holmes' face was working, as he was given furiously to think. 'Do you think that means that the manuscript was on Antony when he arrived for the meeting – that he'd had the audacity to bring it back with him to another meeting – or that whoever killed him had already stolen it, and had taken it along to make a point?' he asked. 'Did you see a briefcase when we took a quick look?'

'Can't say that I did,' replied Garden, his eyes closed in an effort to recall the details of the scene. 'But the murderer could have taken the rest of it away still inside the briefcase.'

'Good point, old boy. Good point,' Holmes encouraged him with a broad grin. That meant the wine was starting to do its work.

'I was going to stay here, originally, because you had a DVD of a Holmes film I haven't seen,' Garden prompted him.

'Another good point, John H. I'll just slip it into the machine, and we shall let things simmer in our brains until after it's over. Like doing a crossword: if you put it down, when you go back to it, your brain's worked out some of the clues that seemed impenetrable before. I'll just open us another bottle, to let it breathe a while, before we need it,' he finished, and trotted off briskly out of the room, enthusiasm for another little tipple in every quick step.

By the time the film was over neither of their brains had done much unravelling, due to the amount of alcohol seeping into them. Holmes attempted to put the DVD away in its case, but finally had to give up; his hands would not cooperate with his eyes, and he was fumbling around like a blind man. He was, however, in the mood for a little light conversation, and put one forefinger to his forehead, to indicate deep thought.

'I was just thinking,' he began, 'That meeting last month, if Dave Warwick's wife hadn't gone into labour, with you there last month, we would have been thirteen for supper – The Last Supper! Don't you think that's ironic, as one of us turned out to be a killer, and did away with one of the other members?'

Holmes found that his glass was still nearly full, a fact that his brain had mislaid in its state of developing muddle, and he drained it in one, as Garden replied, 'That's a bit of a stretch of the imagination, isn't it? Dave Warwick wasn't there, and we don't know for sure that it was one of the Irregulars who killed Antony. We've only been surmising. There's no proof.'

'Of course we do,' replied Holmes, feeling his head begin to spin with this latest onslaught of alcohol on his bloodstream. 'Who else could it 'ave been, Garding?' He'd get his revenge on Streeter by solving this case first.

He was definitely deteriorating if he couldn't even get his partner's name right, thought Garden, and wondered how messily the evening would end. They should never have watched that film or opened that second bottle of wine.

'I-I-I think I've had a good idea, Gra-Gad-Garden,' he slurred. 'I'm goin' to ring good old Greg an' ask him to give me the s, the s, the s-p.'

'Don't you think you might be a little tiddly to hold a conversation?' asked Garden, whose glass had not been so frequently refilled, sitting as it had at a bit of a distance from his partner's and the bottle.

'Jober as a sudge, me, John H. Now, where's his number? Ah, yes. Now, what time is it?'

'It's 11.15; a bit on the late side, don't you think?'

'Rubbish! Never known old Greg go to bed before midnight. He'll be up having a nighty-night nightcap, don't yer know,' replied Holmes rather slushily. His diction had suffered considerably under the influence of the better part of two bottles of wine.

Fortunately for all concerned, his part in the telephone conversation was brief. He managed to announce himself to Greg Wordsworth, but Wordsworth seemed to want to do all the talking, and all that Holmes had to do was agree now and then, and nod or shake his head sagely, an action that did nothing to underline his agreement, as it was just an ordinary telephone he was using.

Making rather an elaborate business of placing the handset back where it belonged, Holmes swung quite recklessly in Garden's direction, swaying alarmingly on his feet as he did so, and said, 'There's been a bit of bad luck for Greg, but it does clari-clafiry-clarify things for us.' He stopped and shook his head from side to side, as if trying to reorder his thoughts.

Leading him to a sofa, Garden asked what Greg had said. 'Said ... 'e said ...' Holmes cleared his throat enthusiastically and tried again. 'He said,' he repeated, slowly and carefully, 'that the'es fire escade – a fire escape – leadin' from that meetin' room, and tha' Street-eet-eeter had found it locked. 'E's gonna get done for that. Poor old Greg.'

Noticing tears of pity well up in Holmes' eyes, Garden gently assisted him to his feet and led him to his bedroom, where he helped him undress and get into his pyjamas. Carefully, he slid the older man under the enormously fluffy duvet – one modern idea that Holmes had grasped enthusiastically, not being a fan of bed-making – and tiptoed out of the room.

He then padded to the kitchen, found a packet of dried cat food, and filled up the plastic bowl on the floor, refilled the water container, checked that the back door was locked, then made his way to his own room. He undressed in the light coming through from the hall, placed his clothes, fairly neatly folded, on a leather armchair against the wall, and, having forgotten to bring a pair of pyjamas with him and wearing only his shirt, slid, with a sigh of relief, under his own enormous duvet. Which, uncharacteristically, bit him on the right buttock.

With a yell of surprise and pain, he sprang upright, throwing back the puffed up cover, thus letting out a lot of the heat the electric blanket had built up over the evening, and exposing what had been a very soundly asleep and contented Colin.

The cat made a lightning swiping motion with his right front paw, drawing four lines of blood from the back of Garden's left leg, shot straight up into the air, and literally flew out of the door.

Garden got out of bed, walked slightly unsteadily towards the door, and slammed it with a growl of fury at being 'got' again by this sneaky and devious animal who obviously hated him. By the time he got back into bed, most of the warmth had left it, and he shivered, curled into the foetal position, until the blanket managed to engender a little warmth back into the mattress and the forlorn figure lying on it.

The next morning, when Garden awoke, he could hear Holmes already up and pottering around in the kitchen, clattering pots and pans and running water. He must have made a remarkable recovery, thought the younger man, as his stomach gave a lurch, and a wave of nausea washed over him. He did not have a strong head for alcohol, and had drunk more than he usually did.

Having disdainfully pulled on yesterday's clothes, he followed the noise and found his friend preparing a fried breakfast, a large cafetière already on the table, and two places set. 'How come you're so chirpy this morning?' asked Garden, running his fingers through his rumpled hair and yawning.

'I haven't the faintest idea, but I slept like the dead, and woke up very refreshed and ready to go on this case of ours,' he replied, putting a couple more rashers of bacon in the pan. 'One egg or two? And one in the eye for that self-important Streeter,' he added, apropos of nothing.

Garden nearly gagged, but took sufficient control of himself to ask, 'What time is it?'

'Don't worry about the time. I've phoned Shirley and told her she can manage for today. We don't get a lot of new business through the door what with the Saturday shopping crowd, so I've told her that if she needs us, she can always ring. We'll be here, solving the mystery of the … of the … of the what?'

'Dead wild bore,' suggested Garden. 'He was a helluva bore, he was absolutely furious at the last meeting when the others wouldn't give his short story a hearing, and he was as dead as a dodo when we came across him yesterday evening.'

'Well done, old chap,' Holmes congratulated him, starting to serve an amazing fry-up. 'There you go, egg, tomato, sausage, bacon, fried bread, baked beans, mushrooms, and black pudding – that'll put hairs on your chest. Just let me pour you a cup of coffee. Get that lot down you and you'll be ready for anything, John H.'

After a few solid swallows of coffee and his first forkful of bacon and egg, Garden found that he already felt better, and tucked in with a will. As he chewed, Holmes said, 'I've just remembered something that poor old Greg said on the phone last night.'

Classing this as nothing short of a miracle, Garden replied, 'Go on.'

'Greg asked all his staff if anyone had been up to the meeting room since his wife had cleaned it, and they all said they hadn't. He said he definitely didn't go up there, so it looks a bit as if we're looking for the invisible man. There's no access to the snug from outside, and the fire-door at the top of the fire escape was locked, so how did whoever did for Antony get up there without being seen? This is a problem worthy of old Sherlock himself, don't you think?'

Garden halted, fork halfway to his mouth, and sat there like a statue, his face screwed up in deep thought. 'Someone else *must* have gone up there,' he stated. 'Did they actually see Antony go up?'

'A couple of them said good evening to him. He didn't like to stay out of the limelight and would obviously advertise his presence.'

'But they didn't see anyone else?'

'No,' replied Holmes, chewing on a particularly succulent mouthful of sausage doused liberally in brown sauce.

'So, who took up the jugs of squash and the plates of sandwiches, then? I can just picture them on the table when we went up there. And there were ice-cubes still in those jugs. I remember them distinctly,' replied Garden, with a smile.

'By Gad, you're right. So can I, now I think of it. But how did they manage it, eh?'

Garden closed his eyes and seemed to go into a trance for a few minutes, then he shot up from his chair with a cry of 'Eureka!'

'What the heck is it, Garden, old chap?' asked Holmes, his eyes shining.

'Who never gets noticed going to a front door? The postman. Who never gets noticed going to a hospital bed? A nurse. Who never gets noticed walking around with a large tray? A waiter or member of staff!'

Holmes' face fell. 'But they all say that none of them went up there.'

'No, I'm sure they didn't, but that doesn't stop an outsider from slipping into the black and white they wear for work, and taking charge, maybe, of their refreshments, which may have been left unattended for a moment,' declared Garden, with a note of triumph in his voice.

Holmes, most unexpectedly, got up from the table and did a little dance round the kitchen, with as much energy as his portly body would allow, then he stopped and glared at Garden. 'If I'm Holmes, then you're supposed to be Watson, and Watson wasn't very bright. But I think you've solved the mystery of how someone got upstairs without being noticed.'

'He could slip back downstairs again, time his moment, and go into the gents, from which he could emerge in his everyday clothes, and no one would be any the wiser. All he would have to do would be to dispose of the black and white he wore.'

'Hang on a minute,' said Holmes, once more looking thoughtful. 'If he only accessorised his black and white, say with a bright tie and jacket – and I've just remembered that all the staff except for Greg and Tilly have to wear baseball caps, all he'd need to do was stash his unneeded items of clothing, and "borrow" a baseball cap.'

'And he could come straight out of the gents' and order a drink with no suspicion whatsoever falling on him,' finished Garden, following his partner's expression of victory, and doing a little war dance up and down the hall. Unfortunately, halfway through this little celebratory dance, Colin shot out of his master's bedroom, and Garden landed unceremoniously on his knees, before he could return to his unfinished breakfast. Colin howled as if he had been shot, at being thus disturbed in his flight to his litter tray, shot off down the hall, through the apartment, and disappeared through the cat-flap as if the Hound of the Baskervilles was after him.

'Get out, you little beast!' shouted Holmes, so flushed with success that he didn't even have time to defend his adored baby Colin. 'This'll show Streeter up for the incompetent fool he really is.'

Garden got up and dusted himself down. 'So, where

does that leave us, then? I'd say that it was probably one of the Irregulars who saw Antony off. Did they go into the pub before the meeting started, *in mufti*, or did they not arrive until after the body was discovered? Can you think of anyone you saw while we were eating, just before we went up?' he asked.

'Leave that one with me and I'll give it some thought,' replied Holmes. 'What else do we know?'

'That the murderer either stole that disgraceful short story from the dead man and shoved the title page into his waistcoat, or he'd already got his hands on it, and brought along the title page to make a point. Whichever way it was, it must mean the story was taken from Antony, because he never let it out of his sight, and could be anywhere by now. Do you have a record of all their addresses?' asked Garden, but Holmes' answer was cut off by the ringing of the doorbell.

Holmes opened the door to find Detective Inspector Streeter and his sidekick, Detective Sergeant Port, standing on the doorstep, an impertinently curled lip displayed, a uniformed constable at the foot of the small flight of steps that led up to the ground floor apartment. Holmes made a face like someone sucking a lemon, and invited them in. 'What can we do for you?' he asked, adjusting his expression to one more akin to that of someone welcoming guests, and less like someone inviting the enemy into the camp.

Streeter came into the hall, followed by the shorter, rather tubbier man, pulled himself up to his full height, gave a smug little grin, then announced, 'Having coordinated all the notes from the questioning we did yesterday evening, and examining all the circumstances very carefully, it is my sad duty to inform you that – oh, Mr Garden is here, too. That makes life easier for me. Now where was I? Apart from advising you to keep your nose out of official police matters that don't concern you.'

'Examining all the circumstances very carefully,' prompted Port.

'Ah, yes. In light of all the evidence we have, to date, we find that our chief suspects are you two. You are the only ones known to have mounted that staircase after Mrs Wordsworth left it, and Mr Richard Brownlow, the barman, says that you didn't turn around and come straight back downstairs. He reckons there was a gap of a few minutes, which we consider was just enough time for you to do away with Mr Antony and wipe off any fingerprints you may have left.' Streeter had enjoyed saying that.

'That's the most preposterous thing I have ever heard in my life!' exploded Holmes, going almost purple in the face with indignation. 'Garden and I are private investigators, uncovering crimes, not committing them. Why on earth should we want to kill someone like him; Garden had only met him on the evening of our last meeting. He'd never seen him in his life before that.'

'Says he,' sneered Streeter, glaring Holmes in the eye, then giving Garden the same Paddington stare.

'Says me, too,' Holmes challenged him ungrammatically. 'And do you have a warrant for our arrest, or is all your evidence just in your own twisted imagination? And we know all about that too, don't we?'

Garden smiled, as if to say, 'take that'. 'Have you spoken to any other members of the Quaker Street Irregulars?' he asked.

Streeter blustered and Port blushed, answering for his superior officer. 'We've not had sufficient time, so far, but DI Streeter wanted to come round here just to mark your cards,' he offered. 'Again.' Then he smirked.

'I think you'll find that I'm holding the aces of spades and clubs, and my colleague here is holding the aces of hearts and diamonds. When I played poker as a younger man, four aces beat anything you could have in your hand,' Holmes crowed in triumph. The man was bluffing.

He'd just wanted to put the wind up them, and it wasn't going to work. They were innocent, and would uncover the guilty party without his help.

Streeter left with his plans in complete disarray, and Port, as he followed him through the door and down the outside steps, looked over his shoulder, and winked at a surprised Holmes and Garden. He wasn't taken in by his guv'nor's behaviour and accusations, either. He rather liked them.

Garden followed them down to the street to have a quick word with the uniformed constable, to find out why he was there in the first place. 'I think he had high hopes of clapping you both in handcuffs and frog-marching you down to the cells,' he explained, good-naturedly. 'Do you know what we call those two down at the nick?'

'Enlighten me,' Garden encouraged him.

'They're known, as a pair, as "Janet".'

'Why's that?' Garden had no idea why this should be so.

'Janet Street-Porter – Janet Port-Streeter. Geddit?'

Garden did, and laughed merrily, going indoors to explain this to Holmes. Of course, he had to explain who Janet Street-Porter was first, before Holmes could become aware of why it was funny, but he got there in the end. And after Holmes had had a quick look on the internet, he laughed until he nearly became reacquainted with his breakfast.

Chapter Four

Holmes did, indeed, have a list of the members' addresses and home telephone numbers – hardly any of them relied on a mobile – these being the only records that the society seemed to keep. Leaving Holmes to ring round to see if the other men could provide alibis for the time before the meeting was due to start, Garden went on to the computer to see what he could dig up.

Apart from the odd 'oh!' 'really?' and 'how very interesting,' Garden more or less worked in silence, tapping away at the keys and making notes on a pad to the right of the keyboard of the laptop that he had, thankfully, thrown into the back of Holmes' car out of force of habit. In their occupation, one simply didn't leave the office without one's laptop, although they had yet to find one that Holmes felt happy with.

Holmes, on the other hand, made quite a bit of noise over his phone calls. Sometimes he spoke to the member himself, at others, to wives or house-mates, and he, too, took copious notes of what was being told to him.

It was one o'clock before they both came up for air, and Holmes suggested a spot of lunch before they compared notes. He was feeling so hungry that he could eat a scabby donkey; not that he counted such an expression in his vocabulary.

After a scratch meal of ham salad sandwiches washed down with a cup of tea, they each took their notebook, and sat opposite each other on the twin sofas. 'What have you got, Holmes?' asked Garden, deciding that the host should go first.

'The chair, Stephen Compton, is a widower and lives alone: retired doctor. Specialist area, the short stories. He returned a spade he had borrowed from his neighbour, however, on his way out, and got talking. By the time he looked at his watch, he really had to rush, and arrived at the pub to find us at the bar hatch, waiting for the Wordsworths to come through.

'Here's the members' list. Could you write in pencil underneath his name, "check with neighbour". Next, we have Ludovic Connor, a forty-year-old single bank clerk. Specialist area, the longer stories like *The Hound*. He worked overtime, and was five minutes late, arriving while we were in the back parlour, from what he tells me, as he remembers us coming back through. Under his name, put "check with employers", although how we're going to do that, I have no idea. You know what secretive buggers – pardon me – bank staff are and how loath they are to give out any information whatsoever.'

'We could always chat up one of the other employees there, and see if they worked late last night or knew of anyone who had,' suggested Garden.

'Excellent idea, Watson, er, Garden: first-class thinking. Next, we have Aaron Dibley, a divorced probation officer: specialist area, just the written stories. He says no one can confirm when he left the house, because he lives alone, so we may have to do a bit of checking with the neighbours there. Make a note: "check with neighbours".

'Next, we have Peter Lampard, gas engineer and single, although I know he lives with another gentleman, and I've never looked too closely at their living arrangements. The other gentleman said Lampard didn't leave until twenty minutes before the meeting was due to start and, although he doesn't live far away, by then we were already on our way upstairs. He's the one that's potty about the series starring Benedict Cumberbatch: thinks it's sheer genius.

Make a note, Garden: "check on relationship", not that it's any of our business what he does behind closed doors. Whether he's telling the truth or not, I don't know. He did sound a little furtive.'

'But if Lampard is gay, he might have felt that the story was written just to get him and to "out" him. Or he may even have felt annoyed that Antony had depicted an obviously straight character as a gay. Some people can be very sensitive about their particular foibles, you know,' said Garden, and winked at Holmes, sparking a memory of the first time Holmes had seen Joanne in full fig, and causing a blush to rise to his face, as he remembered how attractive he thought she looked. This, coupled with the fact that he found Shirley Garden a very attractive woman was something that he needed to keep suppressed in Garden's presence.

He cleared his throat in embarrassment, glad that Garden couldn't read his mind, and continued, 'Rupert Mitchell had been sunning himself in warmer climes, to get away from both his profession and the grimness of the English weather. There's definitely "brass" in embalming!

'Dave Warwick was much too taken up with his new baby to have even considered attending. Similarly, Bob Wiltshire, a generalist, as far as Holmes was concerned, and a social worker by profession, had been called out to an emergency case conference, and wouldn't have turned up either.

'Along the same lines, Christopher Cave, a cabbie whose specialised area was the oddball works about the great detective, had actually dropped a fare off at the pub, then simply parked his car round the back in the car park, and entered the bar just as the clock was chiming the hour.' That was another perfectly good suspect down the drain, thought Holmes. Garden was relieved. They didn't want too long a list when they'd been through everyone, or they'd never get to the bottom of things.

Elliot Jordan, the librarian whose field of expertise was the films, had walked from the library, but he'd seemed to have taken an unconscionable time to get there, but as long as they had confirmation of the time he left the library, there was nothing more they could do, in all reality.

The last one on the list, apart from Holmes himself and the victim, was Kevin Wood, a married teacher who doted on the last series but one. He had claimed to come straight from a staff meeting, without the time to go home and get changed, but that was confirmed by his wife, who happened to be in when Holmes rang his home after speaking to him on his mobile. 'Who does that leave still on the list?' he asked, at last running out of steam.

'If we ignore all the follow-ups and queries?' queried Garden.

'Just so, John H. Who's definitely still in our sights, then? And then you can tell me about what you found out.'

Garden consulted the pencilled notes he had taken while Holmes had been talking, and said, 'The only ones who can't prove an alibi are, firstly, Elliot Jordan, who seems to have taken four times longer than necessary to walk the short distance to The Sherlock. Secondly, there's Aaron Dibley, who lives alone and hasn't anyone to vouch for when he left the house. Thirdly, you seem to want me to include Peter Lampard, because we think his housemate may be lying, and he may be more than his housemate, coupled with what I said about him taking a scunner to the man and/or the manuscript. Who knows, maybe he wanted to steal and peddle it as his own work – the gay re-creator of Holmes.'

'I'm afraid we'll just have to trust our hunch on the last one. It's a gut instinct thing,' said Holmes, twirling the ends of his moustache thoughtfully. 'Where should we start first?'

'I think we should start by leaving any personal visits till this evening. I could do with a shower and a change of clothes, and a lot of people who aren't working on a Saturday go out shopping. These are no fly-by-night youngsters we're looking at, and I shouldn't think they'd be out on the razz on a Saturday night.'

Garden was feeling a bit jaded after their 'bit of a binge' the night before, and a fairly sleepless night with not being in his own bed. 'Just let me tell you what I came across. I think you'll find there's food for thought in it. That's another reason why I don't want to act precipitately. We need to think this through, and not act on the spur of the moment.'

'So, what have you got in that notebook of yours, before you scoot off back to the flat?'

'I checked on the possibility that there were other Sherlock Holmes appreciation societies that might have an online presence, and I found a few.'

Holmes whistled softly, though he had no idea what this could possibly mean. 'Go on.'

'I e-mailed them – hey, *E-mail* and the Detectives!' Holmes looked puzzled. 'Never mind ... A couple of them have actually replied, and confirmed that Cyril Antony turned up at one of their meetings asking to join, sat in on a meeting, and tried to read them his story.'

'So, he was definitely out for some sort of glory, though how he could achieve it ...' Holmes fizzled to a halt.

'I decided to follow this theme a little bit further, and looked on line for recently self-published short stories, and there it was, bold as brass: "A Study in Cerise", available at – get this – six pounds ninety-nine, as an e-book.'

'Scandalous!' spat Holmes. 'What's an e-book?'

'You're pulling my leg, aren't you?'

'Yes,' confirmed Holmes, 'and what a lot to charge for a download where there's no physical product, and it's only a short story.'

'I know. He'll never sell any at that price,' mused

Garden, relieved that he didn't have to describe this particular reading revolution to his older partner.

'I meant that he'd had the brass neck to publish it at all, and inflict that piece of absolute rubbish onto an unsuspecting world.' Holmes' indignation was on the part of Conan Doyle's character, rather than that of a gullible public who were about to be relieved of much too large a sum of money for what had seemed like far-fetched drivel.

Garden calmed down his partner and summed up the situation by stating, 'The way I see it, we've got to check out a divorced librarian – the library doesn't close till seven – a possibly gay gas fitter, and a probation officer who doesn't have a witness to when he left home. I'll come up with a plan, and come back here about six-ish. We can always go to the chippie later.'

'Me? Go to a fish and chip shop?' asked Holmes, in righteous indignation.

'Oh, lighten up, old man. It won't kill you, and you might actually enjoy it,' Garden said, as a parting shot. He then shot out as quickly as he could to the waiting taxi that he had called, as he'd heard the ominous clatter of the cat-flap in the kitchen door, and knew that Colin had now entered the building.

Garden, a veritable study in cerise himself and steaming from his shower, wrapped himself in a thick towelling robe, and padded in his slippers towards his wardrobes. Flinging open a door, he fingered his way through the items hanging there, and finally selected a kingfisher blue blouse and a cream linen skirt before having a bit of a rumble through Joanne's undies drawer. A pair of black ballet pumps would set off the outfit, if he wore his black woollen jacket against the weather.

He dressed and sat in front of his dressing table, selecting the make-up that would go with his chosen items just as carefully as he had chosen the clothes, and treated the choice of his jewellery to the same careful consideration. He wanted to look smart and official, but friendly enough to have a real chat too, for Garden had a plan.

Holmes wouldn't like it, but he didn't know what else they could do. He'd just have to wait until he got back to Farlington Market before he could put it to him, for he didn't want to give him a whiff of what he proposed they should do until he was there in person to judge his reaction.

At half past five, a very different figure from that which had entered by the front door just a while ago slipped out of the back door of the office. The first Holmes knew of his partner's return was a short ring on the doorbell, but when he answered the summons and opened the door, he was puzzled.

Standing on his doorstep was an attractive young woman, quite tall and with blonde hair which was highlighted by the light from the street lamp situated outside the property next door. 'How may I help you?' asked Holmes, noticing that she carried a clipboard. Some sort of survey, perhaps?

The young lady winked at him, causing him even more confusion, then greeted him in quite a deep voice. 'Come on, Holmes, old man, let me in for God's sake. It's perishing out here.'

Holmes' mouth dropped open as he admitted his visitor, who whispered, 'Shut your mouth, Holmes, you look like you're catching flies.'

'Garden? Is that really you?' asked the astonished Holmes. He'd seen Garden in his female gear before, but it never ceased to amaze him how believable he was. And he must have a selection of wigs, because that wasn't the one he had seen him in when he was 'in Joanne's skin' once before. He felt himself reddening again at the thought.

Garden seemed to have the knack of shaving his face so

closely that there was never a hint of a five o'clock shadow or a stray whisker. Maybe that, in itself, should have been confirmation that he was not female, as most women of his age or older seemed to have the odd wiry hair or two protruding from their chinny-chin-chin or top lip.

'I have a cunning plan, Holmes,' announced Garden with a smirk.

'That's just as well, because I haven't thought of any way we can check out what we need to,' replied Holmes. 'Come and sit down for a moment, and you can put me in the picture.'

Once seated opposite each other, the fire blazing away merrily between them, and not a Colin in sight – Holmes had put him out, lest he snag Garden's tights – Garden suggested that they sum exactly what they needed to ascertain.

'We need to find out who killed Cyril Antony,' stated Holmes, simplistically and baldly.

'We also need to find out if the rest of the original manuscript of "A Study in Cerise"' – Holmes winced at the title – 'still exists, but whoever has it in his possession must be the murderer.'

'But surely he'd have destroyed the whole thing,' said Holmes.

'Maybe not if he doesn't know it's out on the internet yet. Maybe he wants to retitle it and publish it in his name, under a new title,' suggested Garden.

'Like what?' asked Holmes abruptly.

'Perhaps ... "The Secret Life of Holmes and Watson".'

'But Cyril had read it to people,' countered Holmes.

'I'd be willing to bet he never got as far as the second page, as he didn't with your group, and only the first few pages may have to be re-written. Or, yes, maybe he just wanted to destroy it. With these two things in mind, I offer you my plan for this evening.'

'Which is?'

'That I represent myself as someone doing a survey, and go inside our suspects' houses, make some sort of diversion, like spilling a cup of tea on the carpet, and have a quick look round inside for any signs that the manuscript is, or has been, there.'

'And what do I do while you're going through all this subterfuge?' asked Holmes.

'Well, I suggest you dress in old clothes, because I want you to go out into their back gardens, search for any signs of a recent bonfire, and go through the contents of their dustbins, to see if you can locate any pages or fragments of it.'

'!' Holmes was speechless for a few seconds. 'What? You want me to go rummaging through people's refuse and old food scraps?'

'If it apprehends a murderer, then it's all in a good cause, isn't it?'

'Do I have to?' Holmes' face had a look of desperation and disgust about this request to go through people's trash.

'I can hardly do it dressed like this, can I?' retorted Garden.

'You could go home and change ... No, I suppose that would take too long,' admitted Holmes, suddenly seeing that there was no way out of his role in Garden's plan for their evening – but he was going to have a very long soak in a lavender-scented bath when he got home, he decided.

'So, remind me of the three members, and what their specialist areas are,' requested Garden, 'so that we can decide what's the most sensible order in which to visit them. If one of them seems a better bet than the others, it's senseless to waste time – especially with your part of the job – drawing out the visits.'

'Thank you so much for your kind consideration,' mumbled Holmes sarcastically, once more picking up his membership list.

'We've got Peter Lampard, specialist area the most recent series starring, what is this fellow's name? – Benedict Cumberbatch? Extraordinary!'

'He's the member whom we suspect may be having a relationship with his male housemate – the gas fitter? To be honest, and taking all things into consideration, I don't think it's likely to have been him. Is he really that sensitive about coming out of the closet? Would he really be stupid enough to think that if he rewrote the first few pages and changed the title page, he could just steal the story? So, why do I think he should be left on the list? What are my reasons?' he asked, as Holmes opened his mouth to do just that.

'Firstly, there is no fire without some smoke, to quote the saying correctly, and if he is in a gay relationship, he's hardly likely to have taken "A Study in Cerise" as a slur and, if I remember correctly, there was some sort of newspaper accusation that the couple in that particular series were closer than it was previously supposed – the characters, of course, not the actors, I hasten to clarify. Maybe he really thought he could make something out of the story. Who's next?'

'Elliot Jordan, the librarian. His specialist area is the films.'

'Again, I find him unlikely, but we'll at least have to take a look round at his place. And thirdly?'

'Aaron Dibley, the probation officer, whose specialist area is just the original books and short stories. He has no interest whatsoever in films or television portrayals.'

They had emptied a pot of tea while they were talking, and Garden looked at his watch. 'If you go and get changed into your tattiest clothes – assuming you have any, which I find unlikely,' he stated, 'I suggest that we start with our librarian chappie, Jordan, then go to Dibley's place, and leave Lampard to the end, because I get the feeling that he's an also-ran, or a red herring.'

'And how are we going to work this thing?' asked Holmes, not having the faintest idea how this was going to work.

'I've got a large-scale local map with me. I'll check out the addresses while you get changed, and explain our strategy to you when you're ready.'

It was a full twenty minutes later when Holmes returned to the room. 'What have you been doing all this time?' asked Garden, who had thought his partner would have returned within five. It was, after all, only throwing on his oldest clothes that he had to do, not getting himself ready to go to the opera.

The older man appeared in paint-splattered trousers, a jumper, the wool of which was covered in minute bobbles, a battered trilby hat, and an overcoat that was crumpled, and rather torn about the hem, but was, thankfully, quite long and black.

'You took long enough,' commented Garden, looking at his watch again and finding that it was just after seven o'clock: at least they should find their librarian at home, now, and wouldn't have to wait for him to arrive.

'I had to go through all the bags I'd got in the bottom and on top of the wardrobe which have been waiting absolutely ages for me to remember, and find the time to take them down to the tip,' explained Holmes. 'I don't actually have any "tatty" clothes that I regularly wear, I'm afraid,' he added, a trifle shamefacedly. 'Now the bags are out, I can probably make time to drop them off tomorrow.'

'Don't be too hasty,' Garden warned him. 'In our profession, you never know when you'll need an out-of-character disguise, and what you're wearing now would be just right for the part of a tramp or a homeless person.'

Holmes glared at Garden at this slur on his appearance, then sighed, and looked resigned to having to keep all his old garments for the sake of the job.

'I've looked at the map, and used my personal

knowledge of where we're going, and I can tell you all the properties, Lampard's included, have rear alleyways for access by the refuse collectors. What I suggest is that I drop you off at the end of each alleyway, you count the houses along, and get in the back way and go through the rubbish …'

'In the cold,' muttered Holmes miserably.

'… While I go in and do my bit inside…'

'In the warm,' Holmes almost growled at the unfairness of it all. Damn it all, why couldn't he have been the one to dress up as a woman? Then he remembered his manly figure – his portliness – and, finally, his magnificent moustache, which was much too luxuriant even for the most hirsute of women to be sporting. With a shudder of horror at the picture this made in his mind's eye, he returned his attention to his partner.

'When you've finished, you can make your way back to the front of the house to where the car will be parked, and wait in that, if I'm not back first – I'll let you have the spare keys.'

'But how will I know which house it is from the back?'

Garden sighed in exasperation. 'We'll drive by the front and count along from the correct house to the end, where the alleyway begins, then you just have to count along the backs of the properties.'

'Stout fellow!' exclaimed Holmes, suddenly understanding what was expected of him. He might not relish the idea, but he was a private investigator, and a private investigator baulked at nothing when it came to solving a case.

Chapter Five

At the entrance to the first alleyway, which ran behind Elliot Jordan's house, Holmes stood lost in thought. Was it the fourth house or the fifth? He couldn't remember, so he'd have to try to look through the back windows to see if he could see Garden. He was so excited at being out in the field undercover that he hadn't concentrated as they had counted along the properties to get to the end of the row, and now he was in a pickle. He hoped Garden didn't find out that he had forgotten where he was going.

The fourth house along, he decided couldn't be the right one, as the gate was bolted from the other side, and a large dog began to bark furiously at his presence, as he stopped just the other side of the fence. Climbing gates and getting attacked by what sounded like a rabid dog had definitely not been mentioned in Garden's plan.

Fortunately, the next gate was unlocked, and he crept inside the boundary of the garden, searching around, at first, for the sign that there had recently been a bonfire. He thought this was a particularly ingenious idea on his part, in case the manuscript had been burnt. Hardly any people had open fires these days, and an incinerator was the best way to get rid of things permanently – and if one didn't have an incinerator, one had a simple bonfire.

Flitting from tree to bush, from bush to half-wall, he made his way round the lawn, ending up back at the end of the garden where the dustbin was located. Taking off the lid gingerly, as the bin was quite full, he began to lift out the contents gingerly, trying to spot anything that looked like sheets or part-sheets of paper, and trying not to get too dirty in the process.

Blast and damn! Jordan, if this was, indeed, his dustbin, must have had a takeaway curry recently, and hadn't wrapped up the remains very securely. Now he had curry sauce all down one sleeve and the front of his right trouser leg. Dropping the package as if it were radioactive, he reached once more into the bin after wiping his hands carelessly down the front of his coat.

Was he absolutely certain this was the right house? Suddenly he wasn't sure. Maybe he ought to just …

'Joanne' Garden had been invited inside by Elliot Jordan, who lived alone, and eyed up this unexpected visitor with an unwelcome lasciviousness, mentally undressing her as she sat down in an armchair.

Had he actually been able to do this, he would have run, screaming, from the room, but his imagination didn't allow him even to consider that this lovely lady might be a gentleman in disguise.

Garden crossed his legs, took a pen out of his handbag, which he set on the floor beside the chair, and looked at his clipboard. This was a busy road, so he used the excuse that he was carrying out a survey about whether a bypass would be welcomed by the local residents.

Jordan very quickly offered his visitor a glass of wine and, when she refused, pressed his offer more firmly. Garden, who had refused without thinking about it, immediately changed his answer to the affirmative, as something liquid would be the ideal way of creating a diversion. 'I'd prefer red, if you've got any,' she said, with a winsome smile, knowing she wasn't chancing her arm, because she knew what was going to happen to the wine.

Jordan quickly returned from the kitchen with two enormous glasses of claret, and put one down on a side-table by the armchair, winking knowingly as he did so, before taking his seat as close as he could get on the arm at the end of the sofa.

Joanne began her questioning about noise nuisance caused by the local traffic then, when Jordan had tipped his glass back to take an enormous gulp, shot out her elbow, and knocked her glass on to the cream, shag-pile carpet, its ruby red contents splattered in a low arc to halfway across the room. 'I'm so sorry,' she purred, her eyes wide and innocent, as she surveyed the mess and turned towards her host.

With a cry of distress, Jordan leapt from his perch and rushed from the room to get some cleaning cloths with which to absorb the defiling fluid, and Garden leapt up and went to stand beside the dining table, which had all sorts of papers lying on its top, with just a small place cleared where it could be assumed that his host ate his evening meals.

As the distraught librarian rushed back into the room and covered the slowly sinking puddle with cloths, his visitor had a quick examination of what was on offer: nothing there to give any cause for suspicion. Jordan then said he was going to open some white wine to use to remove any staining from the spilt red.

As he was getting the bottle out of the fridge and opening it, Garden pulled down the flap of a bureau and had a quick look in that: again, nothing obvious sticking out of the pigeon-holes. Not even noticing her shutting the bureau's flap, Jordan hurried back into the room, finished his mopping, and poured white wine onto the dark pink stain now scarring the pristine appearance of the carpet.

He then turned to Joanne with a leer, and got to his feet with a definite twinkle in his eye, and Garden, inside her clothes, began to panic. He hadn't factored this sort of thing into his plan at all – could not even have foreseen it. As nobody ever seemed to express an interest in him as a man, he had never thought that someone might fancy the pants off him as a woman – and what a grand surprise it would be for them!

At that point, Jordan's face fell, and he pointed at the rear picture window, where the disreputable figure of what looked very like a tramp appeared. 'Who the bloody hell's that in my garden?' he yelled, and tore across the room to chase off the tatterdemalion intruder.

Holmes had only had a little peek to see if he could see either Elliot Jordan or Garden to confirm that he was at the right house, and now made a mad dash for the back gate, throwing the dustbin down behind him to hinder any pursuer.

Garden, in his highest-pitched Joanne-voice, squeaked frantically for Jordan to come back in case he got hurt, and managed to halt him actually in the back doorway. As the householder froze, Garden made a frantic rush for the front door and let himself out, slamming it behind him. He feared he would always remain a mystery woman in Jordan's eyes, but then he'd be a bit more than that if Jordan ever seriously got his hands on him.

He drove the car briskly away, turning round at the corner so that he would be at the end of the rear alleyway, and there he found Holmes, crouched into a ball behind the fence of the end house.

'Thank God you're here,' Holmes said in a loud whisper. 'I thought I'd had my chips, then.'

'With curry sauce?' asked Garden, wrinkling his nose as the smell of jalfrezi wafted across from his partner. 'But it's great that you did look through the window, because that guy was plying me with wine, and was planning to jump my bones. If you hadn't peered in when you did, I think he might be contemplating having got rather more than he bargained for right now.'

Holmes began to chuckle at the thought of Garden's apprehension, then as he thought about it more, he moved on to full-blown laughter. 'Stop that!' ordered Garden, 'You're splattering me with detritus from that dustbin.'

'You just wait until you see the state of me under a street light, never mind the inside of your car,' replied Holmes. 'But I had no idea Jordan was a lech. No wonder his wife divorced him. I'll bet he couldn't keep his hands to himself when they were married, either.'

Dibley's house was the middle of seven and, as Garden pointed out to Holmes, as he fastidiously used a lacy handkerchief from his handbag and a good helping of spit to get some marks off the left leg of his tights, this was hardly a case for getting muddled as to which back garden it might be that he was expected to enter. As he'd stared directly through the back window he had had to confess why he was there, staring balefully into Jordan's house. 'Just count three in both directions, and whatever's left in the middle must be it.'

'It's easy being clever after the event. You don't know what it's like down those dark back alleyways at night, and with no street lights. All the houses seem to merge into one.'

'Don't whine. It doesn't become you,' said Garden, sounding exactly like Holmes' mother, and he pulled up at the end of the row of seven houses and waited for Holmes to get out, which he did, already counting under his breath as he entered the darkness which was the back access alley.

Garden drove round to the front, parked, and walked up the garden path and knocked the door, there being no bell. Aaron Dibley, for it must be he as he was unmarried, according to Holmes, answered the door with a frown at being disturbed during an evening when he had not been expecting visitors.

'What do you want?' he asked brusquely.

'I wonder if I could come in to have a quick chat with you ...' Garden was thinking furiously, because this was not a busy neighbourhood and, so disturbed had he been by Holmes almost getting rumbled, and himself almost getting a tumble, that he had forgotten to have a cover story ready. '… I wanted to discuss what you think of the levels of crime in Farlington Market,' he concluded, quite proud that he had chosen a subject that was likely to be dear to Dibley's heart, he being a probation officer.

'I don't normally take part in surveys conducted by people who come round to my home disturbing me, but I shall make an exception in this case, as I can see no danger in letting *you* into my home, and I have a professional interest in that sort of thing. I'm always telling people who live on their own that they should never let strangers into their house when they haven't someone else with them.'

He stood aside to let his visitor in, and Garden thought it was lucky he hadn't tried to get in here by presenting himself as male. He had acquired a number of false moustaches and eyebrows since he and Holmes had gone into business together, and had even remembered to salvage a few of the drab grey and navy office clothes he wore to his last dreary job, for working undercover in just these sorts of circumstances.

Dibley was quite a forbidding-looking man, with close-cropped dark hair, its short tufts already turning grey, and he wore horn-rimmed glasses, giving him a rather headmasterly look. When Garden was settled, he made a pot of tea, and joined him in the sitting room which, unlike the last house, didn't go straight through to a dining area, meaning it was quite safe for Holmes to ferret around to his heart's content, provided he didn't knock over anything noisy.

An opportunity never presented itself to knock over his teacup, because Dibley kept them prissily on the tray on a low coffee table. There was a bit of rustling discernibly audible from the back garden, but Dibley didn't seem to notice it, just interrupting his monologue on the probation service to murmur, 'Hedgehogs. Nothing to worry about.'

Garden, rather cunningly in his opinion, got him talking about Edwardian policing, and easily steered the conversation round to the subject of the investigations of Sherlock Holmes and Dr Watson. 'I've got a couple of albums of fascinating photographs up in my loft,' he suddenly volunteered. 'They contain photographs of policemen and criminals in the actual time that Conan Doyle was writing. Are you at all interested?'

Garden was so interested, also loving the Holmes and Watson stories, that he almost forgot to use his female voice to answer in a very enthusiastic affirmative, and Dibley trotted off upstairs, where the sound of a loft ladder descending could be heard.

With a jolt, Garden realised that – he didn't know for how long – he had been sitting with his knees apart, as if he were wearing trousers, and not with them crossed in a more delicate, ladylike fashion, and just hoped that Dibley hadn't noticed, and taken it as a come-on.

Pulling himself (and his knees) together, and deciding that he'd have to get out as soon as it was conveniently possible, but not before he'd had a quick search, Garden was off like a shot, going through the wall unit, through the desk, and even taking a peek through the contents of the sideboard in the dining room. Once in there, he started at the sight of an open fireplace, and the remnants of some papers in it. Kneeling down, careful not to ladder his tights, he removed what he could, took a quick look at it, and became very excited.

On one fragment he could discern the best part of the word 'Sherlock'. Dibley had not yet reappeared, but Garden was suddenly aware of a frantic fanfare being played on a car horn, which he recognised as his. Stuffing the paper fragments unceremoniously into his handbag, he fled through the front door and towards his vehicle.

Outside in the darkness of the garden, Holmes had had an

initial swearing fit because there were no lights on in the back room, and he was going to have to search only by the light of the moon and the stars, then a hand in his coat pocket came across a small torch that he used to carry when he had bonfires in the garden, and the batteries seemed to still be in working order.

Shading its light with his hand, he walked round the garden, finding no evidence whatsoever of any signs of a fire or an incinerator. He moved on towards the dustbin, his shoulders slumped. He didn't reckon there was any chance of him coming across any incriminating evidence. He absolutely reeked of curry, his hands and clothes were filthy, and his skin was crawling at what he might come across in this festering collection of household refuse.

The noise Garden had heard had been Holmes trying to smother the sound of the metal dustbin lid as he put it on the ground. Damn these old-fashioned dustbins. Why couldn't everyone have a wheelie bin or a plastic one; it would make this current episode in his life a damned sight easier.

He quietly cursed all these men who lived alone for relying on ready-cooked food, as the remains of a Chinese meal landed on his shoes, and he suddenly remembered that he had forgotten to change them, and these were his good brown brogues. He'd have to take them into the cobbler's to see if they had any magic solution for removing chow mein stains from leather. Blast!

Next, he opened a parcel of newspaper, at first only revealing a pile of potato peelings, and nearly gave up in disgust, when he moved the topmost peelings just to make sure there was nothing else in the parcel, and bingo – there were some fragments of torn and burnt paper, one of them showing the letters 'Wats …'

Just stopping himself in time from shouting with triumph, he bundled up the parcel again and inserted it back into the bin, scooping up the Chinese food as best as he could, put back the lid, and hurried off to the car as quickly as possible. When he got inside it, he began to lean on the horn to get Garden's attention, and it wasn't long before he saw the man – woman – him/herself, streaking down the garden path towards the vehicle.

Garden threw himself into the driver's seat, told Holmes he had evidence in his handbag, thus stealing the older man's thunder, and drove like the very devil himself to get back to his flat, so that he could change back into men's clothing and they could go to the police. They had no alternative, no matter how things stood between them and the official powers that be.

Less than an hour later, they were sitting in the enemy's office, putting their case to him. Garden, still with the slightest touch of 'panda eyes' from his hasty removal of mascara, had handed over the papers that had, not so long ago, dwelt in one of his many handbags, and Holmes was telling him about the contents of Dibley's dustbin.

'This could all be circumstantial,' Streeter hedged, not at all liking the fact that they were way ahead of him in finding the killer. Again!

'But these fragments were actually taken from his fireplace, and the others are still in his dustbin partly burned,' persisted Holmes.

'His specialist interest is the books and stories of Sherlock Holmes, and I bet he knows nothing about e-books. He'd probably think that if he destroyed the original, that would be the end of that. There wasn't even a television in his house, as far as I could see,' added Garden carelessly.

'You've actually been in his house?' This did arouse Streeter's interest.

'Would you, please, just go round to his house and take the newspaper package from his dustbin, then compare any fingerprints on that with any you found on the sheet of paper that was with Antony's body? If they match, and you confront him with that evidence, I'm sure he'll confess,' pleaded Holmes. Nobody must find out about Garden's alter ego, or their secret member of staff would be blown, and they couldn't use him for undercover work in the future.

'And if they do match, and he doesn't sing like a canary?' asked Streeter, looking for some sort of deal as to these two rivals' sources.

As Holmes and Garden left the police station with obvious relief, Garden said to Holmes, 'You know they say fact is stranger than fiction?'

'Yes, old man?' replied Holmes.

'Well, I don't know if that's true, but it's certainly less dangerous than fiction.'

'How do you mean?'

'I read quite a lot of contemporary murder mysteries ...' At this, Holmes raised his eyebrows in disapproval.

'Whatever for?' This was anathema.

'New stories. I can't exist for the rest of my life on Conan Doyle.' Holmes looked scandalised. 'Anyway, when it gets towards the end of the story, the hero or heroine always get themselves into a tight spot with the murderer, and their own life is endangered, then the intrepid policeman, or whoever, comes along and saves them. We've hardly been put in any peril in this case, have we? In fact, when I get to that bit of the modern formula now, I usually just stop reading. It's obvious that the main protagonist isn't going to be killed, and it just seems a bit too formulaic.'

Holmes nodded solemnly, then said, 'We did get in a bit of bother at The Black Swan.'

'I prefer to think of that as the exception, rather than the rule. Let's hope things continue the way they've gone in this case. I don't want to end up with high blood pressure, or a hole in the head.'

'Just so, old chap. Just so,' agreed Holmes, sagely. He could hardly argue with that, could he? 'And we've won the first battle. This is definitely our victory, and nuts to Inspector Streeter.'

The fingerprints did match, Dibley had sung like the proverbial canary, and everything had happened just as Holmes and Garden had surmised, with it later being reported in the local paper that Dibley had entered The Sherlock public house, sneaking in by the outside entry to the gents, where he'd removed and hidden his tie and jacket. He had then gone into the bar and seen the jugs and tray waiting to go upstairs, unattended, in the hatch from the kitchen.

Moving behind the bar, the crush of young people meaning he didn't bump into anyone he knew, he came back out again, through the snug, and upstairs, where he knew Antony to be, having kept watch for him arriving. His crime was, indeed, premeditated.

Having seen off his intended target, and having used the deerstalker that had been hung on the wall of the meeting room, Dibley then left the tray in the upstairs room and calmly came back down again, went out by the saloon bar door, stashed the slim briefcase with the disgusting manuscript inside it in his car, entered by the outside door to the gents for a second time, re-donned his tie and jacket, and came out into the pub as if he'd only just arrived.

It was an audacious crime, but one in which he had carelessly neglected to remove his fingerprints from the title sheet of the story, and the man had been shattered when told that Cyril Antony had already unleashed it on an unsuspecting public in e-book form and that, furthermore, there was nothing he could do about it at all. Once self-published, it stayed published, unless the author unpublished it.

DI Streeter, of course, took all the credit, and just referred to the sudden and unexpected solution to it as 'acting on information received from an unnamed source'. But it still rankled when he thought of the identity of that unnamed source, and the credit he'd received soured in his memory.

Holmes and Garden, meanwhile, seemed to have put it behind them, after a couple of mutual pats on the back, and were interesting themselves in ways to disguise the human face and form. That was much more fun. Maybe they'd get to try it out soon, on their next case. Garden had really been a trail-blazer with his portrayal of Joanne, although he decided he may have to make himself a little less attractive on his next venture out in that persona. He didn't want to be ravished by some macho man who was out for a good time. The poor fellow would end up in therapy.

As he contemplated this ghastly fate, Holmes cleared his throat to get his attention. 'Yes, Holmes, what is it?'

'The battle may have ended, but we must remember we are still at war.'

'Surely not. Haven't we proved something by solving this case first?'

'Not at all, my man. There will be other skirmishes, and we must be triumphant.'

Garden sighed.

THE END

The Curious Incident of …
THE BESPANGLED FUR

Chapter One

The sky was leaden over Hamsley Black Cross, louring and threatening of bad weather to come and lightened only by the growing array of coloured lights that grew daily as December was heralded in by sharp frosts and chill winds, causing the occupants of homes and offices alike to seek the cheer of electric lighting to relieve the mood.

Into such an office, with a cheerful ping of the doorbell, entered Sherman Holmes, dragging a fragrant pine tree behind him. 'Christmas has arrived,' he called joyfully, so that his voice reached not only his secretary/receptionist, Shirley Garden, sitting near the front window, but also her son and his business partner, John H. Garden, ensconced in the rear office.

Shirley got to her feet, exclaiming at the size of the specimen, while John H. put his head round the door to this front office and declared, 'Not already! I thought you could have put it off for just a bit longer.'

'Why?' asked Holmes, propping his recent purchase against a convenient wall. 'Christmas is coming, is it not?'

'Certainly, it is on the way, as there were electricians crawling all over the front of the buildings the other night to get the lights up, and then again last night – nothing but men up ladders, it's been – but you do realise that getting in a real specimen such as that simply won't last. We shall have to replace it before we close for the festive season,' replied Garden.

'And your problem with that is?' Holmes' cheerfulness would not be so easily dented.

'That it has to be decorated and, should all the needles

fall off due to the central heating drying the thing out, that the decorations will then have to be taken off – no easy task, with an office full of needles – and then a new one redecorated.' Garden was suitably gloomy in this prophecy.

'That's no bother for such a happy time of year.' Holmes was equally as stubborn in his mood. He may have hated Hallowe'en, but he positively loved Christmas.

'Then you can do it, for I won't have anything to do with it.'

'Don't be such a wet blanket,' Holmes batted back at him.

'Well, I think it's lovely to have a tree so early.' Shirley Garden came down firmly on the side of the angels, knowing which way her bread was buttered in that Holmes paid her wages – and very good wages they were too, for such an undemanding job.

'There's a box of lights, decorations, and tinsel on the back seat of my car, and a bucket. Garden, if you would be so kind as to bring them in, then go out to the back and fill the bucket with earth, we may commence to give this business a festive touch.' Holmes was on a seasonal roll. Garden's eyes were, too, as he exited the offices and went to Holmes' car to collect the rest of the boss' booty.

'Don't you know anything about fir trees?' asked Garden mutinously.

'Of course I do. I have one every year in my apartment,' replied Holmes, surprised at his partner's attitude.

'And when do you usually buy it?'

'Why, the twenty-third of December. Colin has quite a time, what with knocking off the decorations, and even, one year, having it down on the floor, the whole kit and caboodle.'

'So you don't usually have one around for long?'

'As a matter of fact, I don't.'

'Well, be it on your own head but, as I said, I'm not taking off all the gubbins and doing it all over again with a replacement.' Garden was uncharacteristically adamant on this point.

'It did happen to us one year,' confirmed Shirley, remembering one terrible Christmas in her son's childhood.

'Stuff and nonsense,' retorted Holmes. 'Inadequate watering, I'll be bound.'

Holmes did, indeed, have a box of everything that was needed to make an office or two look seasonal, and had several strings of fairy lights as well as tinsel garlands in his box of tricks, and a giant paper Santa Claus that opened out and could be pinned, in all its three-dimensional wonder, to a wall. 'I'll pick up some holly and mistletoe,' he continued, winking slyly at Shirley, 'when I'm next in the greengrocer's.'

'Don't hang it over my desk,' squeaked Shirley. 'I don't want to be kissed by any old stranger who comes into the offices.' Nor by you, she thought: that would be just too convenient for this ageing lothario. Garden scowled and began to sort out the tree decorations from the general ceiling and office ones, and thought that it would all end in tears.

The end result was a bit like a cross between an explosion in a tinsel factory and a Santa's grotto, but Holmes seemed to be pleased and was quietly humming Christmas carols as he opened the mail: a job that should have been Shirley's, but in a lean period, a task that Holmes took on himself to keep himself out of mischief.

'Oh, just look at this,' he exclaimed, holding up an invitation card for Garden's inspection. 'We've been invited to the HBCRA's Christmas dinner dance.'

'The what?'

'The Hamsley Black Cross Retailers' Association's annual dinner dance, to be held in The Black Swan Hotel.

And guests,' he added, cryptically.

'The Black Swan?' queried Garden, horrified at the opportunity to attend a social engagement at the scene of the first murder they had investigated together. 'And guests?'

'Come along, old man; you surely haven't got a "thing" about that place? And "and guests" means we can each take a partner.'

'No I haven't got a "thing", and neither of us has a partner,' snapped back Garden.

'I shall ask Shirley to accompany me.' Holmes smiled happily at the prospect of swanning in with Garden's attractive mother on his arm.

'Well, I don't think I want to go.' Garden was definitely not in a good mood, and he didn't fancy being a gooseberry to his mother and Holmes.

'Well, that's settled, then.' Holmes resumed humming carols under his breath, firmly convinced that Shirley would jump at the chance of showing off in all her finery.

Chapter Two

A few days later, the HBCRA caused a huge Christmas tree to be erected in the centre of the main shopping street, which was separated by flower beds, with the occasional pedestrian walkway through them. The tree was put in one of these which, although it may have hampered some shoppers, gave more pleasure than it caused inconvenience.

It was really quite impressive when it was finished, with a great number of coloured lights upon it. It was also bedecked with a number of parcels, which were rumoured to be for the local children's home, and destined to be cut off on Christmas Eve. This was only a rumour, however, as such a reality would have resulted in the theft of same, long before that date. It was a heart-warming deception, however, as real presents did exist, and would, indeed, be delivered to the children's ward of the hospital on the twenty-fourth.

The president of the Association was there for the erection and the decoration, as was his deputy, and Holmes made a point of introducing himself in person and informing them that he would be attending the dinner/dance and would like to pay for two tickets, but his partner would, unfortunately, be unable to attend. As only to be expected, he was directed to the Association's secretary, but cordially welcomed by its two representatives, both of whom were well-rounded men who would not have looked out of place in Dingley Dell.

On his way back to the office, Holmes called into Messrs Charles Mott and Son, greengrocer and fruiterer, and purchased a fine brace of bunches of holly and a respectable bunch of mistletoe with plenty of berries which, he hoped against hope, he might be able to remove in exchange for kisses from his secretary/receptionist.

He returned to the office in triumph and informed Shirley of her fate, in that he had arranged to purchase tickets for this sparkling local social occasion, a fate she accepted with all the grace of a horse being offered a beefburger for consumption. Garden was then informed that his declination of the invitation had been passed on to the president of the Association, Mr Henry Morgan, and the vice-president, Mr Robert Findlay. The son was much happier about the situation than his mother, who could see no polite way of declining the invitation.

Chapter Three

A few days before the dinner/dance and coinciding with a dearth of clientele, a young man rushed into the office in a state of mild hysteria. 'You have to help me,' he declared dramatically. 'My father will kill me, after what I've done. Oh, I'm such a fool!'

Shirley directed him to a seat before he swooned, and asked him about his problem, for he obviously had one. 'They've all been stolen, and I thought I was doing the old man a favour. Oh, whatever shall I do?' he squawked.

'Tell me your name and what has happened,' she persisted.

'I can't even remember it, I'm so distressed.' This was a little too melodramatic for Shirley, and she indicated that he should go through to Mr Holmes and Mr Garden.

'I'm sure they will be able to assist you in the resolution of whatever is distressing you,' she assured him, knocking on the door to the rear office.

'Enter,' called Holmes imperiously, and Shirley opened the door and led in her distressed visitor. 'And who is this?' asked Holmes, receiving the mysterious reply,

'I'm afraid I don't know.'

The young man was visibly trembling, and Holmes bade him enter and take a seat before giving details of how they could help him. He duly sat, Shirley retreated, and Holmes asked whom he might be addressing.

It took three attempts before the client could stutter, 'Roderick Fredericks.' Both investigators approached his chair and held out their hands, giving their names as they shook hands with him.

'And how can we be of assistance, Mr Fredericks?' asked the senior partner.

'I-I-I can hardly br-bring myself to utter the w-w-words,' he stuttered.

'I shall arrange for my secretary to bring you a reviving cup of tea, Mr Fredericks, and perhaps you will feel more calm,' stated Holmes, with unbelievable faith in the restorative powers of the dried leaf infusion.

After a few sips, the young man got a grip on his emotions and began to tell his sorry tale.

'I am the son of a jeweller who has a shop in this very street,' he began.

'Ah, yes, Adolphus Fredericks and Son,' interrupted Holmes, and then had to wait a moment or two before Roderick could continue.

'My father, who took over the business from his father, has gone on holiday for two weeks to the Viscount Hotel in Miami' – his father had hammered home his destination enough times since he had booked it – 'and left me in charge of affairs. I'm afraid that I have been very foolish in the way I have conducted them, and lost a large proportion of our stock,' he enlightened them.

Both Holmes and Garden's ears pricked up at this information. 'And you haven't gone to the police?'

'I'd very much rather it was cleared up quietly and privately, without it getting to their ears,' replied their prospective client.

'And how did this calamity come about?' Garden had dragged a chair over to Holmes' desk so that he should not be left out of the commissioning of their services.

The young man turned a fetching shade of scarlet before he continued. 'In the normal run of events, I am responsible for the cleaning of all the second-hand pieces we acquire. We've had rather a lot in, recently, what with the economic climate and Christmas coming, and I decided to take them home with me after close of business on

Saturday so that I could work on them out of business hours on Sunday.'

Here, he swallowed convulsively before continuing, 'I very foolishly went out to a club with a few friends that evening, and when I got home the pieces were gone.'

'Do you not have an alarm system?' asked Holmes.

'I forgot to set it,' replied young Mr Fredericks, hanging his head in shame.

'And who knew about you taking the pieces home to clean?' asked Holmes, thinking what a foolish action this had been: surely far better to go into the shop on a Sunday and work, than expose the pieces of jewellery to the less secure premises of a private house?

'I didn't tell anybody, but I suppose some of the customers may have seen me packing them into a secure case during the last of Saturday's business. I didn't think anyone would know what I was about.'

'You were evidently wrong,' Holmes admonished him and, such was his youth in the presence of someone of Holmes' seniority, that Roderick Fredericks hung his head in shame.

'My father's going to kill me,' he whispered.

'We will come out to your home and your business premises and see if there are any obvious clues but, if we don't turn up something very soon, I really think you will have to report this to Inspector Streeter of the Farlington Market police.' Although the suggestion nearly choked him, Holmes managed to utter it, shuddering as he did so. The inspector had recently 'got one over' on him, good and proper, and he was still smarting from the experience.

'I just can't. My father must never find out about this.'

'I find that unlikely, but we may be able to resolve matters for you. If we are not fortunate enough to be able to do that, though, then you will have to call in the police.'

'Then, heaven help me.'

Chapter Four

The next morning, the one before the dinner/dance, there was a light sprinkling of snow; not enough to hamper road traffic, but sufficient to give the old shop-fronts of the town a delightfully Dickensian air. Its district council was old-fashioned when it came to traditional celebrations and, instead of Slade and Shakin' Stevens blaring out at Christmas shoppers, the sound of old-fashioned carols floated across the cold morning air.

Holmes breezed in with his face glowing from the low temperature, as he had not been able to park nearby, early customers to the retail establishments having bagged all the convenient spaces. 'Come along, Garden,' he exhorted his partner, sitting listlessly at his desk. 'We've got a house and shop to search for clues. This won't get the baby bathed.'

Garden brightened, as he had momentarily forgotten about this prospect, and was thinking, instead, about a parcel he was expecting imminently. He shot upstairs for his coat, but stopped on the way out to have a word with his mother. 'Doesn't the big tree look beautiful,' he declared, as he and Holmes exited, walking to Messrs Adolphus Fredericks and Son, jewellers, gold and silver bought.

The bell pinged as they entered the premises, and young Roderick looked across the counter at them. 'Do you want to look at the case I took the pieces home in?' he asked eagerly.

'You have it here? Did you wear gloves when you brought it back?' asked Holmes, completely oblivious to the fact that the locum jeweller hadn't even bothered with the niceties of exchanging greetings.

'I didn't think about it,' replied the young man, his shoulders sinking at this further display of his incompetence.

'Let the dog see the rabbit,' said Holmes with a sigh of frustration, and then had to explain the remark before he and Garden followed, as the young man put the lock on the door and led them into a back room.

Holmes got out his fingerprint powder from what Garden thought of as his partner's Fisher-Price detectives' kit, and blew some on to the surface of the metal attaché case. Taking a magnifying glass from his beloved bag, he examined the powder-encrusted areas and declared, 'It looks like just one set of prints, which I presume will prove to be yours.'

'Sorry.'

'Would you mind putting your fingers on to this?' asked the scary man with the moustache, as he handed the younger man a sheet of glass which he had just withdrawn from an unmarked envelope.

Roderick did as requested and handed back the now smudged sheet of glass to Holmes, who took his magnifying glass to it. He sighed. 'Yes they look identical to me. Young man, you have been more than careless and foolish.'

'I know.'

'May we have the keys to your home, if it's not too much trouble?' Garden had been listening silently, and knew his partner was feeling defeated, because of his sarcasm.

'Twenty-three Acacia Crescent,' intoned Roderick, hopelessly, as he handed over a bunch of keys.

'And when will your father be back from his holiday?' asked Holmes, anxious to know how much time they might have to find the jewels.

'Evening of the twenty-seventh,' replied the son in a sad monotone, envisaging his eventual fall from grace.

Holmes harrumphed, pulled himself up to his full height – five feet eight inches – and marched out of the premises with a determined air about him, Garden in his wake, not sure how his partner would pull off success in this case.

Chapter Five

Roderick Fredericks' family home turned out to be a large detached Edwardian villa eminently suitable to a family of jewellers three generations in the business.

There were no broken window panes; in fact, the whole place, as expected, was double-, if not triple-glazed. There were no signs of the front door having been forced or any marks around the lock, to indicate that a screw-driver had been used to gain entry.

It was a similar case at the kitchen door and those leading in from the patio. 'If whoever it was wasn't admitted by that young man, then it must be someone with their own set of keys,' stated Garden emphatically.

'You don't suppose that young jackanapes is working an insurance scam, do you?' Holmes was a very suspicious person, and would suspect anyone if they crossed his mind.

'He seemed too genuinely upset and distressed for that to be the case,' opined Garden, thinking back to when the young man had entered their offices.

'It would be a bold move, but typical of the youth of today,' quoth the old fogey.

'I see there's no CCTV on the house,' commented Garden.

'More of a reason to suspect this young man, then.'

'I think you're barking up the wrong tree there, Holmes.'

'Well, let's go in, and you can give me your feelings about the circumstances so far,' he replied.

As they let themselves in at the front door, Garden said,

'I think we need the names and addresses of the friends Fredericks went out with on the evening of the disappearance of the jewellery, and the names and addresses of anyone else who has keys to the property.'

'If you think that necessary.' Holmes simply wasn't going along with this idea now he had his mind set.

'At least appear to play the game, there's a good chap. If you can expose young Roderick as a jewel thief, all well and good; but if it's all down to someone else, then you need to solve this satisfactorily for the reputation of the business.'

Holmes gave another deep sigh. 'If you say so, Garden.'

After a vague wander round, the two self-styled detectives realised that they had no idea what they were looking for, and settled for checking the front door for fingerprints, of which there was a great profusion. 'We really don't know what we're doing, do we?' asked Garden in a defeated voice.

'Nonsense. We'll get to the bottom of this case, you'll see, my boy. We've got until the evening of the twenty-seventh; that's ages away.'

'And all the time the jewels get further and further down a fencing chain,' stated Garden in a doleful voice. 'We'll be ridiculed.'

'Nonsense. Give that young man a ring and ask him who has keys to this property, and for contact numbers for all the friends who accompanied him on his clubbing trip.' Holmes certainly didn't feel downbeat.

'And we'll have to visit all the local pawnbrokers after we've got descriptions of the missing pieces,' added Garden, now feeling that with the application of diligence and a thorough examination of all the facts, they could be successful after all.

Provided with a string of phone numbers and an address for the cleaning woman, they set off in Holmes' new(ish) car to talk to the cleaning lady. It was a car that actually talked to the driver, and of which Holmes was rather proud. Part of its charm was the SatNav, which he could use to get to unfamiliar addresses on cases, instead of getting hopelessly lost, as he was totally incapable of drawing up internet maps, and he now provided it with the address for Mrs Addison.

'Thirteen Mons Avenue,' he pronounced.

'Please repeat instruction,' was thrown back at him.

'Thir-teen Mons Av-en-ue,' he repeated carefully.

'Phoning office,' the car replied.

His mouth dropping open, Holmes uttered a word that barely passed his lips, even in private. 'Bollocks!' he exclaimed.

'Door locks,' replied the car.

'I think it would help if you actually selected SatNav,' suggested Garden and, as the phone rang on The High in Hamsley Black Cross and Shirley answered, he repeated all the contact numbers for his mother to check, whilst they went in search of the Fredericks' cleaner. That would certainly kill two birds with one stone.

'There you are, Holmes. It instinctively knew what was the most efficient thing for you to do, and anticipated your command.' This really was a load of old flannel, but Holmes lapped it up, and thought even more highly of his new vehicle.

As he drove smugly up Mons Avenue, they recognised the just post-First World War architecture and the covering-up of the cracks in the terraced housing with pebbledash. As Holmes braked in front of number thirteen, both of them registered various facts about its exterior. On exiting the car, it was obvious that the lawn had not received its last cut of the season, but that the hedge that peeped over its short front wall was tidily clipped and, although its front door could do with a good coat of fresh paint, the net curtains were white and had been ironed, rather than just washed and hung up again.

'It would seem that our Mrs Addison may not be able to wield a paintbrush or lawnmower, but she is perfectly able to use shears and an iron,' commented Garden, feeling rather in Conan Doyle mode.

'She may have a daughter, and she is not "our" Mrs Addison,' retorted Holmes, his mood instantly soured by Garden's deductive powers. 'She may be an absolute slattern.'

'She's a cleaner, Holmes. How unlikely is that to be?'

'We shall see,' his employer replied darkly, and rapped sharply on the door knocker, for there was no bell.

After a further two knocks, Garden approached the front window and tried to see through the nets, but the only thing he could discern was the fact that no tree lights twinkled inside the room on the other side of them. 'Looks like there's no one at home.'

'Probably hiding upstairs,' grunted Holmes.

'Or gone away for Christmas,' was Garden's opinion. 'Did you ask young Master Fredericks whether she was coming in to clean over the festive season?'

'Stop going all Edwardian on me, and, no, I didn't think of it. Do you want to phone him?'

Garden replied in the affirmative and punched out the shop's number on his mobile, but Roderick could not help him in the slightest. 'I don't know what arrangements Dad made. Mrs Addison just comes and goes. If it's one of my days off, I'm usually still in bed, and don't even hear her. Otherwise, I'm at work when she comes in. Any arrangements she made for while Dad was away were between her and Dad. He didn't say anything to me about her.'

'Honestly,' huffed Holmes when this news had been relayed to him. 'It's like boxing in the dark, isn't it?'

'So, what do you think?'

'I think she has a criminal son who "borrowed" his

mother's keys and went in and half-inched all that jewellery and, is at this very moment, fencing it into the criminal fraternity of the area, or even further afield.'

'God, what an imagination you have. You should be a writer,' Garden told him in amazement. As they drove away, a squat grey-haired figure crawled out from behind the sofa and switched on the Christmas tree lights, which had been glowing away merrily until she had heard a car drive up. What had her Clive been up to now?

The car had to be parked well away from the offices again, and as they walked down The High towards their lair, Holmes commented on the fact that there had been the addition of a number of tiny presents to the town tree, which made it even more beautiful and eye-catching, and that it was a credit to the Retailers Association, which he had now paid a double annual fee for them to join.

When they arrived back at the office, Shirley informed her son that a parcel of some size had arrived for him in his absence, and that she had popped it up outside the flat door. With a whoop of excitement, he went rushing through to the back office and straight up the staircase. He could hardly contain himself.

Yes! It had come! Lovingly, he extracted from its packaging a jacket he had bought on eBay as a sort of Christmas present for Joanne. It had cost him a small fortune second-hand, but it had been worth every penny, he thought as he held it up to admire its beauty.

In his hands was a snow-white faux fur jacket liberally scattered with crystals, which sparkled where the winter sunlight caught them in the light from the window. Oh, how he wanted to wear it! How he wanted to parade in public in such a magnificent garment. Well, fat chance of that. He had nothing planned, so he'd just have to be content with wearing it around his flat, for now.

Chapter Six

The next day, Shirley Garden arrived quivering with nerves at the thought of her outing the next evening with the boss. He was a perfectly nice man, of course, and paid her wages, but she couldn't perceive of him as a date. She just didn't think of him like that, and had, in the past, managed to avoid any occasion on which they could be said to be 'out together'.

Fortunately, the object of her anxiety didn't spend a lot of time in the office, merely grabbing Garden, then making off for all the pawnbrokers in the area, the number of which had grown considerably over the past few years – there was even one in Hamsley Black Cross, and several in the winding streets of Farlington Market.

They began with Z. Scrivett, Pawnbroker, situated conveniently in The High, and immediately ran into a problem.

'Good morning,' Holmes greeted the elderly man behind the counter. 'Do I have the pleasure of addressing Mr Scrivett?' He was unfailingly polite, although he did not approve of such shops. 'Pop Goes the Weasel' had never been one of his favourite nursery songs.

'Zachariah,' the old man declared, holding out a hand. 'And you are?'

'Holmes and Garden, private investigators, sir. We are attempting to trace some jewellery that might have come into your hands within the last few days. May I ask if, er, um, patrons have brought anything of that ilk into this establishment?'

'Why, yes, we've had quite a lot of sparkly stuff

brought in recently. What exactly are you looking for?' And therein lay the problem.

'Well, we don't exactly know. Garden, did that client give you a description of the jewellery we're after?'

'Sorry, no.' Garden wanted a hole to open up beneath him, that it might swallow him whole, at this omission on their part.

'Can you phone our, um, client, and ask if there is photographic evidence of what is missing for, perhaps, insurance purposes?'

Garden slipped outside and made a phone call to an establishment in the same street as they were now enquiring.

When he returned, it was with the information that all the items had been photographed, and that the photographs were in the possession of the legal owner of the pieces. 'Do you think you could be so kind as to ring back our esteemed client and ask if we might be allowed copies of these photographs?'

Garden ducked outside again, once more punching in a number that was becoming increasingly familiar. On his second return he informed Holmes that if they would care to pay a call on their client, they would indeed be provided with photographs of the pieces that were missing.

'Do excuse us, Mr, Zachariaher Scrivett. We'll be back shortly.' Holmes was definitely rattled at their omission.

Outside, Garden commented, 'We're not very good, are we?'

'Just a matter of experience, old boy. We'll get there,' Holmes mumbled, heading for the jewellery shop and hoping that the eyes of Mr Zachariah Scrivett weren't upon them.

The photographic evidence of the stolen jewellery had been retrieved from the interstices of the computer, and was waiting for them when they entered the shop. Garden's breath was taken away by some of the items removed from a small provincial jeweller's home and dreamed of the day when he might get even some good reproductions for Joanne.

'My word, Mr Fredericks, you do carry some pricey stuff,' commented Holmes, on being apprised of the value of the missing stock.

'We have clients in the poshest bits of London, you know,' smirked the irritating young man.

'Well, thank you very much for these,' said Garden, waving the copies of the photographs at the owner's son, and they set out again for Mr Scrivett's establishment, not even considering that he might guess that their client wasn't too far away at their hasty return.

Mr Scrivett smiled an oily smile at their return and, after inspecting the copies of the photographs, admitted that he had not received anything of the class of that sort of thing. 'Unless these are paste,' he added.

'Not to our knowledge.' Suddenly Holmes was indignant at such a suggestion.

'Only asking. It's getting increasingly hard to tell these days, especially from photos,' was his equally indignant reply. 'Look, I'll just put the catch on the door, and you can see for yourselves what I've had through my doors in the last few days.'

In the cramped back office, three trays of jewellery were thrust under their noses, but nothing so fine as was shown in the photographs for insurance purposes.

'Off we go to Farlington Market, then,' puffed Holmes in disappointment. 'Mr Scrivett, thank you so much for your time.'

None of the pawnshops in that town could be of assistance either, and it began to dawn on them that the missing jewels would not be easy to locate.

'We'll have to go to Streeter,' declared Garden in despair.

'I'd rather eat Colin than hand this over on a plate to

that bounder,' stated his partner.

'But we can't deal with this on our own.'

Holmes was adamant. 'Yes, by gad, we can, and we will.'

Chapter Seven

The next day, Mr Fredericks was back, in a similar state of distress as he had been on his first visit to their offices.

'This time the shop's been broken into,' he informed them, his voice a squeak. 'Dad will definitely kill me.'

'Sit down,' ordered Garden.

'Calm down,' ordered Holmes almost simultaneously. 'Shirley, cup of tea required in here,' this last, loudly enough to be heard in the outer office. 'Now tell us, coherently, exactly what has happened.'

'It's the shop, this time. Is there no end to my troubles?'

'What's the shop?'

'That's been broken into. At least, I suppose it has been. It's been turned upside down, but I'm absolutely positive that I set the alarm last night: I know I did.'

'Can you actually remember doing it?'

'Yes.'

'Then someone else must know the code,' Garden insisted.

'But only me and Dad know it,' Roderick insisted, now seeming genuinely scared at what, Holmes perceived, must feel almost like persecution.

'Have you informed your father?'

'No, and I don't intend to either, before he comes back. I can't be held responsible for ruining his holiday as well.'

'And what was taken this time?'

'Absolutely nothing,' he replied in confusion. 'Everything – watches, clocks, chains, rings – absolutely everything was there when I did a quick check of the stock.'

'This is indeed a mystery worthy of the master himself,' muttered Holmes.

'What?'

'Nothing, Mr Fredericks. You just leave everything to us,' Garden reassured him. 'We'll be over later to look for any fingerprints.'

As Roderick Fredericks left the premises to attend to tidying up his shop, Holmes suddenly announced that he had to go to the barber's to have his hair and moustache trimmed for the forthcoming dinner/dance this evening.

'But, Holmes, you can't just swan off. We've got to go to the police on this one,' Garden protested, but in vain.

'I have to look my dashing best for the beautiful Shirley, now, don't I? I promise you that, if nothing's turned up by closing time tomorrow, we'll go to Streeter.' As Holmes uttered this, he thought: and he'd better be wearing black, because it'll be over my dead body.

'Just to disturb his Christmas?' asked Garden.

'If you like to think of it that way, yes.'

There was no further progress that day because Holmes was so distracted with the forthcoming event and, in the end, he went off home early in order to prepare himself for his 'date'. Shirley went off shortly after her boss, snivelling and sneezing into a handkerchief. 'I'm sure I'm coming down with an awful cold,' she told her son, before slipping into her coat and shivering her way out of the office.

Garden locked up that day with relief. At last he could try on Joanne's beautiful new jacket in peace and in costume. He was just slipping a dress over his petticoat when the phone rang.

'Hello, Mother. What on earth do you want? You should be beautifying yourself for your firm's night out with the boss.'

'I can't go, Johnny,' she croaked.

'You can't let him down just because you don't fancy him. What about both our jobs?'

'It's not just because I don't fancy him,' she continued. 'It's because this cold has developed into an absolute stinker. My head's throbbing, my nose is running, and my throat feels like sandpaper: and I can't stop sneezing,' she concluded, matching act to declaration.

'But how on earth are you going to tell him? What were your arrangements?' Garden could see Jobseeker's Allowance on his New Year horizon.

'We were going to meet at the office, because I couldn't face all this "your place or mine" thing for coffee after the dinner dance. I was just going to go, and put up with it, then escape when we came back for our cars. The hotel's only a few steps away.'

There was silence on the line for a few seconds, then Garden replied, 'You just leave it to me. I think I've got a plan.'

'Good. I'm going to bed. If I feel a bit more human in the morning I'll come in, but I'll be bringing some Lemsips with me, and a large box of man-sized tissues.'

Chapter Eight

Holmes had scrubbed his skin until it shone pink, polished his shoes until he could see his face in them, and tripped over Colin, his beloved but Garden-averse cat, twice during his long-winded preparations to look his best for his assignation. On arrival at the office, there was only a low light on, and he entered and cooed, 'Hello, my lovely Shirley. Your beau has arrived.'

A shadow stirred in the half-darkness, and a tall figure arose from a seat through the doorway into the back office. 'Is that you, my dearest?' he called, a little confused by the figure's height, then stared with bemusement as it emerged into the brighter, but still low, lights of the outer office. Who was this tall beauty who awaited him? Had someone from the Association come along to escort him to the celebrations?

'I'm so terribly sorry, but Shirley has been taken ill and I have come instead as your partner,' replied a husky voice.

'That sounds delightful, indeed,' replied the love-sick swain, only for Garden's voice to then reply,

'Don't overdo it, old cock. It's only me, but Mother's got a frightful cold, so I decided to stand in for her so that you wouldn't be disappointed,' and Garden flicked on the full light to reveal the form of Joanne, his alter ego, dressed in her new crystal-adorned faux fur jacket.

'Bugger!' exclaimed Holmes before he could stop himself and, quick as lightning, Joanne replied, once more in her female voice, 'I wonder what your car's computer would reply to that?'

'And just how am I to introduce you to the other members of the Association? I can hardly say you're my secretary/receptionist, can I?'

'You can tell them I'm your partner's sister,' improvised that partner, lying with unsettling ease.

'Oh, come along, then, Joanne. Let's get this over with,' snapped Holmes.

'Get this over with? Have you seen this jacket? It, if not I, deserves a good night on the town.'

Chapter Nine

The food at The Black Swan proved much more inspiring under new management, than it had been when the two detectives had first met earlier that year, and the band was also worthy of its hire.

Holmes spent the evening schmoozing the committee members, while Joanne proved quite a hit with the elderly male members for boogying on the dance floor. In fact, he went so far as to forget himself as far as alcohol went, and when he became aware of his consumption, realised that he had drunk far too much over the limit to drive home that night. Bum! Never mind, Colin wouldn't go hungry, for he had fed him before leaving his apartment, and he could always bunk down with Good old John H. Where was he, by the way, or rather, she?

Holmes giggled to himself at the deception, which owed more to alcohol than it did to the amusement of missing out on an evening with Shirley: that wasn't at all funny, and his chuckles soon subsided into huffs of self-pity. He felt decidedly hard done by, but had he known where Garden actually was, he might have reserved a bit of sympathy for him.

Garden or, as we must refer to him this evening, Joanne, had been strutting her funky stuff on the dance-floor with the greengrocer Charles Mott when that personage had grabbed her suddenly by the hand, and dragged her out of the Hotel and into The High. Joanne was speechless with shock, as Mr Mott commented, 'Such large hands you have, my dear. I do so like a woman with capable hands; so very useful for weighing potatoes.'

Garden risked comment or disapproval. 'Won't your wife be cross at you taking me outside?'

'Nonsense,' he retorted. 'Too busy canoodling with Henry Morgan. She does so admire a man of power.'

'Who's Henry Morgan?' asked Joanne, inexplicably getting a picture of a bottle of rum in her head.

'Why, our esteemed president, of course. '

By this time they had reached the bedecked fir tree that was the town's crowning festive glory, and Mr Mott let go of his companion's hand and removed one of the smaller parcels that had been attached to it. 'I'm not sure what is in these little packages, but may I make the seasonal gesture of presenting you with one as a gift?' he said, an unmistakeable glint in his eye.

Joanne, without thinking, shoved the small parcel into the pocket of her beloved jacket, and then became conscious that Mr Mott's hand was on her right buttock. Without a moment for consideration, she lumped him one round the side of the head, and made her way as fast as her stilettoes would allow her back towards the Hotel.

She found Holmes drowsing on a banquette, and made a desperate effort to rouse him, 'Get me out of here,' she hissed, with some urgency. 'Old Mott's trying to do a number on me.'

'Whassup?' mumbled Holmes, his eyes glazed and staring. He had rather over-compensated for the absence of Shirley and had imbibed well, but rather unwisely. He was definitely not in a suitable state to drive back to Farlington Market tonight.

Putting one of his partner's arms around her neck, Joanne heaved until she had him in an upright position, then began to drag his inebriated body towards the nearest exit. 'Come on, you drunken bum, do make an effort,' she exhorted the almost inert form, in Garden's voice.

'Damned strong filly,' came to her ears, as she became aware of Mott's figure, just inside the door, his cheek reddened by the blow he had received, but a smile still on his face.

'Get a grip,' she hissed into Holmes' ear. 'You've only got to get back to my flat before you can go sleepy-byes, damn you.'

'Wossamarrer?' enquired her burden before, once more, returning to a squiffy silence.

Garden, for it was definitely he again, now his wig was knocked askew, had to put his shoulder under Holmes' behind to propel him up the stairs, then dumped his almost comatose form on to the sofa, before tearing off his wig, his jacket, and kicking off his uncomfortable shoes with the thought that some women had Botox injections into the soles of their feet to lessen the pain of very uncomfortable designer shoes. Maybe he should copy their example.

Without a word, he fetched a sleeping bag from the airing cupboard and covered his partner's inert figure, now sonorously snoring, then went to his own bedroom in a foul temper. His mother's cold had a lot to answer for.

Chapter Ten

The next morning, Garden found himself alone downstairs. Holmes was still sleeping deeply, and would do doubt need some time to recover from his hangover before he came down to the office. His mother had telephoned in sick just before he unlocked the doors and, although the shops were swarming with last-minute shoppers, this being Christmas Eve, he found that no one had any problems that were in need of investigation today.

With all their records up to date, all invoices issued, there was little for him to do except play solitaire on the computer. About eleven o'clock, there were sounds of stumbling footsteps overhead, heading first for the bathroom, then for the kitchen, and Garden presumed that he wouldn't be on his own much longer.

At just before noon, a very shame-faced Holmes tottered down to the office and began to make his apologies. 'I really don't know what came over me,' he said in a very quiet voice, evidently so as not to irritate his throbbing head. 'I acted totally irresponsibly and I ask that you accept my humblest apologies, but please don't speak too loudly, there's a good chap.'

'Apart from having had to lug you home, you got me out of a very difficult situation,' Garden whispered in reply.

'What happened? What did I miss?' Holmes' interest had been piqued, and he lost a lot of his pallor as he asked this.

'That wandering hands merchant, Mott. He dragged me outside and actually put his hand on my bottom.' Garden may have been whispering, but the lack of volume did not detract from the embarrassment of the admission.

'Good God. What did you do?'

'I slapped him round the chops and then rushed back to the Hotel, where I found you blind drunk, and had to get you home.'

'Was I terribly difficult?'

'Yes, but at least it got me out of a very awkward corner. I had no idea Joanne was so attractive.'

Holmes blanched again when he remembered his first reaction to the female figure shrouded in the darkness of the offices the evening before, then made a very flippant comment just to cover his own discomfiture. 'Your mother doesn't know what she missed.'

Remembering Shirley's apprehension about the dinner/dance, and wondering if one could bring on the symptoms of a cold just by thinking about them, Garden thought that she knew exactly what she'd missed, and must be very glad that she had done so. If she'd been there, it wouldn't have been Joanne fighting off the greengrocer, Mr Mott, it would have been his mother fighting off Holmes.

Fortunately it was (again) a quiet morning, and while Holmes merely sat at his desk sulking and consuming large mugs of black coffee, Garden manned the reception desk. When there was absolutely nothing else to catch up with and nowhere left to tidy, he begged Holmes' indulgence while he went upstairs to clear away the evidence of his unexpected overnight visitor.

While he was up in his flat, he put away the stilettoes he had kicked off in so cavalier a fashion on arriving back with his somnolent partner, and picked up his gorgeous jacket to hang it up out of harm's way. One wouldn't want a careless casual visitor to spill a drop of red wine on its pristine condition.

As he picked it up, something made its presence known

in one of the pockets, and he remembered the tiny parcel that Mr Mott had removed from the town's Christmas tree and presented him with the night before. He slipped his hand inside this receptacle and drew out the small, gaily wrapped box.

Out of sheer curiosity, for he didn't really expect there to be anything in this – surely it was merely a decoration? – he picked at the wrapping paper until its contents were revealed. Upon opening the cardboard box, he was bedazzled with an array of what looked like diamonds, or his name wasn't John H. Watson: which it wasn't, but at that moment, he felt exactly like his fictional counterpart.

'Holmes!' he shouted, running down the stairs, two at a time, 'Look what I've found.' Tightly grasping the brooch-cum-pendant, he held it out for his business partner to see, and smiled at the goggling expression on Holmes' face.

'Where in the name of glory did you get that?' he asked.

'It was that Mott. When he took me outside last night, he led me to the Christmas tree and removed one of the little parcels, handing it to me as a gift, just before he copped a feel.'

'This must be from the stolen jewellery. Let's have a look at those insurance photographs again.'

After a quick examination they easily identified the piece, and Holmes' mood changed to one of jubilation; so the caffeine and paracetamol must have done their job, Garden thought.

His face quickly fell again, as he remembered that, although they knew directly from whence the jewel had come, they didn't know how it had got there. 'That's it,' declared Garden, 'We have to go to Streeter now. We can't hold this information back any longer, even if it is Christmas Eve.'

'Bum!' said Holmes.

Chapter Eleven

Inspector Streeter was not at all welcoming, and thoroughly disgruntled because he was just thinking of going out somewhere on some errand or other, and slipping off quietly home. 'What do you two want?' he asked very discourteously.

'We've had reports of two break-ins involving the business of Messrs Adolphus Frederick and Son, and we've got some of the booty from the first break-in here.' With such scant information, Holmes held out the sparkling brooch.

'What break-ins? When? What booty? What have you been withholding from me? That's a criminal offence, you know, withholding information when a crime has been committed. I could charge you both with that.' Streeter frequently relied on this legal-sounding threat as most people would believe it. 'I thought I'd sorted you two out once and for all.'

'I'll start at the beginning, shall I?' asked Garden, feeling that he was the only one of the pair who could explain the events of the recent past to the policeman without resorting to offensive remarks. This situation of stand-off had to be sorted out.

'Orf you go, then.'

'Our offices received a visit, quite recently, from the son of the proprietor; a Mr Roderick Fredericks, who stated that he had taken some pieces of very valuable jewellery home with him for cleaning, whilst his father was away on holiday in Florida.'

'And it got nicked, did it?'

'It was indeed stolen from his house, but without there being any signs of a break-in or the alarm being set off – although Mr Fredericks doesn't exactly remember setting it.'

'Helpful.'

'We feel that that is immaterial. What followed was rather more unusual. The jewellery shop was subsequently broken into and, although nothing was stolen, the place was definitely entered by force although, again, the alarm was dealt with.'

'When did these two events occur?'

'It's all back in our records in the office.'

'And?' Inspector Streeter was now beginning to look more than a little irritated.

'And, these purloined pieces of jewellery were not taken to a pawnbroker's, but wrapped up and hung on the town Christmas tree, hidden in plain view, to be recovered later.'

'How do you know this?'

Garden began to feel flustered. 'I'm afraid that we must protect our sources.'

'I could get a court order!'

Both private investigators were struck dumb by this threat, and Garden, in particular, was in a terrible quandary about what he would do if Joanne's identity were revealed.

'However, I think I have the answer to our little problem.' So, it had become 'ours' now, had it? 'We have recently arranged to be installed some CCTV cameras in The High. On the principle that people will look down rather than up, with the brightness of the shop windows at this time of year when the lights were hung, we sent a crew along to put up the cameras as well, hoping that people wouldn't think anything of it.'

'Good grief!' Garden was almost speechless. 'They must have been the second team of what I concluded were just council electricians swarming over the front of the buildings.'

'How perceptive you are, Mr Garden.'

'But the jewellery was actually stolen from the jeweller's son's family home.'

'But it turned up on the tree. Chances are, then, that the thief put it there. Now,' Inspector Streeter was now beginning to enjoy himself, as he could see a quick wrap-up on the horizon, 'If I'm not mistaken, the tree and the jeweller's shop should be in the range of a couple of our cameras. PORT!

'Ho, yes, we've got good coverage in Farlington Market, but we've had nothing up till now in Hamsley Black Cross. There you are, Port,' he said, as a slightly out of breath DS entered his office. 'Holmes, you get back to your office and let me know which dates we're looking at and, while you're at it, any contact numbers or suspects you have in mind. Port, you're going to be checking some CCTV footage searching until you finish for the day, whether that be before or after Santa Claus flies over in his sleigh.'

'But, sir,'

'You are not a goat, Port; don't "but" me.'

'But, my wife ...'

'Will probably take the children to her mother's tomorrow as arranged, if my memory serves me aright about previous years,' retorted Streeter, mercilessly.

'Can we come back when you've got the dates and probable times?' asked Holmes, as wistful as a child waiting for his stocking to be filled. Considering what had happened between the rivals recently, it would have been churlish of Streeter to refuse this heartfelt plea.

Having phoned through the dates and probable time of the break-in at the shop, the two private investigators made haste to return to the police station in Farlington Market, still the only ones in possession of the telephone number – nay, the very existence – of the cleaning lady and the name of the hotel at which Mr Fredericks Sr was staying. They had to have a trump card, as it was they who had started this hare to run. Of course, these contacts might prove to be a mare's nest, but they couldn't take that for granted.

They found DI Streeter and DS Port hunched over a screen with long sequences of nothing, then the odd scurrying figure. They were looking for the person who had broken into the jeweller's shop, but had not taken anything. They would then try to trace when the extra parcels had been added to the Christmas tree, which they assumed would be during the hours of darkness, and outside business hours for the shops.

With the date, the first was relatively easy to find, and Port was able to isolate a reasonable image of the perpetrator and blow it up. 'Well, knock me down with a feather!' exclaimed Streeter. 'That's our old friend Clive Addison: not long out of stir for breaking and entering. 'I'll get a car to pick him up. Well, there you are, gentlemen; all done and dusted.'

'I don't believe so,' declared Holmes sternly. 'I think you need to prove, without a shadow of a doubt that the parcelled jewel from the tree was put there by him, or find out who the perpetrator really was. If he denies it, you have no evidential proof whatsoever.' Holmes thought this sounded rather good, and puffed out his chest with self-importance.

In the interest of 'good will towards all men' and in light of their recent unprofessional contact, Streeter said that he was willing to lay off interviewing Clive Addison while Port sorted through the CCTV footage for the hours of darkness between when the break-in at the house had occurred, and the break-in at the jeweller's. 'Get searching, Port,' he ordered, then offered his two visitors a cup of coffee and a bun in the canteen.

Port must have struck lucky because, after only forty-five minutes, he came running into the cafeteria shouting,

'I've got him, and it's not Clive Addison.'

'It's not?' queried Streeter, obviously startled by this news. 'Well, who the hell is it, then?'

'I don't know, sir.'

'May we take a look?' asked Holmes, hope soaring in his heart as he realised who it might be.

'Come along then,' Streeter conceded, and they took their place following the two legitimate police officers.

'It's got to be him, hasn't it?' Holmes whispered into Garden's ear.

'Who?'

'Why, Mott the greengrocer, of course. He evidently knew what was in the parcels or he wouldn't have given you, or rather, Joanne, one.'

'No, of course, it's not him, Holmes, it's ...'

But he never got the chance to finish his statement, for Holmes saw the image, enhanced and enlarged on the screen, and exclaimed, 'Good Lord! It's him.'

The image of Roderick Fredericks was clearly discernible. 'Why, the little liar! But he's quite an actor, don't you think, Holmes.'

'And he never even told his father. Wouldn't disturb his holiday,' replied Holmes, still dumbfounded.

'He what?' asked Streeter.

'He wouldn't phone his father to tell him what had happened when the jewellery was stolen from the house, nor after the shop was broken into.'

'Now, that's very interesting indeed, in retrospect. If the little thief had taken the jewels himself from his own home, maybe someone breaking into of the shop was a real shock to him,' suggested Garden, now definitely having a brainwave. May we phone Mr Fredericks senior from your telephone, Detective Inspector Streeter? I have an idea of what really happened, and I think one phone call would sort out the whole business. He's in Miami.'

'A call to Florida?' asked Streeter, thinking of the bill.

'I suppose so, but don't be on there too long.'

Garden dialled the number of international directory enquiries to obtain the number for the Viscount Hotel in Miami. When he'd made a note and ended the call, he made to dial again, and Streeter said peevishly, 'That's two calls.'

'Can't make an omelette without breaking eggs,' Garden offered impishly, and began to dial the long number for the Viscount.

Luckily, Mr Fredericks was in his room – he had not yet got out of bed not surprising, with Florida five hours behind the UK and. In fact, he was doubly annoyed, because his hotel had proved to be just over the road from the perimeter fence of the airport, and he begrudged losing what little sleep he was able to get.

When Garden explained to him that his shop had been broken into, he didn't seem overly surprised. When he told him that his son had been arrested for the theft of the jewels, he became almost incoherent with disbelief. 'But he can't have done. It would have been Clive Addison,' he stated, with absolute conviction.

'And how exactly do you know it was this individual?'

'Because he's got a criminal record, and because he's the son of my cleaning lady. He must have decided that, as I was away, it would be easier to get into the shop without detection. I bet my son forgot to set the alarm.'

'The alarm was disabled with the code-number, Mr Fredericks.'

'I don't know how that happened, but he got away with all that jewellery, which was worth a fortune, I must tell you –'

'No he didn't, Mr Fredericks. The jewels were stolen from your home, and we have visual evidence that your son was responsible.'

And now the whole house of cards came tumbling down. 'But I paid Clive to break in! Why didn't he get the jewellery?' Mr Fredericks seemed to have no comprehension of what he had just admitted.

'Because your son had already faked a robbery from your own home, where he said he had taken the jewellery to clean it whilst you were on holiday.'

Garden looked round, but could see no sign of Streeter. 'When will you be coming home?'

'Not at all, by the sounds of it,' replied the holidaying would-be criminal, who had evidently been planning an insurance fiddle of some considerable value. 'Hang on a minute; there's someone at my door.'

There was the sound of voices, and then someone cut off the call. Garden pressed the end call button and looked round in some confusion. 'He threatened not to come back, then just hung up on me,' he said in dismay as Streeter came bounding through the door with a broad grin on his face – maybe the first one either Holmes or Garden had seen him display: except for their encounter just a few weeks ago.

'The cavalry has arrived, tra-la,' he almost sang. 'I've got a car on its way to Clive Addison's address, and one on its way to pick up young Fredericks. I also got on to the Miami police. They had a patrol car in the area of North-West 36th Street, and they've dropped in to pick up our man, who is, at present, a fugitive from justice.'

'You mean that father and son had both decided, unbeknownst to one another, to rob the business while the father was in the States?' stated Holmes baldly.

'No shit, Sherlock,' replied Garden irreverently, but, fortunately, his partner was too pleased with the result that their joint efforts had achieved to notice.

'Good show, Inspector,' declared Holmes, in genuine admiration at the man's quick thinking, as well as his quick talking.

'We made a pretty formidable team, didn't we – after you'd disclosed the fact that you had a case of which I wasn't aware.'

'We certainly seem to have closed it in double-quick time together,' replied Holmes.

'We could do better if we called a truce,' suggested Streeter, with a feeling of amazement at his own precociousness.

'We could even form an alliance.' Holmes was just as much surprised at his own reaction.

'Well, that's a pact then,' ended Streeter, holding out his hand.

'We'll co-operate in future,' agreed Holmes, shaking hands, and then making way for Garden to do the same. 'By the way, do you really have a DC named Moriarty?'

'It's not against the law, you know.'

Chapter Twelve

Back at the office to lock up for the Christmas break, Garden asked, 'Did what I think just happened happen?' for they had returned to their place of work in silence.

'We seem to have an agreement with the police that they'll scratch our backs if we scratch theirs,' answered Holmes, still rather dazed.

'Is that a good thing or a bad thing?'

'I don't know yet, but it'll certainly be a different thing,' sighed Holmes, only now comprehending what they had agreed to. 'It can't do us any harm. Perhaps now we will get the really interesting cases coming our way. What are you doing tomorrow?'

'Well, Mother's got her sister coming round, so, not much.'

'Would you like to come to my apartment? I should be very glad of the company.'

'Do you mind if I don't?' Holmes looked crestfallen 'But Joanne would be delighted to attend,' carried on Garden 'I don't think she's ever been out to Christmas lunch before, and she does so want to wear her new jacket again, which has, incidentally, been instrumental in us solving this case.'

Holmes stood, lost in thought for a moment. 'I should be delighted to receive her,' he replied, realising that it would still, underneath all the make-up and frills and furbelows, be Garden he would be talking to, and they got on rather well together.

'Do you think Colin might like her?'

'There's no predicting who Colin will and won't like.

Just tell her not to wear her best tights, and we'll tuck her jacket in the cloaks cupboard, out of the furry chap's way.'

'Holmes, is the war definitely over?' asked Garden, with reference to their relationship with Streeter.

'Has been since 1945,' replied his partner, with a wink.

'And you were right about this case from the very beginning. Do you remember, you said it was that young chap all along?'

'Of course I did, old bean. I'm always right. You know that.'

THE END

More Titles
by
Andrea Frazer

Strangeways to Oldham
The Curious Case of the Black Swan Song
Choral Mayhem

For more information about
Andrea Frazer

please visit
Amazon Author page

Printed in Great Britain
by Amazon